Catskill

Catskill

JOHN R. HAYES

Thomas Dunne Books St. Martin's Minotaur New York

THOMAS DUNNE BOOKS.
An imprint of St. Martin's Press.

www.minotaurbooks.com

Grateful acknowledgment is made to Simon & Schuster, Inc., for permission to quote from "A Prayer for My Son," by W. B. Yeats. From *The Poems of W. B. Yeats: A New Edition*, edited by Richard J. Finneran. Copyright © 1928 by Macmillian Publishing Company, copyright renewed © 1956 by Georgie Yeats. Used with the permission of Scribner, a Division of Simon & Schuster, Inc.

Title page photo by James Sinclair

Design by Susan Walsh

ISBN 0-312-28153-6

10   9   8   7   6   5   4   3   2

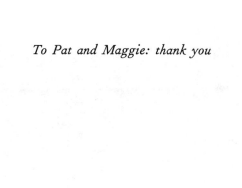

To Pat and Maggie: thank you

Acknowledgments

To: Patricia Hayes, my wife, the eyes, ears, and heart of this effort, who kept me going. Margaret Frazier Hayes, my daughter-in-law, whose perceptive, no-nonsense critique provided early guidance and direction. My mother and father, who passed down so many of the family tales that I have revised, disguised, and pieced together. Judge John J. McQuade, my great-great-grandfather, who built the big white house with the blue awnings at Swan Lake, where I picked blueberries as a child.

To: Ruth Cavin, my editor at St. Martin's Press, who said she loved the book because "I'm taken back to the many summer vacations we spent when the children were little on a dairy farm in Tyler Hill, not that far from Calicoon." James C. G. Conniff, who greeted the original idea as firmly and as kindly as he welcomed my first short story fifty years before. Barbara Tomschin, who assured me that I was on the right track. And Suzan Schwartz, who said straight out that *Catskill* deserved to be published.

To: Alex Hoyt, my agent, who admits he was pleasantly surprised by the first few pages and who so effectively bridged the chasm between manuscript and bound book. And, lastly, James Eldridge Quinlin of Liberty, New York, a fine journalist, who in 1873 told readers of his remarkable *History of Sullivan County* that "all history which is not impartial and true, is a fraud."

COLLINS FAMILY TREE

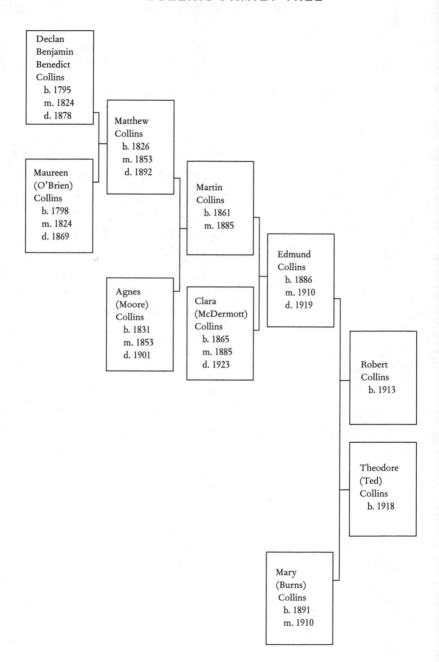

WASHINGTON/BINGHAM FAMILY TREES

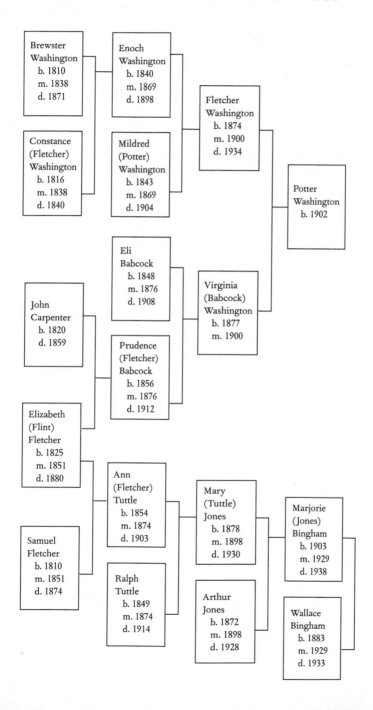

Catskill

PROLOGUE

Declan Benjamin Benedict, the first American Collins, arrived in Boston from Dublin in 1814, a nineteen-year-old journeyman woodworker. In his duffel he had 168 English pounds sterling, a receipt for 2,000 U.S. dollars on deposit in The First Seaman's Bank of Boston, and a hand-drawn map showing him how to walk to the bank from the wharf. All this was a good-bye-and-God-bless-you present from his mother, Elizabeth McNeil Collins.

"I've taken it from my own inheritance," she told her son. "What your father may or may not think does not matter."

His father, the founder and proprietor of Thomas Collins, Cabinets & Fine Joinery, could not understand why a boy with good prospects would elect to live in such a wild un-Christian land.

"All the good Irish wood has gone into English boats," Declan explained. "In America trees grow like grass."

Without a plentiful supply of wood to practice on, a young journeyman's imagination withered. It was as good an excuse as any for leaving home.

Declan's formal education ended at age twelve.

"More Latin than a joiner needs," his father said.

On his last day at St. Brendan's Academy, Brother Arthur Brown, an athletic man with forearms like raw hams, cuffed him on the head "three times for the Trinity" to remind him to be a good boy and to keep his hands out of his pants pockets. On his way to the front door, Declan lit a small fire on the headmaster's desk, next to the old man's pipe rack and not far from his jar of birch switches. The blaze destroyed most of the study, and Declan left for home feeling better.

Seven years later, well trained in his father's shop, he sailed for America.

"May the saints go with you!" Thomas Collins called after him.

"Only if they pay their own way," Declan murmured in reply.

ψ　　ψ　　ψ

Eighteen months after his arrival Declan owned 25 percent of a hardwood veneer company in Brockton, Massachusetts. He had changed his name to Ben and was engaged to the boss's daughter, Maureen O'Brien. They married in 1824. Their first son, Matthew, was born two years later.

During the next decade O'Brien & Collins opened sales offices in Providence, Rhode Island, and Hartford, Connecticut, and formed retail alliances in New York, Philadelphia, and Baltimore. John O'Brien died of typhoid fever in the epidemic of 1828. A year later Collins & Company opened its New York office, and three years later Ben moved the family there.

That Christmas he told Maureen how much they were worth.

"It's not all in dollars but it's all ours," he said. "We are a third of the way to being millionaires!"

ψ　　ψ　　ψ

The passion for wood that led Ben to veneering in Brockton led him to lumber in New York. By 1840 he had a fenced yard on Hudson Street and a block-through-to-the-watershed east of the car barns on the Upper East Side. He built two mills in Ossining in 1842 and 1846, one for rough cut, the other for finished beams and boards. A Collins & Company barge tugged regularly up and down the river. A specialty shop for moldings, veneers, and fine finishes opened in 1852.

"I wish you went to Mass more often," Maureen said to him. "You haven't made your Easter Duty in a long time."

It was her way of saying he was becoming somebody and should be seen more often in church. He thought it good advice. Memories of Brother Arthur and the headmaster's birch switches were put aside if not forgotten.

"Lord, they knew how to make us jump," he said to the archbishop, and they laughed together. He did not mention the fire in the headmaster's study. Over time he came to believe he had had a happy childhood.

※　　※　　※

In mid-nineteenth-century New York, Ben's many talents and his skill at moving forward without pushing into others were noticed where it counted. In less than a generation the family advanced upward and across class lines.

Maureen summed up the family philosophy. "Don't lose your respect for hunger," she said. "And remember that being poor too long leaves scars."

※　　※　　※

The Collinses were drawn naturally toward institutions that reflected the ways they felt about themselves. Early in the century, with Thomas Jefferson's approval, Aaron Burr had built an enlightened political base inside the Society of St. Tammany to offset Alexander Hamilton's elitist Society of the Cincinnati. Burr claimed to favor change, merit, and a free society. Hamilton's people said Burr thrived on chaos.

The sachems, a title borrowed from the chiefs of the Algonquins, controlled the Tammany lodges. A few Tammany sachems served as seconds at Burr's side in Weehawken, New Jersey, the day he shot and killed Hamilton.

From before the Revolution, the Irish, even the Papist variety, had been more or less accepted in New York. But in the late 1840s, the Great Potato Famine began driving the so-called shanty Irish to America by the tens of thousands every year. The new wave was composed of Ireland's poor, refugees from the alleys and the blighted farms, transported with prisoners expelled from Irish and English jails. They arrived on boats called coffin ships.

"They're worse than Gypsies," Maureen told Ben, her nose wrinkled with distaste. "They smell. They steal. They eat goats."

"But they can vote," Ben replied.

Thrown together by accident and by a use for one another, the old and the new Irish became a force that took control of the city of New York for the next one hundred years.

Ben's oldest son, Matthew, earned a degree in engineering from Manhattan College and was welcomed into the Tammany organization. He and Ben served on and off as sachems. Not aggressive by nature, they did the calculating and left the speeches to others. Together they nourished a family fortune that quietly grew and survived.

ψ   ψ   ψ

In 1848 Ben was named, with great ceremony and good humor, a police justice of the city of New York.

"Here's to the Judge," said Matthew in a Champagne toast that won respectful applause. The title stuck and was passed thereafter father to son.

Matthew's son, Martin, was born in 1861. That same year the Collinses began summering with friends in the Catskills, a part of New York Ben had often visited in his never-ending search for fine wood.

In 1867 the archbishop of New York invited Ben to the consecration of St. Peter's Roman Catholic Church in the Catskill town of Monticello. While in the area Ben bought a tract of prime woodland. The following year he and Matthew watched a crew of

Irish workmen lay the cut-stone foundations of Collins House on the bluffs above Lake Repose.

∗ ∗ ∗

Ben died in 1878, having lazed seven well-earned summers on the wraparound porch at Collins House. He left his children and grandchildren a considerable amount of property and money. They, like their friends, made use of it to raise themselves above the vulgarity that surrounded them. They mimicked and mocked a distant aristocracy. They raised propriety to a level that dazzled. They gilded their age. They bequeathed all this to their children with the solemn understanding that it would always be the Judge's task, whoever he might be, to make it last forever.

One

EARLY IN THE SUMMER OF 1926, MARTIN Collins, who was always called Judge by his family, invited Sister Thecla Marie, the Revered Mother Superior of the Sisters of St. Paul, to spend a week's holiday at Collins House on Lake Repose, eight miles north of the village of Chicken Corners in Sullivan County, New York.

The invitation was extended at the urging of Martin's widowed daughter-in-law, Mary.

"She will be sixty-five in November, Judge," Mary had insisted. "Next year, whoever takes her place may not let her go."

"It's not how old she is that worries me," Martin replied. "It's how she looks. We've never had nuns at Collins House before."

"She looks the way a nun is supposed to look," said Mary, tightening her lips. Martin softened quickly whenever Mary seemed upset. She knew he worried about her.

"There are some very jittery people up there, Mary. Someone looking like that could really stir them up."

"It would be you and her together to talk old times again," she said teasingly. He smiled. She felt herself winning.

"You said two others with her. Where would we put them?"

"The rules won't let her travel alone. We can manage," said Mary. "Can she come? *Please, Judge!*"

ψ   ψ   ψ

Sister Thecla had stayed Patricia Dillon until she completed her Paulinas' novitiate in 1879 at age eighteen. Before that, from 1867 to 1875, she had been Martin's classmate at Immaculate Heart Elementary in the east sixties in Manhattan. He had been called Master Martin Collins then.

Young Martin had worshiped young Patricia long into his teens, but she had gone away at sixteen, and over time his feelings had leveled down. The order had returned her to New York six years later, a third-grade teacher and a fully habited nun.

The Paulina habit was based on a sixteenth-century Milanese fashion derived from a Muslim court costume that had been popular in Cordoba a hundred years earlier.

"I wouldn't have known you," Martin said shyly when he saw her in veil and wimple the first time. "You've changed."

"Good thing," she replied curtly. "When we don't, we're dead."

Years later, he questioned her again about the ancient habit.

"It's a discipline," she explained. "It structures our lives. It reminds us we are different."

"*Looking* different is one thing, Patricia," Martin said, unpersuaded. "Looking *queer* is another."

Sister Thecla knew what looking queer meant. At age thirty, as acting principal at an elementary school in Ithaca, New York, she had fought her way through a cordon of angry policemen to pull a second-grader through a burning doorway just as a supporting wall caved in. She lost her left arm.

ψ   ψ   ψ

Collins House was a mid-Victorian country house built on a 1,200-acre tract in the northwestern Catskills in 1871. It was cedar clapboard painted white with a half-screened porch wrapped around both sides. Blue-and-white striped awnings shaded every window on all three floors. The house faced south, overlooking the lake, a hundred yards from a secondary town road.

Most of the Collins tract was still wild. Much of it was still covered with remains of the virgin hemlock forest that had blanketed the region before the bark strippers, working for the tanners, came and killed it. In the 1870s, Martin's father, Matthew, a sachem of Tammany Hall, had cleared seventy almost-level acres on the bluff overlooking the lake, creating a plateau of gentle fields and meadows that were occasionally scythed but never farmed or grazed. The paths through the tall grass followed the wanderings of deer, bears, and children. Martin's wife, Clara, with his parents and grandparents, was buried on the highest meadow in a sunlit corner that was enclosed by a cast-iron fence to keep large animals away. A visiting bishop from the city had consecrated the plot.

From the very beginning Catholic priests of all ranks had been frequent guests at Collins House. They hiked the trails, sailed the lake, often fished and hunted with members of the family. They dozed in the parlors and on the great open porch. With their collars off, wearing flannel shirts or striped blazers or oilskins, they passed for ordinary men.

But inviting nuns to Collins House was a different matter indeed.

ψ   ψ   ψ

Martin and Mary picked up the three nuns at eight on a Saturday morning in front of the main entrance to Mary Immaculate Convent on East Sixty-ninth Street in Manhattan. Martin was behind the wheel of the 1925 Duesenberg touring car. Mary sat beside him. Sister Thecla and Sisters Innocent Marie, sixty-one, and Margaret Marie, forty-four, rode in back.

They made a brief stop for lunch and would have arrived at Chicken Corners by late afternoon if Sister Margaret had not become carsick, and if they had not had a flat rear tire.

ψ   ψ   ψ

Martin was trying to decipher the greasy accordion jack and Mary's shaky reading of the manufacturer's instructions when an ancient green-and-yellow bus, not much larger than a delivery wagon, pulled up on the grass shoulder behind them. A canvas sign, hand-lettered Kaufmann Tours, was tacked on the right side.

The door opposite the driver opened with a kick, and a dark-haired, heavy-eyebrowed young man in his early twenties, the bus's only occupant, climbed out. He was dressed in blue cotton pants and shirt and was wearing heavy brown shoes with high sides and thick soles.

He took the tire iron and jack from Martin's hand, and said, "Please allow me. I am August Kaufman. K-a-u-f-m-a-n."

He very carefully rolled up his sleeves, chocked the wheels, checked the hand brake, jacked the car up, and changed the tire. Then he smiled for the first time, returned to his bus, and drove away. But not before Martin had requested his address—Kaufmann Tours, 280 Third Street, east of Broadway below Cooper Union—and promised he would be in touch.

ψ   ψ   ψ

Nearing Chicken Corners in the late afternoon, Sister Margaret felt queasy again. As they rolled into the village center Martin slowed to five miles an hour and coasted to a stop in front of the war memorial.

The memorial was a small triangle of grass, brightened with summer flowers and shaded by chestnut trees. It was furnished with two concrete-and-oak benches, a small brown howitzer, a flagpole and flag, and a bronze plaque attached to a large block of sparkling granite. The plaque listed the names of the twenty-three Chicken Corner residents who had died meritoriously in the last three American wars. Near the top of the list was the name of Martin's only child, Captain Edmund Collins, missing in action, France, 1918.

Behind the memorial the village sloped to the southeast, where it spread out at the base of a glacier-scoured ramp to a six-mile stretch of deep blue water named Lake Repose. The lake was bordered east and north and partially on the west by steep cliffs. The cliffs were indented by coves that cut deeply into the main shoreline. The Collins tract began at the high bluffs at the north end.

Sister Margaret sat on one of the benches breathing deeply. Sister Innocent inspected the howitzer. Mary waited in the car.

Sister Thecla and Martin studied the four lines of type impressed in capital letters at the top of the memorial plaque. Sister Thecla read them aloud:

GREATER LOVE THAN THIS
HATH NO MAN
THAN THAT HE LAY DOWN HIS LIFE
FOR HIS FRIEND

Three men, seated in straight-backed chairs, watched this tableau from the ground-level porch of Rudy's Country Store, across the road from the memorial. The crucifix on Sister Thecla's breast bounced light at them like a jewel in the declining sun. In all their long lives, the three men had never witnessed anything like it before.

ψ   ψ   ψ

Collins House had nine bedrooms, seven upstairs and two down, and sleeping quarters for a staff of three. Mary set three bedrooms aside for the nuns, partitioning them from the rest of the house but determined to make them feel at home.

"They put their shoes on just like we do, one at a time," she told the assembled staff. "I don't want you treating them like they just stepped out of seashells."

The routine at Collins House was lax and lazy. The sisters got up when they wanted and meandered as they pleased. They stayed up way past their usual bedtime. The summer days were warm and dry. They walked, read, rested, and played croquet on the side lawn. They tried badminton, but found it difficult wearing veils. They did not swim in the lake, but they did take off their shoes and stockings to wade in the rock-bottomed pool below the small waterfall that was the entrance to the ravine behind Collins House.

ψ   ψ   ψ

Radio reception was unreliable, so at night everyone came to the main parlor to play cards. Mary had arranged two lion-footed oak tables in front of the double bay windows, and starting Saturday night they began with every card game that Martin, Mary, and Mary's two sons, Robert, thirteen, and Ted, eight, could remember. By Wednesday, their fifth day, they had graduated from Go Fish and Old Maid through three kinds of rummy to poker. Because only Martin, Robert, and Sister Thecla played poker well, Martin invited Jarvis Evans, an antiques dealer from Chicken Corners who served as town historian, to join the game Thursday night.

Martin, Mary, Sister Thecla, and Sister Margaret sat at the table on the left. Jarvis, Robert, Ted, and Sister Innocent were at the table on the right. The temperature had dropped into the midsixties from a day's high of eighty-two. The cicadas and bullfrogs were singing in a circle all around, the katydids were calling back and forth.

Martin glanced down at the five cards in his right hand, then brought them in tight against his chest.

"I'll take three," he said.

Sister Thecla smiled knowingly. Three meant she had dealt him nothing better than a pair. He thumbed his three discards out blind, watching her watch him. She slid his three replacements across the table.

"Dealer takes one," she said crisply, adding, "Don't misplace those openers, Martin. Your bet."

Ted, the younger grandson, moved from his place at the second table to stand behind his grandfather's chair.

"Two big ones," said Martin. "No peeking, Ted." He separated two pebbles from the pile in front of him and pushed them forward with his left hand.

Sister Thecla came back at him without a pause. "See your two and raise you ten."

"She's bluffing, Judge," said Robert from the other table. "Raise her back."

"When they take just one, that's sometimes to fill a straight or a flush," Mary said softly.

"Sister Thecla doesn't bluff," said Ted.

"Ganging up on me, are you?" Martin muttered.

"Or a full house," said Robert.

"Or a *straight flush*," said Ted. "Jimminy! Can't I look?"

"At hers if she'll let you," said Martin, "not mine. But don't tell me anything."

She nodded her approval.

Ted scampered around to the other side of the table. The players at the adjoining table halted their game and turned to watch the action.

"What do you think, Robert?" Martin asked his grandson. "She got me beat?" He still kept his hand covered.

"Maybe it's a *royal* flush."

Martin shook his head in mock despair. "A few minutes ago, you said she was bluffing."

Sister Thecla smiled sweetly.

"Are you in or out?" she asked.

Before Martin could respond, a glow of light appeared on the front lawn. The curved windows filled magically with little explosions of color that quickly filled out into the plumed tips of a dozen torches spaced out along the edge of the road. In front of the torches a tall cross began to burn, upward from the grass. As their eyes adjusted, the cardplayers could see beside and between the torches and behind the cross a motionless row of figures clothed head to toe in white.

"Well, would you look at that," Martin said. He knew right away what it was. "Are all the dogs in?"

Mary whispered, "Yes, Judge."

"Just sit still," he said. "It'll be all right."

With the cross fully ignited, it was a splendid scene. The torches flickered, the grass glowed, the pure white hoods and robes shimmered beneath a halo of light that pressed up against the dark. The cardplayers sat frozen in expectation, as if they were supposed to know what would happen next but had for the moment forgotten.

Martin turned his cards facedown, moved his brandy glass to the middle of the table, and rose from his chair. He was wearing a finely striped red-and-white shirt with an open white collar, white duck trousers, and soft buckskin shoes. The outfit complemented his graying mustache and snow white hair.

"I need to find out what they want," he said, almost apologetically. "Please, all of you, wait here."

He pushed the screen door open and crossed the porch, pausing with arms folded at the top of the steps. Sister Thecla followed, moving smoothly to his left side, as he knew she would. The door swung closed behind them. As if on cue, five of the hooded figures came forward, lining up before the cross. The one in the center stepped two paces forward. He had red chevrons on his peaked hood and on his sleeves, and he was bent over below the shoulders, as if something was wrong with his back. The two on the ends held torches above their heads.

"You certainly know how to stage an entertainment, Martin," Sister Thecla murmured, as if this was his doing. She spoke without moving her lips and with her eyes forward.

"Now, Patricia, be gracious," Martin replied. "These folks have gone to a lot of trouble."

"Who are they?"

"A few of the neighbors. Come to pay their respects."

"Are they dangerous?"

"They could be, I suppose. Let's not let it spoil the evening."

They locked arms, his left in her right, and together they walked down the six wooden steps and across the flagstone path. They were the same height. As they approached the five figures, she disengaged and moved ahead of him. For an instant Martin was startled. Then, because he knew her so well and trusted her completely, and because it felt right, he accepted her lead and fell slightly behind.

She walked to the figure in the center, smiling and holding out her hand. For a long moment it stayed there, suspended. Then the robe parted and a man's hand slid out slowly and took hers.

"I'm Sister Thecla Marie. Thank you so very much," she said in a loud, clear voice. "The cross is beautiful."

She shook his hand gently. When he tried to pull it free she squeezed harder. He could not disengage without making a scene.

Martin moved quietly to her side, thinking this was one for the books, trying to guess who was under the hoods. He thought the leader, the bent-over one with the red chevrons, was Fletcher Washington, a retired Fredericktown selectman with an arthritic spine. The tall figure standing protectively behind Fletcher had to be Fletcher's son, Potter, an intense young man who supervised the post office substation in Chicken Corners.

"Allow me to present Mr. Fletcher Washington," Martin said to Sister Thecla very formally. "An old and distinguished friend."

Sister Thecla's grip tightened.

"That is you, isn't it, Fletcher?" Martin continued in a friendly tone. "Fletcher, this is Sister Thecla Marie, the Revered Mother Superior of the Sisters of St. Paul."

Fletcher moved his head slightly, a kind of greeting, but did not speak. Sister Thecla released his hand and moved behind him to shake hands with the other four. Martin followed along.

"Sister Thecla Marie," she said to each of them in turn. "Thank you so much. It's beautiful."

They accepted her hand but did not reply.

Behind them the screen door banged shut again, and the other cardplayers arranged themselves on the porch steps. After a moment, Robert came down the steps to take a place at his grandfather's side.

With Robert standing at attention, face stern, arms rigid, the tall figure behind Fletcher suddenly leaned forward, pushed his hood up above his forehead, and raised his right hand in appreciative salute. Robert hesitated, then saluted back. Martin, annoyed, stepped between them, and almost immediately the hooded figures behind the cross began retreating to the edge of the lawn.

The man with the red chevrons nodded again, first to Martin, then to Sister Thecla, lastly to Robert. He signaled the others with a wave of his right hand and a roll of his shoulders, turned abruptly, and walked briskly down the path. On the road, near the edge of the Wild Garden, he swung to the right like a drum major. With a torchbearer on either side he led the string of two dozen Klansmen away and finally out of sight.

They left the burning cross behind.

☙   ☙   ☙

Back in the parlor, Sister Innocent took her seat at the table on the right and stared down at the backs of her cards. The others remained standing.

Robert broke the silence. "Who was the one who showed his face?" he asked.

Martin frowned.

"That was Potter Washington, Fletcher's boy," Jarvis Evans replied, bristling. "Lucky for him Charlie wasn't here."

"Who is Charlie'?" asked Sister Thecla.

"*My* son, Sister. He wouldn't have put up with that."

"Why not?"

"He and those Kluxers don't get along."

"What would he have done?" asked Robert.

"You never can tell with Charlie," said Jarvis. "He's half Algonquin, a Delaware."

"Wow!" said Ted.

"Charlie's mother was Wolf clan. He quarterbacked three years straight for Fredericktown High.

"How wonderful," said Sister Margaret.

"Being an Indian?" asked Ted.

"Being a quarterback," Sister Margaret replied.

"Weren't you frightened out there, Judge?" asked Mary.

"Tell the truth, I was a little uneasy. But when the Revered Mother stepped up front, I thought to myself, My oh my, those fellers are in for it now."

"Oh, hush up," said Sister Thecla.

"How did you think what to do, Sister?" asked Mary.

"I suppose I'm used to it," she replied. Her fingertips touched her empty left sleeve.

"It's ritual, young lady," said Sister Innocent. "No one does it better than Catholics. Vestments. Candles. The altar. The cross. When the time comes, you just go. You're carried along."

"The strength comes from inside," Margaret. "It's knowing God is on your side."

🌿　　🌿　　🌿

Throughout the twenties there were dependably good times to be had at Lake Repose, and if the decade did not exactly roar above the lawns at Collins House there was a steady stream of song and laughter. But entering the thirties, a succession of events that had started with the loss of Edmund in France began to wear Martin Collins down. His wife, Clara, died of diphtheria and grief in 1921. Sister Thecla, his first love, died of cancer in 1928. Tammany no longer needed a man his age in his position, and a series of careless investments, made throughout the twenties, gravely undermined the Collins fortune.

For the first time in his life, Martin found himself facing debts he could not easily pay. With few people of his own generation left to engage him, he felt isolated and alone. He came to believe that he, the Judge, had somehow let the family down. And so, early in the Great Depression, unnoticed at first, Martin began to retire periodically to his book-lined study in Manhattan or to his den at Lake Repose with an ample supply of Irish whiskey to confront the demons of his failure face-to-face.

$\mathcal{T}wo$

AUGUST 1938

THE SOUNDS IN THE CELLAR, A SERIES
of spaced scrapings and grindings, wood on stone and metal on
metal, woke Martin slowly. They seemed to be centered directly
below his cot. He held himself motionless and opened one eye
warily, wanting to be certain there was no one sitting by his side,
watching while he slept. The drapes were drawn. The hooded desk
lamp cast a faint glow at the far end of the room. The door was
closed and bolted. The wooden side chair was still jammed tight
under the doorknob where he had set it Saturday night before he
began the drinking. The desk clock said 2:30, probably Monday
afternoon, he guessed. He was alone.

He sat up gingerly, not sure what kind of shape he was in,
whether it was safe to move at all. He turned his head carefully
side to side. Not bad, not good. It hurt. The air in the room was
hot and stale. His mouth was dry. His hands were shaking. He
could smell himself. He fumbled for one of the bottles on the floor
at the foot of the cot, pulled the cork loose, and took a long
swallow, not bothering to use the glass, something he ordinarily
tried not to do.

He had known right away what had made the sounds: first, the
wooden gun box sliding off the stone foundation ledge where he

had stored it in 1921; after that, one-inch nails screeching as someone pulled them through the metal strapping that held the gun-box
lid in place. His older grandson, Robert, had been with him the
day he had stored it, so proud to be helping. The boy had been
quiet and respectful. Martin could recall the cobwebs, the musty
odors, the mouse droppings, the waxy surface of the heavy box.
Memories of things that had happened years ago were as sharp as
ever.

The box had been very heavy. He had used a farmer's hand
truck, a plank, and a rope to get it down the stairs and inside. It
was made of rock maple, nicely dovetailed and bound with strap
iron, one of a hundred cases designed by the regimental armorer
for senior members of the Regimental Honor Guard. Inside were
six Springfield rifles, thickly coated with protective grease and
wrapped in waxed paper, six leather slings, six cleaning rods, six
cans of cleaning fluid, six cans of gun oil, and a hundred twenty
rounds of .30-caliber ammunition. "Property of U.S. Army" was
stenciled on the lid.

"Why do we need all these guns, Judge?" his grandson had
asked him.

It had been a fair question, but Martin had no answer that would
make sense to an eight-year-old. He could not tell him, "To keep
them from the veterans, to prevent a working-class rebellion,"
which was the truth, the reason why Edmund's regiment had presented six hundred of its surplus rifles to one hundred reliable New
York men for safekeeping.

"Because there wasn't enough room for them at the armory
when the war ended," he told Robert. "We're just minding them
for the colonel." That was true enough.

He had almost forgotten they were there. No one had ever asked
about them. Now, seventeen years later, someone had dragged the
box down off the ledge and opened it. He tried to think why
someone might do something like that, but he soon gave up and
went back to sleep.

At seven o'clock on Tuesday morning the sound of distant gunfire woke him abruptly. He sat up with a start. A sliver of daylight was shining through an opening in the heavy window drapes, illuminating a gold-framed painting of Lake Repose that hung on the opposite wall.

The shooting was taking place at the far end of the ravine, almost half a mile away. Three rifles. One was Ted's Winchester. It made a distinctive snapping sound. He could not immediately identify the other two. One sounded like a medium-weight sporting rifle. The other was heavier, a serious gun with an authoritative bark that he had heard before. Neither of them was Robert's Remington Repeater.

The shots came in bursts of three with long intervals between; time enough for someone to walk halfway out to the printed target, check the placement, walk back, and adjust the sights. First one rifle, then another. They were probably clamped onto the log sighting benches that he and Edmund had built in the ravine above the house before Edmund went away to war and never came back.

Martin stood up slowly and tested his legs. Very weak, very wobbly. Still, the belly was flat. He flexed his fingers and held his arms out to see how badly his hands vibrated. God, this was going to be unpleasant. He had locked himself in to fight his demons only four days earlier. Usually he needed at least a week before he was ready to come out. But there was no time left to spare. He could think of no reason why three people would be sighting rifles so precisely off-season in August, or why one of the rifles would sound like a military Springfield. If one of the people up there was his younger grandson, Ted, with his Winchester, the other would most likely be Robert. And the third gun would be Potter Washington, rubbing up against the family once again.

Very quietly, Martin left his den and tiptoed to the backstairs WC where he emptied his chamber pot, discarded his sweaty, rumpled clothes, and sponged himself clean. Back in his den, he pushed the heavy drapes aside and raised two windows. The room filled with new air, the sunshine stabbed in.

Something was about to happen. It was time to sober up.

Three

"DON'T THINK OF THEM AS PEOPLE,"
Potter whispered. "It might rattle your aim."

"Nothing rattles me," Robert whispered back.

Ted grunted.

It was late Thursday evening, close to sunset. The three men were lying on a hillside in prone firing position: Potter on the left, Ted on the right, Robert in the middle.

Potter had picked the hiding place the day before: a natural cavity in a stack of dead branches and twisted tree trunks piled on a dirt shelf halfway down a hill behind the farmhouse. The pile of wood covered a row of abandoned latrines; six sinkholes, each the length and width of a grave. It was roofed over with trash leaves and pine needles. The front was a lattice of twigs. It offered a clear line of fire.

Potter Washington was thirty-six. He had joined the Fredericktown Police Department in 1931 and had been deputy sheriff for the past four years. Robert Collins was twenty-five and in his second year of law school. Ted was twenty, a junior in college. Late in the afternoon, with Potter leading, they had inched out of the woods at the crest of the hill and wriggled down the slope on their spines. They had burrowed into the woody cover, spread a small tarp on the damp ground, and settled in.

ψ   ψ   ψ

For more than a century the tract had been known as Thornton farm. After the foreclosure in 1930, a succession of bank tenants had abused the house and outbuildings so badly that people stopped calling the place anything at all, sensitive to the feelings of any Thorntons who might still be living in the hills around.

The farmhouse was set on level ground fifteen feet below the base of a pile of wood that covered the old latrines and a hundred yards away. Beyond the house was Thornton Road, two lanes of crumbling macadam that stretched left toward the distant towns of Monticello and Liberty and right toward the villages of Chicken Corners and Thunder Mountain and the township of Fredericktown. Across the road a leased cornfield sloped upward to the wooded edge of a stump mountain.

The building was a two-story, six-bedroom center-staircase box. On the ground floor in back, to the right of the kitchen door, were three large windows. Four smaller windows were evenly spaced on the second floor. Rows of small ventilation windows were set just below the eaves. The kitchen door and all the windows were screened and open, and the windows were curtained with limp, pale cloth. Bare electric lightbulbs illuminated the ground floor, and lanterns glowed in the rooms above.

The clapboard siding was curling, and the chalk white paint had turned a mottled gray, spotted with black mold. The split-cedar roofing was patched with tarpaper and tin. A stovepipe with a pointed cap cover stuck out the side of the kitchen wall.

A medium-sized bus, shiny green and yellow with a black roof and New York license plates, was parked at the left side of the house, facing toward the front. A sign on the back read Kaufmann Tours.

When the sun was close to setting, Potter gave the signal to take positions.

"Ready on the right. Ready on the left," he growled loudly. "Time to scarify some sinners."

Robert mumbled his reply. He was ready. He had heard Potter's scarification litany before.

"We'll wait for the shadows," Potter said softly. "Six shots each, no more. Space them out, half-minute intervals, and roll them into each other. I want it to sound like the end of the world. Remember, there's no cover in there except behind the chimney, so keep your shots high. We want to scare them, that's all."

"I go first?" said Robert.

"Yup. Place your first above the far-left window on the second floor and work across. Ted, you start ten seconds after your brother. Take the ground floor, first shot high above the kitchen door. I'll pick and choose. Wait till I say when. And don't think of them as people."

"When," said Potter, and Robert, who had stuffed cotton balls in his ears, squeezed slowly and let the first one go.

He had never shot at a house before. It made a distinctive sound. Even with the earplugs, he thought he could hear the bullet whine across the open space before it hit the wooden siding. The impact was a *pop-thump*. In one side and out the other, he supposed.

He began counting his half-minute silently. One-one-hundred, two-two-hundred. At ten he heard Ted fire, and ten seconds later Potter. Each shot was followed by that odd *pop-thump*, like a parade drum, after the bark of the gun. He shifted the sights of the Springfield a foot above the second window on the left. At thirty he fired, and this time he thought he could see splinters fly. A woman screamed. Again, above the third window, and a short piece of clapboard jumped loose, leaving a rectangular hole in the siding. The people inside began to come out.

"Well, lookee that," Potter said.

The screen door opened out. A huge man wearing wide-legged black pants and a collarless white shirt with billowing sleeves stood in the lighted doorway, shaking his arms at the darkness. Three figures huddled behind him: a man and woman dressed mostly in black, shielding an older boy between them. The man wore a long jacket and a brimmed hat, set high and level. Thick loops of dark, curly hair dangled at both sides of the boy's face. The big man roared in rage.

"Look at that fat jackass," said Potter. "Who does he think he is?"

Pushed by the growing crowd behind him, the man stumbled down the platform steps and fell forward. Children and grown-ups jumped past him, tripping over those who had fallen before them.

Robert fired his fifth and then his sixth shots carefully, all well above the window line. Ted fired again, and for ten seconds after Potter's last shot, it was quiet. Then those inside pulled the curtains away, pushed the screens out, and began to climb, jump, and lower each other from the ground-floor windows to the shadowed ground below. They picked themselves up, some waiting briefly to reach up for a woman or a child, then ran into the half-darkness. A youngish woman knelt down facing the woodpile, and for a moment Robert thought she was trying to speak, but then she sagged, tilted, and sat down in the dirt. He heard a few shouts and panic noises, but mostly it was done in pantomime, as if the runners believed silence would help to conceal them.

With people still climbing out the door and windows, Robert began counting heads. Deciding that there would be as many Jews going out the front as out the back, he counted in twos, passing fifty before he gave up.

"Lord God Almighty," he said, forgetting to whisper. "It's like Noah's Ark."

"The flight of the righteous," said Potter, and laughed.

Four and a half minutes after saying "When," Potter said, "Time to skidoo!"

Following his lead, Robert and Ted placed their rifles and spent cartridges neatly in the tarp and backed uphill clear of the cover on their hands and knees. They had not rehearsed the withdrawal, but it went as smoothly as if they had.

Halfway up, Potter said, "I'll take it," and pulled the tarp to the side. He rolled it, tucked in the ends, and slung it across his shoulders, the way he would carry a felled deer. They crept upward until they reached the overhanging ledges, where they had to climb. At the top of the hill they turned and looked down. The lights on the ground floor were still blazing, and someone had turned the bus's interior lights on. Small groups of people stood motionless around it in silhouette.

"Idiots," said Potter. "Standing in front of that light. What if my order was shoot to kill?"

"I wouldn't be here," said Robert.

"Me neither," said Ted.

"I only said 'if,' " said Potter. "Let's go."

The car they had used to get to the farmhouse was a black 1929 Nash coupe belonging to Potter's mother. Since her accident the previous year Virginia Washington rarely drove, and Potter knew she would not mind his borrowing her car if she noticed it was missing at all.

They had hidden the car halfway up an abandoned logging trail connecting Thornton Road with a less-trafficked road a mile away. The plan was to be up the hill, down and across Thornton Road, up the trail to the car, and into the village for a quick beer at

Rudy's, well before the people at the farmhouse had pulled themselves together.

After Rudy's they would pick up Robert's car from behind Potter's boathouse. Robert and Ted would be back at Collins House a half hour later.

ⱱ　　ⱱ　　ⱱ

They arrived at the Nash breathing hard from the climb but not tired. The trek had calmed them down. Potter laid the tarp bundle on the floor in the backseat, braced his stiffened arms against the car roof, and began to inhale-exhale rhythmically with his head hung down. The others waited until he was finished. He turned to them and sucked in one more deep breath.

"I think that does it," he said. "For now, anyway. Good shooting. They won't be back."

"Did you see how many?" Ted asked. His voice quavered. "I couldn't believe, all those people?"

"I told you, not people," said Potter. "Just kikes."

ⱱ　　ⱱ　　ⱱ

Below the woodpile in a shadowed cleft buttressed by boulders, Sarah Spray, age twelve, sat with her knees drawn up to her chin, waiting for the noise to be over. She had heard the three men earlier in the day when they dug into the woodpile a few yards above her. She heard the metallic workings of their rifles, heard their muted whisperings, thought she heard a deep voice say "Rattle," "Red right," and "When," and another voice say "Gott and Noah's Ark" as if he were praying. Whenever they had moved forward, bits of leaves and crumbled wood had rained into her hiding place.

When the shooting started Sarah put a finger in each ear and squeezed her head between her knees. While it went on, she hummed a song, a Polish nursery rhyme. When it ended she raised her head and looked down the hill and saw her uncle Carl lying in the dirt at the bottom of the kitchen steps. She had never seen him fallen down before.

After they had moved up the hill, she heard the deep voice say "Shoot to kill." She wondered if Uncle Carl was dead. She twisted around enough to see upward over the boulders and through the woodpile branches. A man was standing high above her in front of a rock splashed with light from the settling sun. His face was shadowed by a bundle he was carrying on his shoulders, a rigid shape wrapped in a brown cloth that hung down at one end like a skirt.

"I will remember you, mister," she whispered. "I will remember you."

Four

used back roads and no lights. After a few miles the excitement of
the shoot faded, and they drove in silence.

"What exactly is a kike?" Ted asked after a while.

"That's what the German Jews call the rest of them," said Potter. "The ones whose last names end with 'ski.' From Russia and
Poland. They don't get along."

"Why not?"

"Different kinds of people. The Germans look sort of American.
They came up here from the city a long time ago, for the summer
and the sanitariums. They behaved themselves. When the kikes
showed up, most of the Germans left."

"How come?"

"Kikes are trash. They're dirty and loud, and they brought the
gangsters in."

"Gangsters?"

"To pay for the resorts. In the twenties they began dumping
their corpses in Swan Lake, and the old German Jews sold out."

"Corpses?"

"Mob killings. Chained to radiators, so they say."

"Where did the Germans go?"

"Saranac, Placid, Saratoga, the Jersey shore. The kikes are taking over here."

"You talk like you hate them."

"It's a war."

∿   ∿   ∿

At the corner table in Rudy's, the letdown set in. Robert and Ted stared at the beer going flat in their glasses. Potter did his best to make conversation.

"Let me ask you, why do you call your grandfather Judge? What I hear, he's just an ordinary lawyer."

Robert and Ted looked up. Potter hardly ever asked about family.

"It's a Collins family tradition, said Robert. "The head of the family is always called Judge. It's Grandfather Martin now. Before Grandfather, it was Matthew. And before him, Ben. Ben came from Dublin. In 1814."

"That early?" said Potter, mildly impressed. "I never knew that."

"My father probably would have been Judge someday if he hadn't died in the war," said Ted. "One day, it might be Robert. Or me."

"Why the interest in Grandfather?" asked Robert. "You never asked before."

"I just haven't seen much of him lately," Potter replied.

"He hasn't been well," said Ted. "He lost a lot of money in '29."

"Who didn't?" said Potter. "The first time I saw your grandfather was at Collins House in 1926. He was with a one-armed lady on your front lawn. I was there watching out for my father. You were next to him, Robert, standing at attention. Ted was on the porch. A little kid."

"I remember," said Robert. "You saluted. That was Sister Thecla. She died a year later, when I was fifteen."

"That was the only time I ever saw the Judge cry," said Ted.

Potter laughed. "I'll never forget her shaking everybody's hands. She was an impressive lady. Shame she had to dress that way."

ψ   ψ   ψ

Driving back to Collins House from Potter's boathouse in Robert's car, Ted said, "I didn't think it would be like that."

Robert did not reply.

"Potter never said there'd be so many kids."

"It was just a warning. Maybe he didn't know about the kids," said Robert.

"I didn't stop. Even after I saw them. I should have stopped."

"You heard Potter. It's a war. It's them or us. We can't let them have Collins House."

ψ   ψ   ψ

The Judge was sitting on the bench at the front door. His grandsons had not expected to see him for another week. He was wearing a red satin robe with black piping and maroon velvet slippers monogrammed MC in gold thread. His white hair was rumpled and he needed a shave, but he looked fully alert. It was after ten o'clock. Ted had his cased Winchester slung on his shoulder. The Springfield was on the floor of the car.

"Good hunting, I hope," Martin said. "It's not season yet, is it?" He smiled, but his eyes were serious. He didn't hunt, himself, anymore.

"Just target practice," said Robert. "We'll be ready when they are."

"It's good to be prepared. I think I heard you sighting Tuesday morning."

His eyes moved to Ted's Winchester, then with concern back to Robert.

"You didn't lose your Remington?"

"It's in your gun cabinet, Judge. You were sleeping. I used Ted's."

"Did you? Just one gun between you? I never let anyone use my guns."

He patted Ted on the shoulder and flicked some leaf fragments off Robert's shirt.

"You'd better brush off," he said. "Your mother catches you looking like that, she'll make you sleep in the barn."

⚜ ⚜ ⚜

Later, after they had hidden the Springfield in the carriage house under a pile of folded canvas and leather trappings, they each had a pull of gin from Robert's pocket flask.

"Lucky he didn't see the Springfield," said Ted.

"Doesn't matter," said Robert. He laughed appreciatively. "He never lets anyone use his guns! The old fox. He knows."

"Knows what?"

"Maybe he heard me in the cellar. And Tuesday, when we were sighting in, he knows what a Springfield sounds like."

"I guess we're in trouble, then," said Ted. He took another swallow of gin. "He came out earlier this time. Maybe he's getting better."

"Maybe the demons weren't as bad," said Robert. "That would be nice."

"I did this mostly for him," said Ted. "He couldn't bear to lose Collins House. Not on top of everything else."

"I did it for all of them," said Robert. "And for us."

He held the silver flask high in both hands. "For all who were, and all who are, and all who will be, *libera nos a malo*."

$\mathcal{F}ive$

ALONG ITS EDGES, THE TOWNSHIP OF Fredericktown encompassed the villages of Chicken Corners, Thunder Mountain, Vandenbergh, and Cooper Place. Two days a week, Wednesday and Thursday, before it got too dark, Charlie Evans, who had been sheriff of Fredericktown for almost six years, ended his day by cruising the roads of one or another of the four villages for about two hours.

This Thursday was Chicken Corners's day and, his tour almost over, Charlie was pointing toward home. He was humming out of tune, thinking about dinner last Sunday with Katy, watching out for sleepy deer, trying to remember what was in the Frigidaire. He had been doing all the home cooking since a hit-and-run driver had killed his father, Jarvis Evans, just before Christmas the previous year.

The Fredericktown Sheriff's Office, like the rest of the country, was short of money and ran on reduced staff. All the equipment was old, and there had been three across-the-board salary cuts and no raises or promotions since 1929. Each of the four villages was supposed to have a full-time constable, but Charlie kept the slot in Chicken Corners vacant. He and Potter Washington, his deputy, both lived in the village, so they split the coverage between them.

Charlie had joined the Fredericktown force in 1927, eleven years earlier. He didn't like being sheriff as much as he had liked being an ordinary cop. At forty he was bored and thinking about a change. He would need a degree in accounting to be considered for the FBI. Maybe the army would take him if they needed commissioned officers for police work and didn't think he was too old. And, of course, he would have to make up his mind about Katy.

He had decided if he didn't run again he would probably let Potter Washington have the sheriff's job. Potter wasn't perfect. He had some personal problems to work out, and he would have to win an election. But he was old family, and with Charlie, the aging football star, out of the way there should be no serious competition.

ψ   ψ   ψ

An hour or so after sunset, having completed the perimeter sweep that threaded back and forth across the Chicken Corners village lines, Charlie made the right turn off Hill Road onto Thornton, a back roads shortcut home.

Six miles from village center, his headlights picked out three of the people who had been in the house at Thornton Farm: a man and a woman with a young girl, about twelve. The man was shirtless; the girl was barefoot. Charlie slowed down, but before he could come to a stop the three of them scrambled through the high weeds lining the road, squirmed through the split-rail fence, and disappeared into a cornfield.

"What the hell was all that?" Charlie asked himself aloud.

Farther down the road two more, both women, showed up in the headlights. He braked the police cruiser, a two-toned 1933 Plymouth with white-and-gold shields stenciled on both front doors, and stuck his head out the window. The women stood still. They were wearing long, light-colored high-necked dresses, and they had kerchiefs on their heads. The smaller of the two looked old.

Charlie opened the cruiser door. They backed away. He pulled his flashlight out from under the seat, turned it on, and hauled himself out of the car. They ran up the road, the younger woman pulling the older one by the arm.

"Hey, wait a minute! Wait!" he yelled.

In the distance beyond them he could see lights at Thornton Farm. He began walking toward the two women, who had been joined in the middle of the road by a bearded man carrying a small child. Charlie felt uneasy leaving the cruiser. His shotgun and other gear were in the trunk. But he did not want to go back to the car and risk losing touch with whatever was going on.

With the cruiser's high beams backlighting him, Charlie realized the people in the road couldn't tell who he was. He shone the flashlight on the silver shield on his shirt, held it there, then moved it up to his face, but only for a moment. Charlie had high Delaware cheekbones and deep-set eyes. He didn't want to spook them.

"It's okay. I'm Sheriff Evans," he called loudly. "*Char*-lie Evans. From Fredericktown. I'm just passing by. Is something wrong? What's going on?"

"Why did you shoot?" the old woman screamed in Yiddish. "Why did you shoot? Why did you shoot?"

"I'm sorry, ma'am. I don't understand what you're saying," Charlie called back. "Please come closer. I need to know what's going on."

More people came out of the shadows. Within minutes there were more than a dozen. A man wearing blue pants and a blue shirt came forward and put his arm around the old woman's shoulders. She continued to chant in Yiddish, "Why did you shoot?" but in a lower, softer voice. Led by the tall man and the old woman, the group moved cautiously toward Charlie, spreading out across the road.

Except for those who stood in his long headlight shadows, the people looked dazzled. They squinted. The old woman cupped her hands around her eyes and shuffled forward, looking down at the ground. When she got close to Charlie she looked up without fear or confidence, saying again in Yiddish, "Why did you shoot?"

"I don't understand you, ma'am."

"She is asking 'Why did you shoot?' " said the man in the blue work clothes. "She does not speak English. Few of them do."

"Why is she talking like that?"

"She is frightened. They are all frightened. I admit, I am frightened, too."

"What does she mean, 'shoot?' Who's shooting? Shooting who?"

"At the house, Officer. It was a while ago. Maybe an hour. Many, many shots. We ran."

More people had come out on the road, and Charlie could sense others gathering behind him. He spoke to the man in blue. "Okay, here's what I want. You tell them what I say. We'll do this together. Tell them all to get behind the car. I'll drive up closer. There's some kind of truck there. With lights on."

"It's a bus," said the man in blue. "I am the driver."

"You're the driver." Charlie had the feeling he was being pulled into this faster than he wanted. "Okay. Tell them to get behind the police car. Then I want you in the car with me. In the back. Down on the floor."

In German, repeated in English, the driver said, "Everyone. This is a policeman. He wants all of you to gather behind his car."

The bus headlights stabbed across Thornton Road and probed dimly into the field beyond. Its interior lights illuminated a large area to the right of the house. There was a car parked in the shadows in front at the left. Charlie thought he knew it. More light came from the downstairs windows and the open front door. He stopped the cruiser a hundred feet from the driveway and dimmed his lights. A baby was crying.

"Are there more people?" he asked the man on the floor behind him.

"Yes. Many."

"Where was the shooting?"

"From outside. In back. At the house."

Why was this man only answering when he was asked? It was like pulling teeth.

"Who was shooting? C'mon, tell me. Fill me in."

"I don't know."

"How long did it last?"

"Only minutes, I think."

"Was anyone hurt?"

"I do not know."

Charlie switched on the swivel spotlight on the roof of the cruiser and played it over the front of the house and as deeply into the surrounding darkness as the beam would go. He did not know what to expect. Maybe the light would start someone shooting again, but he had to do something. He left it focused on the front door.

"This isn't covered by the manual," he said to himself. He had a feeling he was doing this wrong.

"What's your name, mister?"

"August. August Kaufman. One *n*."

"Okay, Mr. Kaufman, it's like this. I can't call for help, because my two-way's busted. I can't *go* for help, because I can't leave these people alone. So the first thing is to find out if anyone's hurt in there."

"I understand."

"Nothing's happened for the past half hour, so I'm guessing whoever it was is gone. I'm going to look around. You stay here. Anything happens, like a shot and I don't come out, or ten minutes pass and I'm still inside, you drive this car straight down that road."

"To where?"

"First right, just past a big rock painted white. Second left, a nice wide road. That'll bring you into the village, about five miles. Any place you see open. Probably a place called Rudy's. Get help.

If nothing happens when I go in, wait until I come out. But no more than ten minutes. Got it?"

"I understand. Shall I find the rest of them? Tell them who you are?"

"No. I need you with me. They'll have to work things out themselves. Here're the keys. Stay in the car. Remember, Rudy's."

֍   ֍   ֍

He thought about the shotgun, but decided that with it or without it if someone in the house wanted to shoot him there was really nothing he could do about it. He took the Smith & Wesson out of the holster because he felt obliged.

"Not proper work for one man," he muttered as he moved forward.

He glanced again at the car in the shadows. He knew that car. The front porch of the house had been pulled down long ago. A thick flat-topped stone was the only step up. A little splashboard projection had been nailed over the entry. Both the main door and the screen door were open. The screen door had been pushed back so far that the spring had stretched around the frame and caught so that it couldn't pull the door closed.

For a minute he thought maybe he should walk around the house first, but he decided that was just loss of nerve pretending to be reason. When he stepped inside the house, a board squeaked and the screen door whipped around and slammed behind him. If the Smith & Wesson had not been on safety, he might have fired at the floor. All told, he was gone seven minutes.

He came out holding the pistol limply at his side. A large crowd was gathered around the cruiser, blocking most of the light. August Kaufman sat inside, not moving.

"Someone is dead, Mr. Kaufman," said Charlie. "On the stairs. She's not one of yours."

He looked down at the pistol, put it away.

"She's one of mine."

※　※　※

The change in Charlie seemed to affect the people behind August. They began murmuring to each other. Charlie held up his hands, and they stopped.

"Her name is Marjorie Bingham. I know her," he said to August. "I don't know what she's doing here or what happened. That's her car in front. She's lying at the bottom of the stairs upside down. I've got to do something different now."

"I should turn off the bus lights. They are weakening," said August. "There is another battery, but it may not be enough."

"Will it start? You can drive into town."

"I do not have the keys. They are not in the bus. Whoever turned the lights on, when the shooting stopped, must have taken them."

"This is crazy," said Charlie. "Who are you people, anyway? Why did that lady say I was shooting? What language was she speaking?"

"It was a kind of Yiddish, sir."

"Charlie. Not sir. I'm the sheriff."

"She speaks Yiddish. Many of them do. It's something like German, with other languages mixed in. I was speaking true German. I do not think she meant *you* were shooting. 'You' to her means the whole world."

"The whole world?"

"She is troubled. They are from the city. I drove them here this morning for some fresh air."

"God, I saw her this morning. Marjorie, I mean. I passed her on Mill Road. She's in real estate. She waved right at me. Big smile."

"Are you certain she is dead?"

"Part of her head is gone. Look, we're going into town. You and me. In the cruiser. I can't leave you here. Tell them to stay where they are until we get back. I know that's hard, with the kids and all. But no one goes into the house."

He paused pensively.

"I need to see your license and registration, please. Just procedure."

☙ ☙ ☙

A mile down the road, they met Potter Washington driving the deputy cruiser.

"What's going on, Charlie?" Potter asked. "Someone heard shots and called the desk. They couldn't get you or me, so they called my mother."

"My two-way's broke again. It's Marjorie Bingham," said Charlie. "At the old Thornton house. She's your cousin, isn't she?"

"What about Marjorie?" asked Potter.

He turned to stare at August Kaufman, who was sitting up front in the cruiser.

"She's dead, Potter. Someone shot her. This is August Kaufman. He drives the bus."

August opened the cruiser door.

"You stay inside, feller. You just stay there," snarled Potter with his hand on his holster.

"Easy, Potter. He's fine," said Charlie

Potter deflated.

"I guess we go back there, huh?" he said. "You lead, Charlie. I'll follow."

When they got to the farmhouse, the door was still open, the lights were still on. Marjorie was head-down at the bottom of the staircase, but the bus and the people were gone.

Six

BEFORE THEY HEADED BACK, CHARLIE called in on Potter's two-way and released the overlap night shift. It was after eleven. His secretary, Rose Vanderhoff, said she'd wait around until they got back. August rode in Charlie's cruiser, up front.

Charlie wanted to hold off questioning August until morning, but Potter was insistent.

"Tomorrow's too late," he pleaded. "I need to know what happened. Marjorie was family. Tomorrow I'll have to tell my mother something."

"Okay," Charlie said, "but you go easy with this guy. He's our only witness. All we know he did was drive the bus."

"That's what he says. But don't worry. He's a Jew. I understand these people."

"That's what makes me worry," said Charlie.

Rose had put August in Potter's office with a diner sandwich, cole slaw, and coffee, and showed him where the john was and how to use the phone. August called the Kaufmann depot in Long

Island City, where he knew his father would be anxiously waiting. He told him about the missing bus and promised to come down by train the next day. Following Potter's instructions, he said very little about the shooting. He did say that the police might call later that night or in the morning. Potter monitored the call at the switchboard.

August was seated behind Potter's desk when Charlie, Potter, and Rose came in. He stood up.

"No, stay right there," said Potter. "That's the best chair in the house."

August sat back down.

"I know it's late," said Potter, "but we need a few answers. We'll put you up tonight at The Coach and Anvil at town expense. Great blueberry pancakes. If all goes well, you can head home in the morning."

"I will look forward," said August.

"When we're finished talking, I'll call your father," said Potter. "He owns the company, right? Buses."

"He and the investors. We have four buses and seven limousines. We do trains, the airport, restaurants. Also, theaters, weddings, religious gatherings, occasions like that. Mostly in the city."

"Chicken Corners is a long way from the city," said Potter, raising his eyebrows.

"Does that mean I am suspected?" August asked in a soft, flat voice.

"No," said Charlie. "He didn't mean it that way."

"We have some distance contracts. To New Jersey, Rhode Island. Some resorts and sanitariums up here. Even in Chicken Corners, cars sometimes for Mr. Collins when he has important guests."

"*Martin* Collins?" asked Charlie. "You know him?"

"Once I helped him to change a tire. He and my father are now good friends. He has invested in our company."

"Small world," said Potter. "Getting crowded. Jacob Kaufmann, right? Two n's."

"My father attached the second *n* at the immigration. To be fancy," August explained. "I took it off again, to be more American."

"Nothing to be ashamed of," said Potter. "Lots of Jews change their names."

Charlie interrupted. "Why don't you just tell us what happened," he said.

"Start with a little more about Kaufmann Tours," said Potter.

ψ   ψ   ψ

The family had come over from Germany just before the 1914 war. August was an only child. Jacob started the company with a used van in 1923.

Kaufmann Tours had grown into a small-to-medium-sized operation. Even with the economy badly depressed, the business was getting by. The office was on East Third Street in Manhattan. They kept the idle buses and cars in a fenced lot on the Queens side of the Fifty-ninth Street Bridge.

The run to Chicken Corners was part of a new summer contract. Except for Martin Collins, it was not Kaufmann's usual kind of business, or their usual kind of passengers. Jews on the Lower East Side didn't ordinarily order limousines and tour buses. The few that had that kind of money didn't need Kaufmann.

The client was a referral, a new neighborhood organization, the Shofar Foundation. The East Side was even more overcrowded than usual. Refugees were pouring in from Eastern Europe and Russia. The poorer Jews from Germany were following the rich who left earlier. Summers in the tenements were always bad. This year they were unbearable. The Shofar Foundation was offering some relief.

Beginning in late June, Kaufmann's had averaged two runs a week for the Shofar account, big and little buses, on Thursdays and Sundays, almost all of them into Sullivan County, mostly north and west of Monticello. Destinations varied, but they were always old houses like the one on Thornton Road, places that the foundation had fixed up quickly. No luxury and still crowded, but cool and out in the country. They gave a few days away from the pavement. Places where children could play safely, where maybe they could see a cow.

"Tell us what happened at Thornton farm," said Charlie.

⚜   ⚜   ⚜

Ordinarily August would not have been the driver, but the man who was supposed to do the run had called in sick. August had picked up his thirty-eight passengers—six men, eleven women, and twenty-one children—in the parking lot next to the synagogue on Mott Street at 10:00 A.M. on Thursday. Six of the children were babies. He had names for all the adults, but no addresses. The synagogue wasn't involved in the contract. Its parking lot was handy.

The men passengers carried identical suitcases, heavy black cardboard with copper rivets and black metal corners. The suitcases looked brand-new.

All of those waiting for the bus that morning were recent arrivals from Europe, a mixture of country and city people. Few spoke any English. They were standing in clusters, and the groups didn't seem to know one another. The foundation had put the busload together, picking families from this building and that, using its own rules of selection. The people were talking quietly when August drove up, the men standing close to their women. When they boarded, conversation became muted.

On the bus they sat men on one side, women on the other. The women had food wrapped in newspapers, but they did not offer any to August. They would not acknowledge his presence until the men gave approval. Two of the babies cried most of the time. The bus was two-thirds full. They stopped once at a big roadhouse to use the rest rooms, but not to eat because the food was not kosher. The manager ordered them away.

"You didn't talk to your passengers?" Potter asked.

"You must understand," said August. "These people do not easily trust strangers. On the outside they were not friendly, even to each other, and I was to them an American and a stranger."

"You, an American?" Potter asked.

"An American from Germany. Some of them knew German. I learned this later. They understood what I said, but they were not ready to talk. They needed time. They are foreigners. Everyone comes from somewhere else."

Potter grinned.

"Everyone but the sheriff," he said. "His folks have been up here from the beginning of time."

ψ   ψ   ψ

August showed Charlie and Potter a hand-drawn map he had used to get to the farmhouse.

"Who drew it?" Potter asked.

"Carl," said August. "Carl Rozkopf. I was to meet him at the house."

They let the name pass for the moment.

The bus had arrived a little after four. There were another twenty people already there. Some of them knew some of his passengers. The newcomers were shown around, but no one seemed to be in charge.

"Did you see Mrs. Bingham?" asked Potter. "A pretty blonde. She would have stood out in that crowd."

"No, I saw only Jewish blondes," said August.

Nor had he noticed her car. He thought it was not there when the bus arrived, but perhaps it was. He could not be sure.

An outdoor meal was set up in back of the house on oilcloth-covered tables made from wooden sawhorses and old floorboards from the barn. The mood became friendlier. The men decided to accept August. It was now a big joke, not feeding him on the bus. They asked him to join them. The food was very good. They passed around a bottle of plum brandy wrapped in a paper bag. The women pretended not to notice. No one drank too much. Everyone became relaxed. The younger children chased each other around. The older ones explored the barn. While they were still eating in back, around six, August heard a car come to the front of the house.

"Did you see it?" Charlie asked.

He only heard the tires on the gravel and the car door slam. Someone may have gone inside. He thought he remembered hearing the screen door slap shut. He could not be sure. He was playing word games with some of the children. They thought his German was funny. They wanted to know the English words for things. One boy, ten or eleven, sang little bits of songs. August translated the words into English and sang them back to him.

When August finished eating and playing, he went inside. It was beginning to get dark. He was looking for a man named Carl Rozkopf from the foundation who was to tell him if anyone was to go back to the city that night. He had asked for Mr. Rozkopf earlier and had been told that he was upstairs, busy.

"He was the guy you said drew the map. He was upstairs with Mrs. Bingham?" Potter asked.

"Yes, the one who drew the map. I do not know with whom he was."

"So you never met this Rozkopf before?"

No, but he had heard the name from his father. He went inside the house to look. Inside it was strange. Seven rooms had been made into bedrooms with mattresses covering the floors. Women and children were upstairs, men down, married or not. The black cardboard suitcases were stacked against the walls. It was neat and clean with sheets on the mattresses, but the people were packed tight. Army-style woolen blankets were folded on each mattress, but there were no pillows. Men and some older boys were sitting on the mattresses with their backs against the walls. A few were lying down. There was no place inside to sit formally except on some chairs in the kitchen or on the stairs.

Through the railings at the top of the stairs he had looked quickly into two of the second-floor bedrooms. He saw women and children. The upstairs lighting was poor; kerosene lamps, standing on the floor and hanging from hooks. The door to one of the rooms in back was closed. A cardboard sign tacked on it read Private. He did not go all the way up. He did not want the men to think he was spying on the women.

"Get to the shooting," said Potter.

August was back in the kitchen when the shooting started. He had just located Carl Rozkopf, a big man, well over 250 pounds, wearing a white shirt, standing by the stove. The shots came from the back. He was sure of that. Everyone froze, shocked. No one moved until the second shot. Then they moved in all directions. Some just fell down. Rozkopf began to roar, like a lion in a cage. He charged through the screen door, still roaring, as if he were attacking. Some of the others followed him.

August stayed where he was, trying to understand what was happening.

"The shooting was not so much, but steady. Very disciplined. It lasted only minutes."

Some of the bullets went right above his head. He did not remember being frightened then. He was frightened later. He remembered one part of his mind questioning why he was standing straight up. He bent over and went into the front room, still very calm. Once the room must have been the dining room. A bare lightbulb hung on a cord from the ceiling. He saw two of the children he had been playing word games with. They were clinging to two of the women, who were sitting in the corner with their legs under them. He told everyone to lie down. They stretched out on the rows of mattresses along the front and side walls. He stayed beside them until the shooting stopped. There was a large picture of a swan hanging above his head. It bounced each time a bullet came through the wall.

"You can skip the swan stuff," said Potter.

"Let him tell it his way," said Charlie.

When the shooting was over he waited a few minutes, then went out the front door. He had not looked back at the stairs. He could not say whether a woman had been lying there. There was a car parked on the right. He wandered around, calling out, trying to calm people down, trying to coax them out of the fields and the hedges, not sure what to do next. Then he saw the car lights. He walked forward and put his arm around a woman who was screaming words in Yiddish, and that was when he met Sheriff Evans.

"You went out the front door, right?" asked Potter. "Past the stairs. Did you see her there?"

"It was dark in the hallway. I saw nothing."

"Jesus! A body probably right there, and you didn't see it? How about cars?"

"Only the one you say was hers."

"How about the one you heard earlier? The door slamming?"

August shrugged his shoulders. *What do you expect of me?*

ψ   ψ   ψ

Charlie explained that Rose would try to have a typed-up draft of her notes ready the next morning so that August could read and okay an official transcript before he left for the city.

"We'll want to see that passenger list before you leave," said Potter.

"I left the list on the bus," said August. "It is gone."

Potter stood up, looked first at Charlie, then at August with disgust.

"Enjoy the pancakes," he said. "I'll be here all night."

Seven

CHARLIE WAS IN AT SEVEN FRIDAY MORN-
ing, two hours early. Rose was already at work on August's transcript.

"Have someone drive him to the train after he signs it," Charlie
told her. "I'll be with Potter."

Potter was shaven, but his face was puffy and he looked tired.

"The city police found the missing bus this morning," he told
Charlie. "On the Lower East Side. Next to a hydrant one block
from Kaufmann Tours. Nothing in it. Especially no passenger list.
Just garbage."

"There's a flock of reporters outside," said Charlie, shrug-
ging. "Tell the desk man to hold them off a few hours till I get
caught up."

※   ※   ※

At eleven-thirty Potter found room for seven reporters in his
tiny office, two stringers with city papers, the *World-Telegram &*
Sun and *The Daily Mirror*, a stringer with United Press, and staffers
from *The Sullivan County Courier*, the *Monticello Sentinel*, and the
Fredericktown Flame.

Charlie's girlfriend, Katy Bower, was covering for *This Month*. Potter didn't consider Katy a real reporter because *This Month* was just a local monthly, and she was its only full-time employee. Besides, being so close to Charlie, he assumed she wasn't a problem.

Charlie sat quietly in a corner behind Potter's desk, watching his deputy at work. The investigative squad on the Fredericktown force consisted of three detectives, all the same class. On paper all three reported to Charlie. But little by little Charlie was letting Potter take over. He figured that as long as Potter wanted to be the next sheriff he should be given a chance to show his stuff.

☙ ☙ ☙

"I went out there this morning," the UP stringer complained. "To that farmhouse. Your people wouldn't let me in."

"We're still going over the scene with county," said Potter. "I'll arrange something for you tomorrow. For now, let's follow procedure. First time you ask a question, please identify yourself."

He knew most of their names, but the manual said with interviews to take control early.

"O'Donnell, UP. What will I see tomorrow?"

"A battlefield. Whoever it was really shot the place up. Last night, in the dark, we couldn't count all the holes."

"Fabian, *Daily Mirror*. What about the lady they killed?"

"Marjorie Bingham," Potter snapped. "Real estate broker, part-time records clerk for the township, thirty-five. Gunshot wounds to the back of the head. Never felt a thing."

Abruptly he stopped talking, lowered his head, and closed his eyes. Charlie leaned slightly forward, not wanting to interfere unless he had to. A dozen seconds passed. The eyes opened and Potter sat up straight, in charge again.

"Perpetrator unknown. Motive unknown. Her presence there unexplained. Medical examiner's report should be out soon. Her car was parked in front. She had the keys, so we're assuming she drove it. It was unlocked. No car thieves in Chicken Corners."

"Just lady killers," said *The Daily Mirror*, not looking up from his notes.

"Katy Bower, *This Month*."

"I didn't mean you, Katy," said Potter. "You're one of us."

The Daily Mirror grinned. Katy winced.

"She was related to you, wasn't she, Mr. Washington?" she asked.

"That's getting into the personal, Katy," said Potter. "You folks want to talk *personal*, put the pencils away."

They went through the motions.

"Yeah, we were related. Marjorie's mother's mother was my mother's mother's sister," he said, then smiled at the blank looks on their faces.

"Or, to make it simple, *my* maternal grandmother, Prudence Fletcher Babcock, was *her* maternal grandmother's sister. *Her* name was Ann Fletcher Tuttle. That made Marjorie and me second cousins."

"Thanks," said *The Daily Mirror*, "You make it sound like something I could learn. So she was from around here?"

"Chicken Corners. Good family. Her maiden name was Jones. A good name in these parts if it's from the right line. Her mother was a Tuttle. Her father's mother was a Fauconnier, and there was an Evans in that line way back."

He paused.

"I believe there was a Bridges somewhere on the Jones side. Maybe even a Livingston."

"Married? Kids?"

"She married Wallace Bingham, a banker. Not from around here, but good family, too, far as I know. He died a while back. No children. Nothing wrong with Marjorie's background anywhere."

There was a moment of uncomfortable silence.

"You sure know your family trees, Sheriff. Tommy Thompson, *The Courier.*"

Potter glanced sideways at Charlie and smiled.

"Thanks, but just deputy for now," he said. "Family history is a hobby of mine."

"You said Evans," said Katy. "Does that mean Marjorie was related to Sheriff Evans, too?" It seemed odd to Katy, Charlie sitting right there in the corner and no one even asking who he was.

"Could be," said Potter. "Aren't we all?"

ᔕ   ᔕ   ᔕ

Marjorie Jones accepted Wallace Bingham's proposal of marriage when she was twenty-six and he was forty-four. Relatives and friends were glad for her. Another few years, it was understood, and her chances of making a good match would quickly fade away.

"True, he is quite a bit older, but sometimes that's for the best," said Ginnie Washington, Potter's mother. "His prospects are excellent. And, Lord knows, her folks can use a leg up. Poor as church mice."

Marjorie was Ginnie's first cousin, once removed.

Wallace had transferred to the Fredericktown branch of State-wide Savings & Loan assured that he would be a vice-president and director in five years or less. He died of a heart attack judging a three-legged race at the Congregational church's summer outing at the age of forty-eight.

Wallace left seven thousand dollars in savings, enough insurance to bury him, and a medium-sized mortgage on a small house not far from the Washington estate in Chicken Corners.

"Now we'll find out what she's made of," Ginnie Washington announced.

Having no previous business experience and no office skills, Marjorie decided on real estate and discovered she was good at it.

Wallace's colleagues at the bank provided estate tips and referrals, and a number of his old friends, bank people from the city and around the state, stayed in touch.

"You're still an attractive woman," Ginnie Washington told her. "Keep your eyes open and your war paint on. You don't want to work all your life."

Marjorie liked working more than she had liked marriage. Her real estate commissions and the small salary she got for helping with tax assessment and land records kept her going.

"Pulled her socks up. Good blood always shows," Ginnie said. "Fletcher and Jones, not Tuttle."

ψ　　ψ　　ψ

"What about witnesses?" asked *The Daily Mirror*. "I hear you let about a hundred get away."

"That was me did that," said Charlie from the corner. "It was closer to fifty."

"And who may you be?"

"I'm Charlie Evans, the sheriff. You're a stranger, so you're excused for not knowing."

"He likes to listen in when I'm with the press," said Potter, grinning. "And he didn't let anyone get away. His two-way was busted. He couldn't know I was coming. I wouldn't be happy reading anything about witnesses getting away."

The reporter smiled.

"Then why not tell us what really happened?"

"Just between the two of us, I wish to God I knew," said Potter. "That's it for today."

ψ　　ψ　　ψ

When the conference ended, Charlie and Katy went back to his office. Potter stayed at his desk, staring at nothing. He still had trouble believing it. He and the boys had placed each shot with so much care. He tried to imagine Marjorie inside while the firing was going on. It must have been awful. What was she doing in there? None of them had aimed anywhere near the stairs, but bullets sometimes bounce. He wondered which of them had hit her.

Potter's mother had been up and awake when he got home from Rudy's. She had given him the desk complaint about the noise at the Thornton place, and he had decided to drive back out there. It would strengthen his story that he had been on the road beyond radio range when the shooting happened.

He had been all right with the reporters, but now, sitting alone at his desk, he felt like his head was bound in strips of lead. He still hadn't told his mother about Marjorie. The two women had been very close. They'd often had tea together. He would have to call her. If she heard it from anywhere else, she would be that much more upset.

As he sat staring at his phone, the phone in Charlie's office rang. Minutes later Charlie opened the door and came in. Katy stood behind him in the doorway.

"It's polite to knock," said Potter.

"It isn't what we thought, Potter," Charlie said. "That was the medical examiner. Marjorie was killed by three small-caliber bullets, probably twenty-twos. The killer wasn't on the hill. He was inside."

Potter looked at Charlie a long time without expression. Then, to Charlie's amazement, he smiled.

ψ   ψ   ψ

Mary heard about Marjorie Bingham Friday morning on the seven o'clock news. She mentioned it to Ted when he came down at eight. When Robert arrived, he and Ted went outside for some air.

"She's got all the party-line gossip, too," said Ted. "They found

Mrs. Bingham on the front stairs. That's where I was aiming, so it must have been me. It couldn't have been you."

He sounded shaky.

"Don't think like that," said Robert. "We don't know where she was when she was hit. The chimney is probably next to the stairs. One of mine could have ricocheted, hit a pipe."

"I sort of knew something bad had to happen," said Ted. "Now it has."

"It could have been any of us. We don't know where Potter was aiming. Besides, it was an accident."

They had almost finished breakfast when Martin came into the kitchen. Mary was more surprised than they were. He wasn't due out for a while.

"Good morning," he said. "Hope I'm not too late."

When no one responded, he asked, "Why all the looks?"

Flustered, because no one ever talked openly about the Judge's drinking problem, Mary turned up the volume on the shelf radio. The news was being repeated.

". . . on Thornton Road, riddled with bullets," the announcer was saying. "The body was identified as that of Marjorie Bingham, a prominent real estate broker and long-time resident of Chicken Corners. An official statement is promised later today."

"Dear God. Marjorie," Martin muttered.

He turned to his grandsons, who were staring at their plates.

"I hope you've left me some of that coffee," he said. "I'll need a pot of it today."

Eight

LATE ON SATURDAY MORNING MARTIN met Rose Vanderhoff at the Imperial Diner in Fredericktown. Martin had been seeing Rose's mother, Hilda, for almost a year after Clara died. Before it had enough time to become serious, Hilda had sickened and died, too. Martin and Jarvis Evans had stood on either side of Rose at the graveside, and together they had helped her put her life back in order. No one in town would be very surprised to see Rose and Martin having a late breakfast together.

The diner was art deco, all curled chrome and black enamel. They sat in a back booth. At fifty-two Rose was a pretty woman, almost still a pretty girl, with a milkmaid's skin and electric blue eyes. She had never married. She thought Martin was the nicest man in the world. He fit her notions of a father, a husband, a lover, or just a best friend. With so much to imagine, she was never quite sure how to act with him. Lately she had tried flirting, and he seemed to enjoy it. So did she. It made things easier.

Rose ordered the full breakfast with hollandaise sauce. Martin settled for English muffins, toasted, no butter. He needed two hands to lift his coffee cup to his mouth.

"Mom used to recommend a bit of the hair," said Rose. She recognized the symptoms.

"A wise and wonderful woman, your mother. But that's not the right remedy this time, love."

"If mom had lived? . . ."

"Then you might be my stepdaughter, and we'd have to behave ourselves."

"But I'm not, and we're both single, and we can behave however we please."

He took a long sip.

"Ah, to be sixty again!"

"Stop talking old. You're the best-looking man in town, and you know it."

The English muffin tasted surprisingly good. He managed a second cup of coffee one-handed and got to the point.

"The boys are in some kind of trouble. One of the Springfields the division gave me to mind isn't in its box. So, before I lose my mind entirely, can you tell me what's going on around here?"

Rose always knew what was going on. She passed a manila envelope under the table.

"They questioned August Kaufman, Jacob's boy, Thursday night. A copy of the transcript's in the envelope. The medical prelim is in there, too. She wasn't shot with a rifle, Martin, if that makes you feel any better."

"Half my worries are over," he said, sliding the envelope into his side pocket, "but the half remaining will keep me awake at night."

"I wish I could help. Potter's acting peculiar. I think Charlie's worried."

The early luncheon crowd was beginning to fill the booths around them.

"If Charlie's worried, there's got to be good reason," said Martin. "It sounds like there's work to do."

He put two quarters on the table and picked up the check.

"Sometimes it helps to visit Edmund," he said. "Will you come along?"

THAN THAT HE LAY DOWN HIS LIFE
FOR HIS FRIEND

Martin sat on the stone bench, reading the papers Rose had passed to him in the diner. August and Jacob were old friends. But Carl Rozkopf was an unfamiliar name. And he could not imagine the Marjorie Bingham he had known in the company of any of them.

Rose had placed a little bouquet of wildflowers at the base of the memorial and stood silently before it. Martin knew she was saying a prayer for Captain Edmund Collins. He wondered if that was proper, if that was what memorials were for. When he came here, he talked with Edmund. He never thought of praying.

"Once upon a time I could call back all of Edmund's faces," he said, loud enough for Rose to hear. "From when he was a baby to the day he went away. All I had to do was close my eyes. All his voices, all his smiles."

Rose turned to look at him.

"Now it's hard to see him for more than a second."

She came and kissed him gently on top of the head.

"Those two are Edmund's boys, Rose. He left them with me, and I didn't give them the attention they deserved. Another of my failures. I'll need your help."

"I know," she said. "I know."

Back at Collins House, Martin split a pile of kindling with a hatchet on a loose stump behind the woodshed. When he was sweating and the blood was flowing strong again, he walked back to Collins House, leaving the wood pieces scattered for the boys to pick up and put away. With the setting sun at his back, he thought about Robert's faces, about the box of Springfields, and about Mary, who would pay no attention to any of this until it slipped like a star from the sky. He would give anything to keep them safe.

Back in his den he read a bit of Yeats.

> And may departing twilight keep
> All dread afar till morning's back
> That his mother may not lack
> Her fill of sleep.

He would wait until something else happened, he decided. It always did.

ψ   ψ   ψ

Later that afternoon the telephone wall box in the foyer rang four times, the Collins's call number. Martin reached it first. Mary was weeding in the herb garden. The boys were still not back from their hike.

If anyone but Martin had answered, Jacob would have hung up.

"Martin," he said, "forgive me. I hope you are feeling well. I am loath to disturb you, but I do not know where else to turn."

"This is a party line, my friend," said Martin. "We may have an attentive audience. Let me do the talking. I'm glad you called. I'm feeling just fine. Is August all right?"

"He is fine. He came home yesterday. But he is upset still."

"Understandably. I know something about your problem, but I need to know more. We should talk face-to-face. Would it help if I came to your office?"

"Martin, that is so much to ask, but I would be grateful. There were others at the farm. A man is here with me now. They are looking for him. And there is a child."

"Enough, my friend. I will take a morning train and be with

you tomorrow afternoon at four. There's no staff at the city house this week. Would you make a reservation for me in the Village? There is a little hotel on Waverly Place called the Baronet. They know what I like."

"Of course. It will be done. Thank you, Martin. I am grateful. I look forward."

"As I do, my friend. Good-bye."

He replaced the earpiece on the side of the wall box and stood in silence, studying the telephone, trying to remember if he had spoken Jacob's name. He didn't think so. There were six other parties on the line, each with its own number of rings. People were supposed to pick up only when it rang for them. Trust versus temptation.

The thoughts ran around in his head. *A lawyer needs privacy, even an old one who doesn't practice anymore. Would Jacob be so grateful if he knew where I stand? Right now I may know more about all this than anyone, except whoever did it. If it comes to choosing between friends and family, whom will I defend?*

Someone shot at the Jews. Marjorie Bingham is dead. Jacob and August are involved somehow. And so are the boys.

Ah, Jacob, he thought, *you can turn to me, but where in God's name do I turn?*

Nine

SHORTLY AFTER MARTIN LEFT COLLINS
House to meet Rose, Robert drifted over to the carriage house.
Ted followed a few minutes later. It was not a safe place to keep
the Springfield. They couldn't put it back in the gun box all cleaned
up where someone might find it. They would have to get rid of
it and take their chances with the Judge.

"We'll hike up to the Slide this afternoon and drop it off the
bluff," Robert said. "The lake's supposed to be bottomless there."

From the top of the Slide the view of Lake Repose stretched
southward unobstructed, the surface of the water changing from
black to blue to almost white as far as Robert and Ted could see.
They sat on the upper edge of the smooth slope, their canvas
knapsacks low on their backs, hugging their knees the way they
had when they were boys.

"Remember on Potter's boat, his asking if the lake was *really*
bottomless, how come all the water didn't run out?" Ted remi-
nisced. "That was the first day he taught us to sail."

"Except for him, I wouldn't know anything," said Robert. "Not
how to camp or hunt or play tennis. Not even how to tie a decent
knot."

"The stuff Dad would have taught us," said Ted.

He picked up the Springfield and sidled down the burnished surface to the point where it got too steep to go farther. Bracing himself, he held the rifle at the muzzle, whirled it twice around his head, and let it go. It hit butt-end on an overhanging boulder near the bottom, sprang into the air, and splashed cleanly into the lake below.

"He was okay," Ted said when Robert had climbed back up. "Potter, I mean. Wasn't he?"

"I suppose so," said Robert, breathing hard. "He was all there was."

♦   ♦   ♦

On a Saturday morning early in the summer of 1927, Potter and Robert were standing in line at the counter in Rudy's Country Store. It was the first time Potter had seen the boy since the Kluxers had burned the cross at Collins House the previous year.

"Good morning," he said cautiously. "You're Bobby Collins aren't you?"

Robert knew who Potter was, from the post office in Chicken Corners. He replied politely but firmly.

"My name is *Robert*, Mr. Washington. I don't like the nickname."

"I apologize," said Potter. "My first name is Potter. I don't care for mine either."

Robert wondered only an instant what he meant. Then he grinned.

"Pleased to meet you, *Potter*," he said, and they shook hands.

"I've been working on the boat. Ran out of spar varnish," Potter explained. "Do you and your brother sail?"

♦   ♦   ♦

On Independence Day in 1930, a drizzly gray morning, Potter found Robert standing alone in front of the Chicken Corners war memorial. Robert was seventeen. A token parade, a salute to the flag, and some speech making by the first selectmen were scheduled for later in the day.

During the night someone had smeared the word *merde* in brownish yellow paint on the bronze plaque, defacing the list of Chicken Corners's war dead.

"My father's name is on there, Potter," said Robert.

Potter heard an anger he had not heard before.

"I know," he said. "He was a fine man, Captain Collins. We were proud of him."

"Some people said it didn't belong there, because we're summer people. But we made them change their minds. The American Legion said he had a right, and Governor Smith sent a letter, so they put it on. Whoever painted that word went right over it."

"A damn shame," said Potter.

"You're a policeman now, Potter. Can you find out who it was?"

"I don't have to, Robert."

"Why not?"

"I already know."

"Will you arrest him?"

"I can't prove it."

"That's not right," said Robert. "Tell me who it is. I'll fix him."

"You meet me here at eight tonight," said Potter, "and we'll do something about it together."

         ᛉ   ᛉ   ᛉ

At eight-thirty Potter and Robert were parked in a tractor slot near the gravel pits on the far side of the lake.

"He's younger than you, fourteen or fifteen, and he's half-wild," said Potter. "He doesn't go to school. He and his mother are squatting on my family's land."

"That French kid?"

"That's him. A half-breed. He'll get in serious trouble someday if he isn't straightened out. They're mixed bloods from Maine. Drifters who came down from Quebec."

⚓   ⚓   ⚓

Antoine du Sault lived with his mother and sometimes his older sister in a derelict house trailer set on cinder blocks near the B & W gravel pits on the eastern side of Lake Repose. They had moved in without notice in the spring after the pits had been shut down.

Antoine's mother roamed around the area in a battered Lincoln hearse with satin window curtains. It belched thick black smoke. Antoine made do with a size-fourteen girl's bicycle with no fenders. When he tried to get a job delivering for Rudy's, Rudy Jr. had said no-and-don't-come-back-you-little-thief.

Mrs. du Sault was rarely at the trailer, but she saw to it that there was always enough food and water. Her men friends stopped by to make sure the kerosene stove was working properly, to fill the gasoline drum out back, and to check on Antoine. Being part Indian and a reject made Antoine interesting to Charlie Evans. Canadian Mohawk, he figured, or maybe Abenakis. Charlie came by a half dozen times but never found anyone at home.

In September the county planned to put Antoine in a foster home. If somebody could catch him.

⚓   ⚓   ⚓

"A scare will do him good," said Potter.

He handed Robert a cotton sack with cutout eyes.

"Put this on like I'm doing and don't talk. If he puts up a fight,

I'll hold him still while you tape his eyes. Come in behind me when I get the door open."

Antoine didn't fight. He crouched in the corner, burrowed into a pile of blankets, blinking at Potter's flashlight. He wore only a pair of khaki shorts. No shirt, no shoes or socks. The trailer was hot and damp.

Potter cradled a shotgun under his left arm and clutched a cut-down buggy whip in his left hand.

"He's seen enough," he said as Robert wrapped two-inch cloth tape around the boy's head. "Get him outside."

He spoke in a deep, theatrical voice, spacing the words out dramatically. Outside, the night air was damp and cool.

"You shouldn't have done that, Frenchy," he said.

"Done what?" said the boy.

"Don't lie. And keep your hands down. You want to find out how a buggy whip feels?"

"Leave me alone," the boy said.

"The war memorial. We know it was you."

He began to slice the whip through the air.

"Hear that? Know how it feels? Answer me."

"Yes. I mean, I hear."

Potter snapped the whip once across the boy's back. The boy screamed and began to shake.

"Don't, don't, don't!" he said.

"Listen, you little tramp. Tomorrow morning you pedal over to the Evans's house on Farragut. You ask whoever's there for some turpentine and a stiff brush and some rags. You tell what you did and say that you're sorry. And then you clean it. Like new. Say anything about what happened here and I'll come back and burn this rat's nest down. With you and your mother inside."

The whip began hissing again.

"Okay." The boy was starting to cry. "I will. I will."

"Okay what?"

"Okay, sir."

"Now the second thing. I'd like a little song."

The boy snuffled.

"You know 'My Country 'Tis of Thee'?"

"Yes, sir," said Antoine. He could barely talk.

"Then sing it."

The whip hissed.

" 'My country 'tis of thee, sweet land of liberty . . . ,' " he sang.

" 'Of thee I sing,' " said Potter.

" ' . . . of thee I sing.' "

Ten

THE TEN O'CLOCK WAS THE SUNDAY FULL service at the Fredericktown Congregational Church that the best people in town went to. There was always room for them.

The building had the stark feel of a classic American church: a box filled with light, lines that pulled the eyes up, anchored to earth. Potter sat in the second pew on the right side where the Babcocks, followed by the Washingtons, had been sitting for more than ninety years. His mother, Ginnie, sat beside him. The church was full to overflowing. All the regulars and a high percentage of occasionals had come to hear what the Reverend Thomas A. Dalton would have to say about the passing of Marjorie Bingham.

The service was routine, and Reverend Dalton's sermon, "What He Expects of Us," was bland. When he had finished the weekly announcements, he folded his hands on the pulpit, hunched forward, and fixed his eyes on the congregation for a long time.

"This is very painful for me," he finally said.

"Five years ago, when Wallace Bingham fell dying in the field behind this church, I was among the first to reach his side. It was a beautiful summer day. His eyes were open. He was moving his lips, but he could not speak. I felt I knew what he wanted to say. Of course, he wanted to say, 'Help me!' as all of us will someday.

"He wanted to say, 'Take care of the children.' The little ones were circled around us, their eyes like saucers. He had been judging their games only moments before.

"He wanted to say, 'I am ready, Lord!' as we all hope to be. He wanted to say, 'Take care of Marjorie!' He wanted to say 'Good-bye' to all of you.

"Now Marjorie is also gone, without a chance of her own to say good-bye, and we must mourn for her."

What a senseless loss, thought Potter. *Who did this to you, Marjorie?*

"When Wallace died, I prayed as much for Marjorie as I prayed for her husband," the reverend continued. "I'm sure many of you did the same. A young widow, so fragile, so vulnerable. We feared she might be overwhelmed. But Marjorie surprised us. She emerged from her grief strengthened. She rose among us filled with purpose and ability, determined that tragedy would not hold her down."

I will miss you, thought Ginnie Washington. *You were so strong. I wanted you for Potter. He needs a wife. He needs a son. And now it is too late. Good-bye. Good-bye.*

"She was a model," said the reverend. "She showed us what virtue and determination can accomplish. There is much to learn from her example. Surrounded by evil and misfortune, He was her salvation, as He can be ours."

What were you doing in there, Marjorie? Potter wondered, his eyes suddenly brimming with tears. *Mixing with all those awful people? Why?*

Eleven

EARLY SUNDAY MORNING MARTIN DROVE the '34 Chrysler Airflow over to the town of Callicoon on the east bank of the Delaware River. He parked the car behind the Western Hotel where he knew it would be safe overnight. The Western was a stately Victorian building with a columned veranda, a widow's walk, a mansard roof, and an ornate dining room. He and Clara had celebrated their thirty-seventh wedding anniversary there in 1922. It was a place he sometimes went to by himself to ponder their last good-bye.

He caught the early morning express to New York.

He was feeling almost back in form but tired. Alone in the plush parlor car, he ordered the complete English breakfast and nodded off between Parker's Glen and Pond Eddy while awaiting his third cup of coffee. The white-jacketed waiter, Bill Campbell, an old friend, quietly cleared and removed the table, gently tipped the lounge chair back, and covered Martin with a light wool blanket. Hours later he woke him with a velvety "Here we are, Judge!" as the train neared the Lackawanna Depot in Hoboken, New Jersey.

Because the air was unusually cool and he was not weighed down with luggage, and because he had been looking forward to a leisurely stroll through the Village, Martin chose the smaller, slower Christopher Street Ferry for the ride across the Hudson. He arrived at Waverly Place at five to one.

ψ   ψ   ψ

The Baronet was a small, tightly run hostelry on the north side of Waverly Place, just west of Washington Square Park. It had been a favorite no-questions-asked hideaway for politicians and theater people around the turn of the century. As Martin was signing the register, he caught himself recalling breakfast with Rose the day before, and smiled.

A little spark still glimmers there, he thought, not really surprised.

In his junior suite, third floor front, he enjoyed his second bath of the day and changed into lighter city clothes from the more-than-adequate wardrobe Mr. Conrad, the hotel manager, kept on hand for him. Poised ten feet in front of the full-length mirror on the closet door, he released the spring-loaded short sword from his ebony walking stick.

"En garde, villain!" he said icily.

He parried left, disengaged, parried right, and lunged. *Gotcha!* He glided to attention, wiped the blade with his handkerchief, and graciously saluted his fallen foe.

He had fenced varsity foil for St. John's College at Fordham in the Bronx in 1882–83.

In the front restaurant off the lobby, he ordered a light salad lunch and iced tea. The harpist, who rarely spoke, mouthed a silent "Hello!"

"You're looking very well, Mr. Collins," Mr. Conrad called out from behind the reception desk.

He did make a smart appearance. Seventy-seven, but still spry. Spiffy, a man to notice.

"As are you, Mr. Conrad," he replied.

Mr. Conrad, who looked like a stage butler, dated to the lonely years after Clara died.

"The Presidential Suite is available, sir," he said in a conspiratorial voice.

"The President won't be needing it today?" Martin inquired, eyebrows raised, a ritual response.

"Very unlikely," said Mr. Conrad.

"Alas, I won't either," said Martin.

They both smiled as he moved across the lobby to the open glass doors.

As he cut diagonally across Washington Square Park he swung the walking stick jauntily, enjoying the sunshine, admiring the tall brownstones on the north side, remembering Henry James.

He continued eastward, then down Broadway to Third Street. Jacob Kaufmann's neighborhood, west of the Bowery, looked sadly defeated. It had been decaying for forty years. The cast-iron Corinthian facade of the building that housed Kaufmann Tours was beginning to corrode. The tall plate-glass windows were whitewashed on the inside.

A waist-high counter stretched wall to wall across the outer office. The waiting area was decorated with tired vacation posters and furnished with battered metal chairs.

"Martin Collins to see Jacob Kaufmann!" Martin announced.

The counter clerk knocked twice on the wooden door behind him. It opened seconds later and Jacob, with a radiant smile and hands extended, stepped out to welcome Martin, his good friend and silent partner in Kaufmann Tours since 1928.

ψ　　ψ　　ψ

The inner office was furnished in the more delicate form of Empire style called Biedermeier, a furniture design Martin greatly enjoyed. Jacob had brought a few pieces with him from Germany in 1912 and had collected the rest over the years. Charlie's late father, Jarvis Evans, who dealt in antiques, had found two of the pieces for him.

"Business must be better than the peeling paint outside suggests," said Martin.

"Martin, if our customers see everything looking fine, they will want lower rates," Jacob admonished.

A pre-Raphaelite painting in a gold-leafed frame hung above Jacob's desk. It featured a very tall, forlorn maiden with limpid eyes, clothed in a pale blue tunic and soft leather sandals, cross-laced to her knees. Her fingers were curled delicately around the jeweled hilt of a double-edged great sword.

Martin waved a hand at her. "Good day to you, Princess," he said, thinking again of Rose.

"She misses you," said Jacob.

"I could not love her half so much," said Martin, looking up.

"Loved you not honor more," said Jacob, and they laughed at an old joke together.

Martin smiled a silent hello to Jacob's son, August, who stood attentively at the left of his father's desk. To the right, a large man in a black suit slouched uncomfortably in a delicate satinwood chair, studying Martin with half-closed eyes. He rose when Jacob turned to him but did not come forward.

"May I introduce Carl Rozkopf? The police are looking for him. August, of course, you know."

Martin shook August's hand and nodded politely at Carl, who remained a distance away. Carl sat down. Jacob, Martin, and August took their places in matching chairs close by.

"Carl does not trust easily," said Jacob, "even when he must. I have explained that you and I are as close as brothers, and he accepts that. But he is slow to rely on strangers."

Carl smiled slightly. Martin smiled back.

"Before you tell me anything more, Jacob, I must make a lawyer's speech," said Martin. "Although I am licensed to practice in the state of New York, I have rarely represented individual clients. My professional life has focused on legislative activities, here and in Albany. I retired from that work seven years ago. Your situation is not at all my specialty. I will help however I can. But you should be aware of my limitations. Also, as you may have noticed, I am not as young as I used to be."

"I place myself and my son and my friend entirely in your hands, Martin," said Jacob. He turned to Carl, who nodded his assent. "Good. Then let us start. Carl?"

"I had just come into the kitchen from the front room looking for August when the first gun was fired," said Carl. "The others said he was asking for me. I have known Jacob for some years, but I had never before met August.

"I have been shot at many times before. I should have performed better than I did. My first thought was, 'They have found me!' My enemies, and I had no weapon. The bullets were making holes high in the wall.

"The kitchen was filled with women and children. I felt this anger. I ran out the door. I was yelling, 'Here I am! Shoot at Rozkopf, you bastards!' And then I was pushed off the porch by the people behind me, by some children, and I was lying on my face in the dirt. So, I was Rozkopf, the clown. I stayed there, not moving. When I got up, it was all over."

"Did you see anyone?" asked Martin. "Whoever was shooting?"

"No one. At first it was too dark. A young man turned on the bus lights. A foolish thing to do, I thought, I should turn them off. I took the keys from him. But the shooting was finished. I left them on.

"People came to the bus. Some were crying. A few were smiling, as if this was an entertainment, a prank, not wanting to believe. It can be like that after a battle. I talked to them. I looked at the car in front of the house. I went inside. I saw the dead lady on the stairs. I went out again to the fields to coax them back. There was no discipline until the police car arrived."

"You saw only the dead lady? No one else?"

"No one."

"You did not speak to the sheriff? His name is Charlie Evans."

"No. I did not know who did the shooting. I thought I would wait to see. From the darkness I watched August and the policeman. When they drove away, I thought we should leave also. I gave orders, and they obeyed."

"You make it sound military," said Martin.

"I am good with orders. I was Reichswehr."

"Reichswehr?" Martin asked.

"It is Wehrmacht now. Herr Hitler changed our name."

"What I meant was . . . a Jew in the German army?"

"In the war many of us served our Fatherland," said Carl. "People today do not understand. *We thought we were Germans!*"

"You should have waited at the house, Carl," said August. "We were going for help. I went because the policeman had to have one of us with him."

Carl shrugged. "I did not know where you had gone. I thought you were perhaps arrested. Bullets had come from the darkness. We could not protect ourselves. I thought, maybe they will come back. A woman was already dead. Could we stay there?"

"You did the best you could," said Martin. "All of you."

"We filled the bus quickly. I counted heads. They were all present, except Sarah. I went back to the house calling for her. She came immediately down from the hill. She had been up there all that time!"

"On the hill where the shots came from?" asked Martin.

"Yes. She is a very brave child. On the bus all of us sat on top of each other. I drove. I went the other way from August and the police car. It was a long time, but I know about these roads. I brought them home."

He slumped forward, his hands and arms dangling between his spread knees. He looked up. "That was all."

"All?" Martin asked. He did not ask how Carl knew about these roads.

Their eyes locked.

"All for now, I think," Carl answered.

"While Carl asks himself if perhaps there is more, I will tell you about Sarah," said Jacob soothingly. "Sarah is now twelve. Three years ago, 1935, Sarah was found by good women at the railroad terminal in Warsaw, Poland. A young man was with her. He ran away and left her there alone. The women protected her. In her hand was a note giving her first name and the name of a village, and saying that she was Jewish, but nothing else. It had no signature. Sarah would not tell more. She came by special means, first to London, then here."

"Where is she at this time?" Martin asked.

"I have hidden her," said Carl defiantly. His voice softened. "Now she calls me *Uncle* Carl. Soon it will be *Papa*."

Jacob rapped on the wooden leg of his chair and continued.

"Something has happened to make Sarah like two little girls in one body. One of our Sarahs learns very fast. She speaks good English. The other Sarah has little education. She speaks a low Polish. This Sarah trusts strangers even less than Carl. Our search for her people tells us some things, but Sarah keeps her secrets."

"I will need to see her," said Martin.

"If you must, you must," said Jacob. "First let me tell you what more we know. She is from a small village near Warsaw that is no more. Destroyed. Her family name is gone with the Jews who lived there. Sarah, of course, knows her name, but she plays a game with us. She says her name is Spray. Sarah Spray. Like a wave makes, or rain when the wind blows. She took this word, we think, from a soap wrapper in London. A new name to make her clean, no?"

"It is perhaps better forgotten," said Carl.

Jacob frowned.

"Her parents were peasants. They did not own the land, but the family had perhaps lived there a long time and had some rights.

Poland today makes a big show of treating Jews better. So these people perhaps had some way to protect their right to stay there."

"Sounds like serfdom," Martin said.

"Perhaps a little better. I am told the new laws now allow Jews to buy land in Poland. But who would want to own something that could be taken away tomorrow?"

"Does he need all this?" Carl asked.

"If he is to talk with Sarah, I must explain her," Jacob replied. "Everywhere is this Depression. Except in Germany. Hitler gives the German people hope. We must accept that. National Socialism has improved German life."

"Hope is a thing with feathers," said Martin.

"Which means?" asked Carl.

"Sorry," said Martin. "Something Clara used to say."

"Hope in Germany also gave hope in Poland," said Jacob. "The value of German land went up. Poles began to think like Germans. Landowners. Bankers. Noblemen. Get land. The village where Sarah lived is a miserable place for two hundred years. Suddenly it becomes valuable. The owner does some magic, and the village is gone."

"And months later Sarah is found at a train station in Warsaw," said Carl. "So now you know what we know."

"What happened to the villagers?"

"They all disappeared," said Jacob. "In Europe these things happen. No one has ever come to find Sarah. That is all we know."

"The night of the shooting," said Carl, "she was on the hill. She often looks for a place to be alone."

"She does not know how to play," said Jacob.

"She climbed the hill in the afternoon and found a place to look down at the others. The shooting began close to her. She hid in the rocks until it was over."

"So, she saw who did it?"

"She heard two men, and she saw one of them for a moment

from far away. She remembers some of their words. One said, 'Shoot to kill.' The other, who she thinks was younger, she heard say, 'Gott, Gott,' which was probably 'God, God.' She thought he was praying."

"And someone said, 'Red right,' " said Jacob.

" 'Red right?' That's odd. You're sure?"

Jacob shrugged. "Communists here?" he asked. "But I don't think so."

"Where do you and Sarah live, Mr. Rozkopf?" asked Martin.

"I have a flat, a small apartment, near here."

"And also you have Upstate," said Jacob in a reminding tone.

"Yes, and Upstate I have my farm," he said, frowning at Jacob. "Above Liberty I have forty-five good acres. Land I cleared with my own hands. I sell vegetables wholesale. It has taken me many years to make this business."

"And the cabins," said Jacob.

Carl glared at him.

"Yes, also some cabins to rent. Near a stream with fish. And a small camp for families. For vacations."

"And to teach Jews to shoot," said August. "It does no good to make faces, Carl. A lawyer should be trusted."

"Before we go on," said Martin, "a formality. If I am to represent you, I must know if any of you had anything to do with the shooting at the farmhouse? Or with the death of Marjorie? Or do you know anyone who did?"

Without hesitation all three said no.

"Do you know *why* any of these things happened?"

Carl frowned. "Let me think more about that," he said.

"Just let me know before we talk with the sheriff," Martin replied.

Twelve

SUNDAY WAS CHARLIE'S DAY OFF. AS usual, Katy came by in the afternoon and he cooked an early dinner. A venison stew in Finger Lake red wine with wild mushrooms, baby carrots, and home-baked bread. The chunks of meat had been soaking two days in Charlie's special marinade: lemon vinegar, salt and pepper, a spoonful of horseradish, and a touch of thyme. Charlie browned it and set it to simmer very slowly Saturday night. While he puttered in the kitchen, Katy made the salad and set the table. She placed a low bowl of wildflowers in the center and a tall white candle at each end.

"Your father's best china and silver," she called out, standing back to admire. "The way he liked it Sundays."

"My mother's folks ate with their fingers," Charlie called back. "Off flat stones and bark plates when they had them. Seven days a week."

"I grew up somewhere in between," Katy said to herself.

Katy and her uncle had moved to the western Catskills from Atlantic Avenue in Brooklyn in 1930 when she was twenty-two.

He had entered a tuberculosis sanitarium three years later and was not expected to return. She had been seeing Charlie for four years.

With part-time help from two schoolteachers, Katy wrote, set, printed, and delivered *This Month*, a journal of community news and high-level gossip aimed at the residents of Fredericktown and its four villages. The back two pages were devoted to for-the-record information on such things as births, deaths, permits, licenses, taxes, arrests, convictions, land sales, and foreclosures. She had an office in the cabin her uncle had built in Thunder Mountain on the Chicken Corners border, but she rarely used it. She spent most of her work time typing at a courtesy desk provided by the township just outside Marjorie Bingham's office in the Fredericktown Public Records Building next to town hall.

ᗶ   ᗶ   ᗶ

"Your father was one of a kind," Katy said during dinner.

Jarvis's hand-printed picker poster was still tacked to the wall behind Charlie.

ANTIQUES ANTIQUES ANTIQUES
JARVIS EVANS
91 Farragut Street
Chicken Corners, N.Y.
FRedericktown 683

WANTED
Old furniture, China, Glass, Books, Photographs, Legal Documents, Ledgers, Letters, Stamps, Coins, Paintings, Picture Frames, Jewelry, Gold & Silver, Brass, Ivory, Rugs, Toys, Baskets, Quilts, Needlework,
ET CETERA, ET CETERA, ET CETERA
CALL OR WRITE
BEST PRICES

"I really miss the old fox." She sighed.

Charlie grunted.

"Don't you?" she asked. "You never say so."

"It's unlucky to think about the dead," said Charlie. "About people you know. Even my father."

He could tell she really wanted an answer.

"Okay," he said, pushing his plate to the side. "That last night, before he went out, we were sipping applejack together. He got to talking about bloodlines again. He thought I didn't pay my ancestors enough respect."

"He thought you were special," said Katy. "Even Potter acts like you are."

"Potter's just jealous," said Charlie. "Dad traced my tree further back than the Washingtons', and that bothers him. According to Dad, I'm descended on his side from John Evans, captain of the man-o'-war *Richmond*. Old Captain John practically owned the Catskills in Queen Anne's time. My mother went straight back to Teedyuscung, king of the Algonquins, and Pemeranaghin, chief sachem of the Esopus. Poor Potter's just an all-white Congregationalist. He can't match me."

"An English pirate and a couple of Indian chiefs," said Katy. "Very romantic."

"When I was twelve, Dad sent me to Ohio for a month to stay with my aunt Copper Pot. She was Minsi, the refugee tribe the Shawnees took in after the French and Indian War. I came home from the reservation not sure who I was and not much caring. I didn't like looking backwards. All I wanted was to play football and become a cop."

"What about your mother?"

"She was dead by then."

"You never talk about her."

"She was pure Algonquin. Wolf clan of the Delawares. Some of the neighbors never forgave Dad for that."

"For what?"

"Falling for an Indian. Marrying her. Muddying the family line."

"Whose line? The captain's or the king's?"

Charlie got up and walked to the far side of the room.

"When the phone rang I was standing right here with a glass of jack in my hand. I thought it was a business call. Someone with an antique to sell. He told me he'd be back in an hour or so. I went looking for him around eleven. We finally found him in the lot behind The Coach and Anvil. Whoever did it drove over his head."

Katy went to him and wrapped her arms around his chest from behind.

"When I'm working on his files, I think about him," she said. "There wasn't any warning. It's like he's still around, lost inside those papers, and I'm trying to get him out."

"I worry about you," said Charlie. "You've got that same ferrety streak he had."

ψ   ψ   ψ

In addition to being the unpaid Fredericktown historian, Jarvis was a picker-dealer. Picking is the beginning of the line in the antiques business, and every Tuesday and Thursday, Jarvis picked for a living. Crouched behind the wheel of a battered pickup with slat sides and a canvas top, he prowled the county back roads, eyes flicking side to side, alert for throwaways.

A network of scavengers, mostly housewives, prepicked for him. He scheduled his tours to haggle prices with them, and between stops he searched for places that looked promising: old houses that had attics and fieldstone foundations with barns and storage sheds. When a door opened, he presented a letter-sized copy of his picker poster and tried to start a conversation.

As Fredericktown historian, Jarvis viewed himself as guardian and custodian of the town, the villages, and all the hills around. He founded the Chicken Corners Historical Library in the old parsonage that also housed the offices of the first selectman and the permits clerk, and he lectured on local history to any adult or child who would listen.

His hoard of old documents—land grants, love letters, and gum wrappers—was stored in stacks of file boxes in the house he left for Charlie. Some people were maybe a little worried about the contents of his collection. That had always amused him. He thought something in there would someday make history.

Thirteen

CHARLIE ARRIVED AT THE SHERIFF'S office in Fredericktown at nine on Monday morning, an hour early. Katy drove her own car to her office cubicle in the Public Records Building.

Potter had come in at eight to bridge the night shift. He had been working at his office or out at Thornton farm most of the weekend, and he told Charlie that he had divided the shootings into two distinct although possibly related cases. Charlie was relieved to find Potter's behavior almost back to normal. Thursday night and Friday morning he had been grim, tight jawed, almost in shock. Now he was clowning with the office staff and teasing Rose, who called him a twit, her ultimate expression of annoyance.

"He's been this way all weekend," she told Charlie. "Like a frisky kid. What happened to the grieving second cousin?"

"Go easy. Marjorie's death hit him hard."

"So? She's still dead," said Rose, unimpressed. "Why the sudden change?"

"I'll meet you at the farmhouse at eleven-thirty," Charlie told Potter. "I'm picking up Katy."

"What for?" Potter asked, clearly annoyed. "The other reporters will scream. That's favoritism."

"She not coming as press. Katy worked next to Marjorie. Maybe she'll notice something we'd miss."

"Speak for yourself," said Potter. "I never miss anything."

 ⚘   ⚘   ⚘

Katy had been surprised at the invitation, too.

"How come, lover?" she asked. "Why the special treatment?"

"I want someone around I can trust," said Charlie.

"Isn't that what Potter's paid for?"

Charlie took time with his answer. "He's too personally involved," he said evasively.

Katy thought that over. Personal in what way? And why was that bad? Charlie would tell her what he meant when he was ready to.

"If you need a woman's viewpoint, why not bring Rose?"

"That's complicated, too," said Charlie. "She's too close to Martin Collins."

"Martin's got to be a hundred," said Katy. "You're full of surprises."

"The two of them had breakfast at the Imperial Saturday morning," Charlie said, as if that explained something.

"So?"

"I know he was close to her mother, but something funny's going on. I don't trust Martin either."

 ⚘   ⚘   ⚘

Charlie and Katy entered the farmhouse through the back door. Potter was waiting inside. Charlie pointed to the wall above the kitchen door and window. The holes punched out of the plaster were the size of fists. The holes in the opposite wall were smaller and a few inches lower.

"Heavy rifle," he said to Potter. "Not a twenty-two."

Potter did not respond.

Upstairs in the room with the Private sign, Katy said, "Look at this place. All those old, dead dreams."

It had been a child's bedroom once. The walls were papered with a faded and stained print of bunny rabbits in dresses and overalls hopping around flowers, chasing a ball.

In the middle of the room was an oak table. On it were a candle in a Coke bottle and three pencils and a gum eraser in a Hellman's jar. At one end were two press-back oak chairs with cane seats.

On the floor was a wooden box with a hinged top. An advertisement on the inside of the lid read, "Frank Siddall's Soap. Does away with the Wash Boiler Nuisance." There was a picture of a smiling man kicking a metal boiler and a smiling woman scrubbing laundry in a wooden tub. The box was half filled with papers, envelopes, and cards.

"That was Marjorie's travel box," said Katy. "She said it kept her reminded how much she hated housework."

A sweater was lying on the seat of a chair, white cotton with red trim.

"She must have left in a hurry," Katy observed. "That was her favorite sweater."

Potter checked the label.

"Wanamaker's," he said. "A Christmas gift from my mother. I'll give it back to her. A remembrance."

He fingered the sweater thoughtfully, then draped it neatly over the back of the chair.

"I want this guy bad, Charlie," he said. "I called the troopers this morning."

"You should have talked to me first," said Charlie, frowning. "They get a foot in the door, they'll try to take over. What did they say?"

"Funny," said Potter. "They didn't seem interested. Just asked me to keep them informed."

"Maybe they know something we don't," said Katy.

"Like what?" asked Potter.

"Not *what*," said Charlie. "Like *why*."

♅   ♅   ♅

"So, what have you got that's new?" Charlie asked.

"We can't locate this Shofar Foundation," Potter replied. "That's strange. We should be able to find them easily. Kaufmann, two *n*'s, dealt with them directly, but he doesn't know where they live. They paid him on time. Seven envelopes in all, every week or so, by mail. Cash, big bills. That's unusual these days. He's more used to checks that bounce."

"Did they ask for a discount?" Katy asked.

"Not a cent. A charity that doesn't plead poverty. Must be loaded."

"What about the passengers?" Charlie asked.

"Always poor Jews," said Potter, "bottom of the barrel. Kaufmann got sent a list of names each trip with the time and place. The passengers were there waiting for the bus. They weren't people he knew."

He lifted the soapbox onto the table and stirred the papers with his fingertips.

"There is one thing you should know about."

He kept playing with the papers in the box.

"A woman's name. At the foundation. Emma Brown."

He looked up to catch their reaction.

"She's the one set it all up. She found the Jews. She sent the names, the notes, the maps, the money. Kaufmann saved most of it, even the envelopes, but he didn't copy the passenger lists. The drivers probably threw them away."

"Brown, huh?" said Katy. "Nice family name. Like Smith? Or Doe? Or Jones?"

"You got it," said Potter. "More like Jones." He barked a laughed.

"A good name in these parts," said Katy. "If it's from the right line."

"Kaufmann and this Emma Brown talked on the phone. He met her once, in his office."

He paused, closed his eyes, then opened them resignedly.

"In her early forties, five-five or six, brown eyes, a little plump, blond hair, maybe dyed, attractive, well dressed, educated. Poised, very confident, firm in a ladylike way."

"Marjorie Bingham," said Katy.

"Probably. Yeah, cousin Marjorie. The one with the good family background. Not so sweet and innocent after all."

He slammed the soapbox cover closed, threw up his arms.

"How'd she ever get into this? It makes me sick. You grow up with someone, you think you know them, you don't know them at all."

He tapped on the lid with his fingertips.

"This stuff has all been gone over. The stationery is rubber-stamped Shofar Foundation but there's no address. The stamp's in the box. From some Five and Ten. There are some pages from *The Herald-Tribune* on the bottom, May eighteenth last year. Probably just lining, but maybe it tells us when some of this started. There's a few electric bills and two lists, hand- written."

"Handwriting?" asked Charlie.

"Looks like hers. I'll show it to my mother."

"Lists of what?" asked Katy.

"One is addresses. Eighteen, all of them in Sullivan County. The farthest is over by Narrowsburg, near the marshes. Old man

Kaufmann says six are places he sent buses to. Run-down dumps like this one."

"The other list?"

"People around here. Sixteen in all. My mother's name is at the top. Number two is Martin Collins, Kaufmann's silent partner. Mine is there. Yours, too, Charlie. It's sort of a Who's Who in Chicken Corners. Not you, Katy. I guess you're not famous enough."

He picked up Marjorie's sweater.

"There was a cup and saucer with some tea leaves on the table. And a slice of toast on a blue plate with one bite out," he said. "The toast, not the plate."

He threw the sweater across the room. It slid down the wall to the floor. Katy picked it up and brushed it off.

"Stupid bitch," said Potter. "This is embarrassing."

"So are you sometimes," said Katy.

"Let's go downstairs," said Charlie.

ψ   ψ   ψ

They were careful not to step on the clots of blood. It had dried brown, black at the edges. A chalk outline on six of the steps and risers showed where Marjorie's body had been.

At the bottom Potter turned and looked up.

"Don't misunderstand me, Katy. She did something stupid and I'm embarrassed, but she was still family. We grew up together. So I care."

He pointed to the slanted ceiling above the stairs.

"One slug exited above her forehead. They dug it out up there. Two stayed inside and rattled around. Low velocity, made the usual mess. The hair at the back of her head was singed. Rapid-fire, *bang-bang-bang*. No kick to a twenty-two."

The mattresses were still on the floor of the room to the left of the stairs, but the blankets August mentioned were gone. There were holes in the front and back walls. The two above the front windows almost touched the frames.

"It must have been a wild scene," said Charlie.

"Real wild," said Potter.

A hand pump was attached to the kitchen sink, and a wood-burning stove vented out the side wall. A stack of kindling and a bag of charcoal leaned against the wall at the right. A shiny new electric toaster with an extension cord was plugged into the overhead light socket. The bullet holes in the back wall, four of them, were just below the ceiling line.

"Good country shooting," Charlie continued. "Follow that trajectory."

He held his left arm in front of his face, bent at the elbow with the hand flattened, tilted slightly, fingers pointed uphill.

"Starting down at that angle, the slugs dropped about twelve inches the width of the first floor, back to front, before they went out the other side. Shooting like that, they couldn't hit anyone shorter than six foot eight."

"Meaning what?" Katy asked.

"Meaning whoever it was didn't want to hit them," said Potter.

"Sounds sort of familiar," said Charlie.

"Familiar?" Katy asked.

Potter smiled.

"Charlie will explain," he said.

They walked out the back door, down the steps, and up the hill, through the trampled grass. They looked down into the pile of wood and over it at the house below. A thicket of spicebush and blackberries partially shielded it from view uphill. The downhill sides were overgrown with timothy and rye grass three feet high.

"I'm not dressed for this," said Katy. She wrinkled her nose. "It smells like someone had the runs around here."

"Some of them probably did," said Potter. "This used to be where the outhouses were. The pits are filled in, but they get soggy when it rains. The brush on top is to keep wandering cows away."

"This is where the shots came from, huh?" said Charlie.

"One shooter, two, maybe more," said Potter. "Eighteen shots minimum. No cartridge cases, no slugs recovered yet. They're still looking."

He slid a few feet down the incline toward the brush pile, bracing himself on the heels of his hands.

"Nothing left behind. The ground's messed up. Some scuff marks where the leaves are scraped away, some broken branches. Looks like something heavy was dragged partway. A sack or a duffel, something like that."

He looked to the top of the hill.

"It's all rock up there. He, or they, probably crossed over to the road. Maybe someone was waiting."

"Young Kaufman said it lasted four or five minutes, no more," said Charlie. "That's a lot of work for one shooter. He'd have to reload a few times unless he had something special. He covered a lot of wall."

"He, if it was a he, knew what he was doing," said Potter. "No mistakes. No tracks. No clues." He paused. "Except for the slate."

"The slate?" said Charlie.

"A little piece of black slate," said Potter.

He dug in his pocket and held out his hand.

"One of the county guys found it yesterday. On that stump, right where he was supposed to. Poison Seas slate. Two initials scratched on. TQ."

"Tom Quick," said Charlie. He spat after he said it, as if the words tasted bad.

"Looks that way," said Potter.

He turned to Katy.

"I think that's what Charlie meant by 'familiar.' "

⚘   ⚘   ⚘

"This'd be a pretty farm fixed up again," Katy said. "Better than my place."

Above the woodpile was a low outcropping of ledges and gravelly slopes with a few small pin cherry and black birch trees sprouting out of crevices. From the top of the hill they could see over the house, across the cornfields to the second-growth woods covering the mountainsides beyond.

"This was once a floodplain," said Potter. "See how the rock strata alternate? Flood leavings, then soil, then leavings again. This whole ridge was shoved up here by ice."

"How come you know so much about rocks?" Katy asked.

"It's my family's business, Katy. Rocks. B and W, Babcock and Washington. Gravel, bluestone, fieldstone, marble. Acres and acres of it, place your order. It's cheap nowadays. I was supposed to run it, until the Depression came along. My mother's in charge."

"Weren't you in the post office once?"

Potter smiled.

"From mailman to policeman. The start of a brilliant government career."

He ran his hand over the surface of the outcropping.

"Here's a rock with a real history, Charlie. Old red Catskill sandstone. Devonian. Paleozoic. Been right here three or four hundred million years. It's named after Devon, in southwest England. They have the same rock there. English Devonian."

He picked up a chip and held it at arm's length.

"Some of my family came from Devon, near the city of Exeter. The Washingtons, the Fletchers. Two hundred and thirty years ago. They followed the Dutchmen up here, and look what they found. Devon rocks. Kind of like coming home."

Behind the wheel of the cruiser, Charlie steered with his wrists, palms up. The piece of black slate felt cool and alive, like a coiled snake. He shifted it gently from hand to hand.

"So who's Tom Quick?" Katy asked.

Fourteen

TOM HAD NOT MOVED FOR THREE HOURS.
Just before dawn it rained for four minutes, a downpour so heavy that the water seemed almost to displace the air. He had wrapped a fat-soaked rag around the breech of the flintlock rifle to keep the powder dry, but the rain had soaked his buckskins through. They dried on him, hard and tight. If he moved, they would crackle.

He had picked Butler's Rift, a narrow point in the river, because he knew that sooner or later one of them would come by. At this hour of the morning they would most likely come from the right, heading north. He would have preferred a quick kill in the woods. An ambush stiffened the bones and took time, and he did not have the patience anymore.

They knew he was back. They were shying away from Lumberland. They were being careful, even the young braves who were always hunting him, who wanted the glory. He had not killed one of them in a long time.

The first sound he heard was the blade of a paddle lifting out of the water, about two hundred yards downstream. Tom was wedged in the crotch of a fallen tree, behind a screen of reeds on a muddy bank. He saw the canoe glide around the bend slowly and silently on his side of the rift. It was a family, five of them.

The man with the paddle was half kneeling, nervous, ready to spring. He was naked from the waist up. One boy, about five years old, knelt up front, his black hair just visible above the curved prow. Another boy, about seven, stood behind the man, his fingertips touching the man's shoulders. The woman sat in the back, leaning against a twig mat, suckling an infant. It was large, not a newborn. Tom saw all this in seconds.

When the canoe was twenty yards away, Tom rose stiffly to his feet, toes dug into the cool mud, the long barrel of the flintlock leveled at the man's chest. The man rippled the paddle on the off side of the canoe, to slow it and keep it pointed straight. It began to drift closer to shore, closer to Tom. Their eyes joined. All their eyes were fixed on his eyes, above the barrel of the gun. They knew who he was.

He cupped the fingers of his left hand to motion them in. The canoe sucked into the soft mud, and the man with the paddle stood up. He was wearing a breechcloth and a leather apron, nothing else. The boys were naked. The woman was wrapped in a red blanket, open in front. The baby was curled around her, resting on a green bed of sassafras leaves. It had stopped sucking. The canoe was only a dozen feet away and still drifting.

"I am going to kill you, Delaware," Tom said to the man. He said it in English, then repeated it in Lenape-Algonquin, the language the Delawares had taught him when he was a boy.

The man had a tomahawk with an iron head hanging by a leather thong from his right shoulder. He knew the trick of dropping it into his hand with a small twitching motion even as his arm began the arc of the throw. He knew he would still die. He could not beat the gun. But a good throw might hit the gunner, giving his family a little time. The paddle in his right hand was in the way. He would try anyway. He had no choice.

When he did, Tom shot him in the head. As the man fell, Tom stepped forward, catching the tomahawk in his right hand before it hit the water. He moved very fast. The water was above his knees. There *was hard gravel beneath the mud. The canoe was tipping. He dropped the flintlock into it, gripped the bentwood gunwale with his left hand, and pulled the canoe steady against his left thigh. Almost in the same motion, he sank the blade of the man's tomahawk into the woman's head just behind her left ear.*

When he turned to the boys they backed away. The older one snarled a word Tom did not know. The younger one began to whimper. The tomahawk flashed six times.

"They squawked just like young crows," Tom said years later, when he told his nephew how he had killed them.

The infant was tangled in the woman's lap, its head between her parted knees. It was crying. The woman had fallen forward at the waist and bled on it. Tom pushed her back and scooped the child into the crook of his left arm. It was a girl. She stopped crying and looked up at him. Big brown eyes, almost no whites. Later, he admitted that he had wavered, just for a moment. Then he drew the razor-sharp edge of the tomahawk across her throat.

"Nits make lice," he explained.

He hid the bodies by weighting them with stones tied together with strips of basswood and sinking them with the canoe in the middle of the river.

Before he turned back to the woods he stood, legs spread, in the shallows where the water ran fast and white and clean again. He tipped his head back, looked up at the towering Catskills, and screamed his name once, for all the Delaware to hear:

"Tom Quick!"

٭ ٭ ٭

Tom's people were Dutch. They arrived in Nieuw Amsterdam in the seventeenth century. They were respectable, hardworking settlers, well regarded and well off. Sometime before 1689, after the English had captured their city and renamed it New York, Thoomas Quick, Sr., Tom's father, moved his family north into

Ulster County, where he bought a tract of woodland from Harmon Hekun, a Christianized Indian. He cleared it, farmed it, and prospered.

Thoomas sold the Ulster farm in 1733 and took his family farther west to the Pennsylvania border. There he cleared another farm and built a mill at a place that became known as Milford. It was wild pioneer country, and the Quicks were among the first to settle it. It was the homeland of the Minsi Algonquins, the Wolf clan, also called Delawares, a French name for both the valley and the river that drained it.

Young Tom grew up among the Delawares. He learned their ways. He became a backwoodsman, a mock Indian, as comfortable in the wild as the Minsi. He had no formal schooling. He spoke two languages: a crude blend of country English and Low Dutch, and Lenape Algonquin, the language of the Delawares.

ψ　　ψ　　ψ

During the French and Indian War, some of the Quicks ventured out to cut bulrushes by the riverbank and were ambushed by Indians. Old Thoomas couldn't run as fast as young Tom and the other men. An Algonquin mercenary named Muskwink caught up with him and dragged him down. Tom watched from the safety of the cabin door as Muskwink butchered his father, took his scalp, and cut the silver buttons off his coat. The day that happened, Tom lost a part of his mind. He took an oath that for the rest of his life he would kill Delawares.

ψ　　ψ　　ψ

Tom's favorite killing ground was eastward across the New York border into the lower Catskills in an area called Lumberland. The heart of Lumberland township was within an angle of land formed by the Mongaup and the Delaware rivers. It was there that Tom earned his whisper name, the Indian Slayer.

After the defeat of the French, those Delaware clans that had joined them in the war against the English were driven farther west. Muskwink stayed behind. He drifted back to the lower valley of the Neversink, where he lived the life of an alcoholic vagabond. One evening in Decker's Tavern, three-quarters of a mile northeast of Port Jervis, Tom watched as Muskwink boastfully reenacted the murder of Thoomas Quick.

"You don't believe?" Muskwink growled at the crowd of hunters and trappers around him. He untied a soft leather pouch and poured the contents on the bar. "I got his buttons. See!"

Tom took an unloaded musket from its place above the mantel, scooped up the silver buttons, and ordered the drunken Muskwink outside. Walking along the main road between Kingston and Minisink, on the way to Carpenter's Point, he cleaned and loaded the gun and shot Muskwink through the spine.

Year after year, Tom killed Indians whenever and wherever he found them. Drinking in a tavern, eating at a campfire, walking by a neighbor's house. In the woods, he shot them without warning and moved on.

Generations of Delawares hunted Tom in turn. The name of the brave who killed the Indian Slayer would never be forgotten by his people. Many young braves died trying. Older men stayed out of the forest if Tom Quick was known to be around.

Over the years, the legend grew. Some settlers in New York and Pennsylvania who had grievances or ambitions of their own spoke approvingly of Tom. But to most of the people of his time he was just a crazy renegade, the worst of a bad kind.

Fifteen

WHEN POTTER WASHINGTON WAS A BOY, Tom Quick was the ghost in his closet, the shape in the shadows when the candle went out, the devil underneath the bed. Home from school, lying sick in bed, Potter could trace Tom's outline in the cracks of the ceiling: a lanky phantom in buckskin with a flintlock rifle and long, dark hair.

"Tom'll get you if you don't behave," Fletcher warned his son. "He's got fiery eyes and fingernails sharp as butcher knives. He'll chew you up and spit the splinters out."

ψ   ψ   ψ

In July 1913, on Potter's eleventh birthday, Ginnie baked a cake and made black raspberry ice cream, Fletcher's favorite. After dinner the three of them sat side by side on the creaky metal glider on the back porch, having a little party. Potter was gently working the bolt of a birthday present: his first rifle, a single-shot .22 caliber Remington.

"This is an important day," Fletcher said. "Eleven is the beginning of a man."

"I think it's too soon," Ginnie said.

Fletcher ignored her.

"He's ready. Aren't you ready, boy?"

"Yes, sir. I mean, I'm ready," said Potter solemnly.

Fletcher twisted to face Potter, who was squeezed in the middle.

"Then it's time you learned the truth about Tom Quick."

☙ ☙ ☙

"We are fighting a war, Potter. A secret war. We are fighting for what is ours. The fight is about land and struggle and pride. It's about a promise the Lord has made to the righteous."

"Yes, sir."

"It's about duty and justice and punishing the wicked."

He brought his face closer to Potter's.

"It's about the real Tom Quick."

Potter shivered. Fletcher smiled.

"Does that name still frighten you?"

"A little," said Potter.

He shivered again. The sun was down, and the shadows of the mountains were crawling across the lake.

"That's foolishness, boy. Tom was the first of us. We followed in his footsteps. My father, Enoch, and his father, Brewster, they were Tom Quick. I am Tom Quick. Someday, when I am gone, you will be Tom Quick, and your son will be, too."

☙ ☙ ☙

On Monday afternoon, three days before Thanksgiving, in November 1915, Fletcher was stretched out on his stomach on the dining room table, wearing only the bottom half of his long johns. Ginnie had cushioned the tabletop with blankets covered by a rubber sheet.

Potter was standing on a footstool at the side of the table, kneading his father's aching back. He was thirteen.

"Thanksgiving is a schoolbook lie," said Fletcher. "Turkey and cranberries and pumpkin pie. Rubbish! Real Indian history is about cheating and stealing and fighting and killing and dying."

"Killing who?" Potter asked.

"The Delawares. The Lenni Lenape. The ones who were here before us. They rolled in from the West with the Mengwe like a thunderstorm a thousand years ago. They destroyed anything in their way."

"Why?" Potter asked.

The table legs creaked with the rubbing.

"To cleanse the land. Their gods said everything from what we call New England to Georgia was theirs, so they took it."

Potter dug his fingertips deep into the knots of muscles that lined Fletcher's spine. The boy had strong hands.

Fletcher's head rose, his shoulder blades came together.

"The Mengwe split up. They became the Hurons above the St. Lawrence and the Iroquois from the Great Lakes to Lake George. The Iroquois are a foxy people, Potter. And cruel. Specially the Mohawks. If you come across one, run the other way. They eat their captives raw."

"Raw?" said Potter.

"They ate the Jesuits." Fletcher cackled. "They were a great people!"

Ginnie's liniment combined beaver-tail fat with a patent medicine containing camphor and opium. Fletcher claimed it was the only thing that eased the pain in his back. Potter liked the smell.

"The Mengwe were best at fighting and trickery. They made treaties and broke them. The treaty they forced on the Algonquins turned them into women. The Mengwe called them petticoats after that."

Potter poured more ointment on.

"But we beat them all. It's our land now, Potter. Our blood sanctified this ground. We had the leaders. James Clinton. John Sullivan. Moses Van Campen. George Washington. They led the way."

"And Tom Quick?"

"And Tom Quick. Visit graveyards, boy. Read the names on the stones. Those are the chosen ones."

"What about the others?"

"We let some of them stay. Even some Delawares. As long as they obeyed the rule."

"What rule?"

"Do what you're told. Become like us."

"What if they didn't want to?"

Fletcher twisted faceup on the table, his torso propped on his elbows. The ointment that had run under him pooled in the crease between his belly and his chest. His eyes blazed.

"If they didn't want to, they got scarified away."

Sixteen

CHARLIE, POTTER, AND KATY WERE BACK at police headquarters a little after noon. Rose spread a lunch from the diner on the worktable in Charlie's office: a platter of sandwiches, a bowl of potato salad, a jar of sour pickles, and a pitcher of root beer.

Charlie motioned Potter aside.

"I want Katy to stay," he told him. "Rose, too. And both of them in the conversation, not just taking notes."

"Why Rose?" Potter growled.

"She probably knows more about policing than you and me put together," said Charlie. "I want her on my side."

Rose had joined the Fredericktown force as a file clerk in 1913. Her father, Hank Vanderhoff, had served with the former sheriff when both of them were starting out.

"She's only a secretary."

"I couldn't run this place without her."

"I'd be willing to try," said Potter.

"Whodunit time," said Potter.

"Who done what?" asked Rose, her mouth full.

"That's the question," said Charlie. "Let's start with the shooting from the hill. Friday we thought whoever shot up the house also killed Marjorie Bingham. Now we know that isn't so. We seem to have two separate cases. So, what did happen?"

"Well, the two cases have to be connected, don't they?" said Katy. "I mean, it couldn't be just coincidence, one party shooting up a house at the same exact moment some other party is murdering someone inside."

"Depends on what you mean by 'connected,' " said Potter. "Can you imagine the inside guy staying inside if he knew what the outside guy was about to do?"

"Maybe Mr. Inside knew *what* but not *when*," said Rose.

"Or maybe Mr. Outside knew Mr. Inside was there but didn't give a damn," said Katy.

"Let's say neither one knew," said Potter. "Where does that leave us?"

"Back to coincidence, maybe" said Charlie. "What about this guy Rozkopf? The man who roared."

"I've got something there," said Potter.

He pulled a sheet of paper from his file.

"NYPD found a small arsenal in his apartment. Listen to this: Three shotguns, two heavy rifles, a Thompson sub, and three handguns, a thirty-eight, a forty-five, and a thirty-eight/forty-four heavy duty with enough ammunition to fight a war. Plus four range targets. Taped on his living room wall."

"Range targets?" said Rose. "What for?"

"Ready on the firing line," said Potter, extending his right arm and squinting his left eye. "Practice, I suppose."

"Any priors, any warrants out?"

"No record of any handgun licenses, so they think they might get him on possession. But for now it's just wanted-for-questioning."

"Could he be Mr. Inside?" asked Katy.

"Not if you believe young Kaufman. He places Rozkopf in the kitchen the whole time," said Potter.

"Suppose he did it before Kaufman got there?" Rose suggested. "Shot Marjorie, then ran around the house and in the kitchen door?"

"Not enough time, and Kaufman would have heard the shots. There wouldn't have been any rifle fire to drown them out."

"What else do we know about Mr. Rozkopf?" asked Charlie.

"Another German Jew, like the Kaufmann-Kaufman pair. In this country a long time. Some kind of businessman. Food and stuff. According to Kaufmann, he made all the arrangements."

"Arrangements?"

"He supplied the necessities for the houses Kaufmann has been busing his Jews to," said Potter. "You know, flour, sugar, salt and pepper, coffee, toilet paper. They bought perishables and extras locally after they moved in."

He paused for attention.

"We don't know for sure who did the butchering."

"Butchering?" said Rose.

"Chickens and sheep mostly. On the back roads at night or early in the morning. Real messy. Lots of complaints."

"Roads in Chicken Corners?"

"All over. Wherever the buses went," said Potter.

"And you're saying Rozkopf did it? Or the Jews from the city?" Charlie asked.

"Maybe. One or the other."

"Why would they do something like that?" Katy asked. "On the roads."

"I said *maybe* them. As for why, because they had to. Their religion says meat has to be killed a certain way. They were up here with no facilities. So they did it the hard way. Followed the basic rules. *Maybe*."

"They could have made other arrangements," Rose said.

"Look, these people are trash," said Potter. "They aren't civilized Jews. Kaufmann's bus drivers are Jews, but they're different. They were brought up better. Remember the guy young Kaufman replaced? I checked. He wasn't really sick. He just couldn't stomach another run. How would *you* like to take people like that shopping?"

Charlie interrupted.

"We'll find out more about this later," he said. "What about the electricity?"

Potter went back to his notes.

"The Thornton place was hooked up July twelfth. There's no interior wiring. Someone ran live lamp cord right off the new fuse box. Upstairs they used lanterns and candles. Glad I didn't have to sleep there."

"I don't think you would have been invited," said Rose.

"What about that piece of slate?" said Katy.

"Poison Seas slate," said Potter, "formed on a stagnant sea bottom a million years ago. You've got clay and silt under tons of pressure from above. With all the oxygen squeezed out, nothing can live in it. No fossil traces. That's why they call it poisoned."

"Just the right stuff for Tom Quick," said Katy.

"What's that screwball got to do with this?" Rose asked.

Charlie showed her the piece of slate.

"I didn't even know his name," said Katy. "Charlie told me about him in the car."

"You have to have grown up around here," said Rose. "The Indian Slayer, the Avenger of the Delaware. A homicidal loony they buried near Port Jervis a long time ago."

"Milford, Pennsylvania, 1796," said Potter. "Born 1734."

"That's what he's known for? Killing Indians?"

"*Famous* for," said Rose. "Which wasn't easy, considering the competition. Killing Indians was what people used to do around here for fun."

"Or to earn a living," said Charlie.

"How so?" asked Katy.

"It paid better than hunting. Ask Aunt Copper Pot. In 1764 William Penn posted the prices: One live Indian male over the age of ten, one hundred and fifty dollars. One dead male, scalped, one hundred and thirty-four dollars. Any live male or female under ten, one hundred and thirty dollars. One dead female over ten, scalped, thirty dollars."

"Scalped? Little girls?"

"The government held on to the scalps. To make sure a corpse didn't get claimed twice.

"Tom never scalped anyone," said Potter.

"He killed Delawares for free," said Charlie. "About a hundred of my ancestors, according to Aunt Copper Pot. All ages, both sexes. He was never charged, never tried, never punished."

"They say he had friends in high places," said Rose.

"You're taking sides, Charlie," said Potter. "Tom Quick was respected while he lived. Still is. The settlers in the Delaware Valley built him a fine monument."

"A monument for a baby killer? You're kidding!" Katy said.

"In 1889," said Charlie.

"You should go see it," said Rose. "It sits in the middle of a street in Milford, flowers and ribbons on it all the time. They hold prayer meetings there sometimes. God bless Tom Quick!"

"How could they?" asked Katy.

"People thought a lot about Indians in 1889," said Charlie. "The country was still mourning Custer. There was gold out West and plenty of empty land."

"Except for the Indians," said Rose.

"Some of Tom Quick's descendants had become real prominent," said Charlie. "Rich and powerful. They didn't relish being kin to a homicidal maniac."

"So they turned him into a hero," said Rose.

"There was a big dedication, with a parade," said Potter.

He looked as if he were remembering.

"The governor made a speech. The New York papers came. His bones are there under the monument."

"And now he's in Chicken Corners, shooting at Jews?" Katy asked. "Wow!"

ψ   ψ   ψ

The speaker's platform, heavily decorated in red, white, and blue, stood next to the monument, an obelisk set on a small island in a side street at the edge of town.

"He did the Lord's work," the speaker intoned, almost like a prayer. "He kept his vow. He purified this valley. He showed us what God expects of men."

Suddenly the wind picked up and shifted. The Stars and Stripes, flying atop a tall pole, snapped briskly a few times, then whipped around to the other side, pointing due west.

"The Creator is sending us a sign!" the speaker screamed in excitement. "He has changed the wind's direction. It blows now from Plymouth Rock to the Pacific. God offers this whole continent to the white race. Let us pray we have the will and the strength to bear the burden!"

ψ   ψ   ψ

"Once they made him a legend, he wouldn't stay dead," said Charlie. "Law-enforcement offices in this part of the state have active sheets on him going back to 1800. Thornton farm is just the latest."

"So we're looking for a ghost?" asked Katy.

Potter smiled.

"We get maybe one complaint a year. They're all pretty much the same. A man roughs up his wife and kids too often, he finds a dead cat on his doorstep. The note says, 'Stop the beatings. Tom Quick.' Whoever he is, he generally helps keep the peace."

"A defender of women and children," said Rose. "The Lone Ranger. Without faithful Tonto, of course."

"There's no proof he ever hurt anyone," said Potter. "At least no one who didn't deserve it. Some of the folks he scared away, we're better off without."

"It isn't always just scare stuff," said Charlie. "When it's about religion or skin color or a man's last name, something he won't or can't change, it gets rougher."

"Rougher how?"

"Dead livestock. Bullets through the wall at night. A fire under the family car. A note that says what could happen to the kids. Some people who didn't do what they were told had their houses burned down."

"There's no proof of that," Potter protested. "Who knows for sure when it's Quick or not."

"He has a certain style," said Rose. "When someone shoots up a houseful of Jews and leaves his initials, that's him."

"Let's move on," said Charlie.

"Case number two," said Potter. "Who wants to go first?"

"Kaufman says he never heard the twenty-two," said Rose. "But he wasn't everywhere."

"The rifle fire covered the sound?" asked Katy.

"Probably," said Potter. "It couldn't have been earlier. Three shots inside the house would have caused a panic. And it couldn't have been later. Kaufman would have noticed. A twenty-two sounds different."

"Describe what you think happened," said Charlie.

"I see her at the top of the stairs, the killer behind her. Hiding there, waiting for her? Maybe. Someone she knew, wasn't worried about? Again, maybe. Someone who had been in the office with her? Why not?"

"Any struggle?"

"No sign of one. She didn't turn around. He fired, she fell forward, slid all the way down, face first."

He turned to Rose and Katy.

"Broke her nose, took out some teeth, almost tore her left breast off."

"You don't sound very grieving anymore," said Rose.

Potter shrugged. "I'm just describing what happened. It wasn't pretty, but she made her own bed."

"Whatever that means," said Rose.

"What about her car?" said Charlie.

"The one you saw in front when you got there was hers. Kaufman doesn't remember seeing it there when he arrived, but he isn't sure. He says he heard a car drive up while he was in back. Hers? Some other one? We don't know."

"Was there time for the killer to get down the stairs and out the front door before Kaufman reached the hall?" Charlie asked.

"I guess he could, assuming both shootings were at the same time, which I think they were. He only needed a couple of minutes."

"So, where did the killer go?" asked Katy.

"You tell me. He ran into the woods. He mixed with the crowd. He drove away if he had a car. No lights, up the driveway, gone before Charlie got there. It would have to be before the bus lights were turned on. Maybe some of Jews saw something. But we don't have the passenger list."

"I didn't see any car except Marjorie's," said Charlie, "but that was maybe an hour later."

"More questions than answers," said Rose.

"One thing's certain," said Potter. "Whoever it was, it wasn't Tom Quick."

ψ   ψ   ψ

There was a gentle knock on the office door.

"I'll see who it is," said Rose.

She was back in two minutes.

"There's a Mr. Rozkopf," she said, smiling.

"I'll take it," said Charlie. He reached for the phone.

"No," she said. "He's right outside, with a little girl. Martin Collins and a Mr. Kaufmann are with him."

She turned to Potter.

"Two *n*'s," she said.

Seventeen

"I PUT THEM IN BRIEFING," SAID ROSE.

Briefing was short for the briefing room, a narrow, windowless conference room at the far end of the corridor that Potter sometimes used to interrogate vagrants.

"Let's play this casual," said Charlie. "You go first."

The room was set up for a party. Four folding tables, placed together, were covered with wide strips of white paper sprinkled with colored confetti. Party things were stacked in the middle: paper plates and napkins, poppers and feathered noisemakers. A cluster of balloons hung from the chandelier.

The three men were seated on folding chairs behind the party tables. The girl stood in back of a chair, facing the door. She was thin and pretty with dark brown hair braided loosely at the back of her neck. She had a pink-and-yellow noisemaker in her hand. As Charlie and Rose entered the room, she blew into it. It snaked out at them and made a blatting sound.

"Cute kid," Rose said in a low voice.

Charlie tipped his head questioningly toward the balloons.

"I forgot," Rose replied. "Freddy's birthday. We're short of decent space."

Freddy was the day janitor, a popular man.

Martin and Jacob stood up.

"Welcome to the party, Mr. Collins. Your friends, too," said Charlie.

"Good afternoon, Sheriff," said Martin. "Sarah, gentlemen, permit me to introduce Charlie Evans, the esteemed sheriff of Fredericktown. And just behind him, Miss Rose Vanderhoff, his trustworthy assistant."

They all smiled sociably, except Carl and Sarah.

"Sheriff, this is Jacob Kaufmann, the head of Kaufmann Tours. He is an old friend. You met his son, August, last week. August is minding the store."

Charlie nodded acknowledgment. The table was too wide to easily shake hands.

"With Jacob are Mr. Carl Rozkopf and Miss Sarah . . . Spray. Miss Spray is Mr. Rozkopf's ward."

"Very pleased to meet all of you," said Charlie. "Please sit down."

He took two chairs from the stack against the wall and unfolded them for Rose and himself. Sarah remained standing behind her chair.

"To what do we owe this unexpected visit, Mr. Collins?"

"Good citizenship," said Martin. "Mr. Rozkopf heard that certain inquiries are being made, and he wishes to cooperate. He contacted Mr. Kaufmann, who contacted me. Miss Spray is with us because she saw and heard some things at Thornton farm that may be of interest."

Sarah's eyes moved from speaker to speaker, her face giving nothing away.

"We are much obliged, Mr. Collins. I assume you represent these folks. Should I, then, consider this visit official?"

"*Semi*official. We would like to keep it informal. A friendly chat with you is preferable to a meeting with your colleagues in the city."

"Understandable and well put. We'll give it a try," said Charlie. He turned toward Sarah.

"May I make a suggestion? Katy Bower is waiting in my office. Suppose she takes Miss Spray over to the diner for some homemade pie and ice cream while the rest of us get better acquainted?"

Carl looked at Martin, who nodded his approval. Sarah put the noisemaker back on the table.

"You may call me Sarah, Sheriff Evans," she said very politely.

Charlie acknowledged the gift with a slight bow and turned to Rose.

"Would you please introduce Sarah to Katy? And bring Potter back with you. He ought to be in on this."

He turned back to the visitors.

"Potter Washington, my deputy," he explained.

As Katy and Sarah headed for the door, Martin said, "I recommend the peach pie, Sarah. And the pistachio ice cream."

When the door was closed Potter said, "So everyone's Jewish but you, Mr. Collins?"

Rose groaned.

"You have some difficulties with Jews, Mr. Washington?" Carl asked softly.

"Not to speak of," said Potter. "Why?"

"When the first thing asked is am I Jewish, I wonder is all."

"I asked because someone around here is shooting at Jews. We're trying to find out who and why. There was nothing wrong with the question."

"Some people do not like Jews, Mr. Washington."

"That's their problem, not mine," said Potter. "How about you? You got any problems with policemen?"

Carl leaned forward, his fists clenched.

"Not to speak of," he hissed.

Rose groaned again. Charlie shook his head but did not interrupt.

"This is not a very good beginning," said Martin. "Suppose I speak for my clients."

"That might be an improvement," said Charlie. "Please do."

Martin quickly summarized Carl's account of the shooting at the farmhouse.

"Seems to fit," said Charlie.

"As far as it goes," said Potter.

"For the record," said Martin, "neither Carl Rozkopf, Jacob Kaufmann, or August Kaufman are aware of anything that might explain either the shooting at the farmhouse or the death of Marjorie Bingham. They do not know who committed either act or why either act was committed."

"The girl was on the hill. Did she see anything?" asked Potter.

"Perhaps she *heard* something," said Jacob. "A voice, not so much a face."

"You must ask her yourself," said Carl. "But understand, it was becoming dark, and she was hidden. She saw only one man for half a second, and she heard just pieces of words."

"The information you've given us is already helpful," said Charlie. "It tells us there were at least two shooters and maybe more. These words Sarah heard don't mean anything to me now, but if she can identify voices, that may help later. Now, let's go back to Mrs. Bingham and this Shofar Foundation."

"By all means, Sheriff," said Martin.

"Well, let me say right off the bat," said Charlie, "that something's wrong there. Around here, we're used to seeing poor people from the city. All kinds of charities send them up. Protestants, Catholics, Jews. Boy Scouts. Girl Scouts. The *Herald-Tribune*. Even the big resorts take some of them in."

"There are lots of organizations and plenty of room," said Rose. "Tourists with money are scarce this summer."

"That's what's got me puzzled," said Charlie. "Any interested group can find good summer housing in this area without any trouble. Camps, bungalows, empty hotels, you name it. Cash is always short. Donations for food, bedding, transportation, salaries, that's always welcome. All these groups have their hands out. But space is not their problem. So if someone has the money and wants to bring a few thousand people up from the Lower East Side, he or she doesn't need to rent abandoned houses."

"And he or she doesn't need a Shofar Foundation," said Potter.

"Your turn, Mr. Collins," said Charlie.

"Let's both drop the pretense, Sheriff," said Martin. "The Shofar Foundation isn't real. We all know that. Emma Brown, or whomever she worked for, invented it. A shofar is a Jewish trumpet made from a ram's horn. A kind of rallying device. A good symbol for a charity."

"Mrs. Brown was lying," said Carl.

"Please, Mr. Rozkopf, let me do the talking," said Martin. "Two key points: One, the Shofar Foundation does not exist. Two, Emma Brown, who is now assumed to be Marjorie Bingham, was a fraud. Can we agree on that?"

"Sounds reasonable," said Charlie.

"Fine. And, three, can we agree that her relationship to Kaufmann Tours was strictly business, limited to securing transportation? That Jacob was not involved in anything else?"

"Maybe," said Charlie, turning toward Carl. "Is Mr. Rozkopf part of Kaufmann Tours? An owner or an employee or whatever?"

"No. Mr. Rozkopf was just an intermediary," said Martin. "He provided routine assistance to Marjorie Bingham, whom he knew as Emma Brown. He recommended Kaufmann Tours to her."

"Why Kaufmann?" Potter asked.

"He and Jacob know each other from the neighborhood."

"But Rozkopf did represent the Shofar people, right?" asked Potter.

"An interesting question," said Martin. "How could he represent something that we just agreed does not exist? He sometimes relayed Mrs. Bingham-Brown's instructions to Kaufmann Tours. At other times she did it herself. She used notes mostly and telephoned once or twice."

"So, she didn't want anyone getting too close," said Potter.

"I agree. For Kaufmann Tours the job seemed a little unusual, but not complicated. Shofar paid well and on time, and these days money is money. They were not paid for the last bus they sent to Thornton farm."

"Did you ever meet Mrs. Brown, Mr. Rozkopf?" asked Potter.

"I will answer that for him," said Martin. "He met her six or seven times. The first time was in April. April twelfth. Two days after she called him at his farm."

"Farm?" asked Charlie.

"Mr. Rozkopf has a small commercial farm north of Liberty. Mrs. Brown telephoned him there. She told him he had been recommended by friends of her late husband."

"You have the friends' names?" asked Charlie.

"A banker in New York, an attorney in Liberty," said Martin. "I spoke with the attorney this morning."

"Jewish?" asked Potter.

"That's not important," said Charlie, frowning.

Carl smiled.

"The attorney's name is Peter Carlson," said Martin with annoyance. "I believe he's Lutheran. The friend is Stephen Collier. He's with a big Wall Street investment firm. Probably Presbyterian. Perhaps Episcopalian."

"Carlson owns land close to mine," said Carl.

"Marjorie asked Mr. Carlson if he knew someone who had connections with Jewish refugees in the city. She said she was using the name Emma Brown to remain incognito and to insulate the donors. He saw no harm in that. She dropped a few names. A law firm in Albany, an investment bank in the city, a few socially prominent people."

"I'll need those names, too."

"I'm afraid I don't have them," said Martin. "Carlson feels he can't release references without Mrs. Bingham's approval, and of course she's dead."

"How uncooperative of her," said Potter.

"Carlson recommended Mr. Rozkopf. Mrs. Bingham told Mr. Rozkopf that she and her associates wanted to focus on European refugees, meaning Jews. She said they were horrified at what was happening on the Continent. They were concerned that recent immigrants were worse off than earlier arrivals and that they were being neglected."

"I am not neglecting them," said Carl.

"She said she had access to funds and some properties up here. Mr. Rozkopf's role would be to locate the refugees, put them on the buses, arrange local transportation, and get them comfortably settled in. That's all. She would provide all the housing. He would bill for his time by the hour. Was that the way it happened, Mr. Rozkopf?"

Carl nodded again.

"What qualified Mr. Rozkopf to assist?" asked Potter.

"Experience," said Martin. "Trust. Contacts. Mr. Rozkopf is well known. He has the farm up here, a produce business in the city. He's involved in relief work. He mingles. He supplies fresh vegetables to some of the resorts."

"What about the butchering, Mr. Collins?" Potter asked.

"What butchering?"

"The meat they ate. Who butchered it?"

"Can you answer that, Carl?" Martin asked.

"All meat and poultry was supplied commercially by the same companies that supply the Jewish resorts."

"They didn't do any butchering themselves?"

"They were not qualified."

"You're sure of that?" asked Charlie.

"Of course," Carl answered. He looked perplexed.

"I've got to butt in," said Rose. "Everything you're saying about Marjorie is nonsense. This isn't the kind of thing she'd do. Marjorie detested poverty. She never gave a cent to charity. She didn't like children. She despised foreigners. And you're making her sound like my fairy godmother."

"Then what did she want those Jews for?" asked Potter. "Why would she get mixed up with them? She was a Tuttle."

"That is for you to discover, Mr. Deputy," said Carl.

Eighteen

MARJORIE TUTTLE BINGHAM WAS RE-cruited in September 1936 in a Victorian-style bed-and-breakfast two blocks behind the boardwalk at Atlantic City, New Jersey. It was as far from Chicken Corners as Marjorie could travel in a day, leaving early and getting there quite late. Her partner for the long weekend was Stephen Collier, manager of a blind-trust portfolio for the closed-end investment firm of Arnold, Rolf, and Adler, her late husband's first employer. Stephen was twelve years younger than Wallace had been. She told family and friends she was attending a four-day course in commercial real estate.

✳   ✳   ✳

Stephen was propped in a pile of pillows at the upper end of the four-poster bed. Marjorie sat cross-legged at the bottom.

"You are exactly what I have been looking for," he said, trying to sound businesslike.

"Looking for, Stephen? You've already *had* me three times."

"That was seduction. This is recruitment. And it's not polite to count."

"Do recruits get paid? Do they have to be beginners?"

"They are paid quite well"—he smiled—"but not for that. And no, they don't. Now *listen*. The people behind this are important and powerful. They're top drawer in finance, government, *and* high society. Say yes, and I can tell you more."

"I'm all ears," she said, uncrossing her legs and stretching them out.

"You're . . . impossible. How in the world am I supposed to keep my mind on serious things? Let's talk money. The offer is cash now or a small piece of the action with the payout later."

"How much cash?" She pushed her left foot between his legs and wiggled her toes.

"*Stop that.* I'm authorized to offer you ten thousand dollars, spread over a year. Or what, in effect, would be a junior partnership. Meaning, no money now, but a lot more in years to come."

"If we must talk money, I'll take three thousand three hundred dollars by the end of next week, plus a two-third's piece of all the action I can get."

She straddled him in a quick, gliding movement and pushed him deep into the pillows.

"Now, what do I have to do to earn it?"

Nineteen

"LET'S MOVE ON," SAID CHARLIE. "WHAT about the guns they found in Mr. Rozkopf's closet?"

"He's had them so long," said Martin, "he practically forgot they were there. He does not carry guns on his person. However, he does carry large amounts of money, so he would qualify for handgun permits if he applied. The rifles and shotguns are not a violation."

"What about those range targets on the wall?" asked Potter. "What are they for?"

"Decoration," said Martin. "A matter of taste."

"That's ridiculous," said Rose,

Martin smiled apologetically.

"Handguns aren't for hunting. Who *was* he planning to shoot?" asked Potter.

"No one. Mr. Rozkopf had some unpleasant experiences in Germany years ago. He had to leave in a hurry. For a long while afterward, he felt a strong need to protect himself. The guns are just left over."

"Anything else?" asked Charlie.

"I don't think so," said Martin.

"Then let's call it a day. We all have other work to do. I'll need a formal statement in their own words, Martin. Your initials on Rose's notes will serve in the meanwhile. If you trust her shorthand, that is."

"With my life," said Martin, and they both smiled.

"Can you come by tomorrow morning?"

"If you wish."

"With the girl. I'll need her description of what she saw and heard."

The door opened slowly. Sarah stood in the doorway with Katy behind her.

"Are we interrupting?" Katy asked.

Sarah's eyes moved quickly to Potter, then away.

"Sarah, this is my deputy, Mr. Potter Washington," said Charlie. "Potter, this is Miss Sarah Spray."

"I'm pleased to meet you, Mr. Washington," said Sarah.

Potter nodded in reply.

"Would ten A.M. be convenient?" Charlie asked Martin.

"Fine. We'll all be at Collins House tonight. A question: will we have any further problems with your colleagues in the city?"

"No promises, but I'll talk to them. I doubt he'll get all his ordnance back."

"Let's hope he has no use for it," said Martin.

ᴪ   ᴪ   ᴪ

"What do you make of it?" Charlie asked.

He was back in his office with Potter, Katy, and Rose, studying each of them closely.

"If it wasn't for the alibi young Kaufman gave him, Rozkopf would be my pick," said Potter. "Maybe they're working together."

"I recognize you were riling him intentionally, but you went too far," said Rose.

"It doesn't take much," said Potter. "He has a temper and a thin skin. But he's been around. He won't give anything away."

"He doesn't like you very much," said Charlie.

"That just means he's normal," said Rose.

"So, what did we learn?" Charlie repeated.

"We learned that cousin Marjorie was a busy and mysterious lady," said Rose. "That there were two or more shooters. That little Sarah can maybe identify one or more of their voices."

"You really think she was that close to them?" asked Potter.

"I'd say ten feet from their cover all that time," said Charlie.

"A very sweet, very tough kid," said Rose.

"I wouldn't want her mad at me," said Katy.

"Meeting's at ten A.M.," said Charlie. "We'll find out how much she remembers."

When Potter and Rose left, Charlie shut and locked the door and called Janey Planck. Janey was first cousin to the former sheriff's sister-in-law. She was also supervisor of operators at telephone central and a staunch supporter of law and order. When Charlie was elected sheriff, he inherited Janey's special service: eavesdropping on phone calls.

"I need you to bend the rules again, Janey," Charlie said. "It's really important. Martin Collins's phone in Chicken Corners. All calls going in and out for the next few days. Every word that's said if you can get it."

"Yes, sir, Sheriff," said Janey. "Happy to help. Gregg or Pittman?"

"You pick it. I'll read the transcriptions."

"Hold on while I try to rewire."

Charlie fiddled with the piece of slate while he waited.

"Someone's calling Collins House right now," said Janey. "You want to listen in?"

Martin was calling from the Sinclair station on the corner.

"Mary! Is Robert there? Or Ted?"

He waited.

"Robert, I'm glad I reached you. Just listen. Don't say anything but yes. I am bringing some special guests to Collins House tonight. Your mother knows they're coming. This would be a good night for you and Ted to camp out. Please leave right away. Be gone all tomorrow morning. When you return, we will have a talk. Tomorrow afternoon or evening, I hope. Or the next day if need be."

"Yes, sir," said Robert. "Good-bye."

Janey came back on.

"Did you get it?" she asked.

"I heard it," said Charlie, "I'm not sure I get it."

⚜   ⚜   ⚜

Rose joined Potter in his office to tackle the annual inventory. Two hours later she was feeling the strain. Numbers for everything: cars, guns, typewriters, fountain pens, tables, chairs, shields. She wondered how many of the good people of Fredericktown knew about the stack of crowd-control shields in the subbasement. Thirty curved metal rectangles with helmets and batons to match, moldering down there since 1880, ordered for a riot that hadn't happened yet.

Potter tipped back in his oak swivel chair and carefully crossed his feet on the corner of his desk.

"It's impolite to show the bottoms of your shoes," Rose said wearily.

"Why?" asked Potter. He took his feet down.

"I don't know. Something my father used to say."

"Sounds like old Hank," said Potter.

"Mr. Vanderhoff to you," said Rose.

Potter began to doodle on his inventory pad.

"Mr. Vanderhoff didn't like me, either," he said. "How come?"

"I guess by 'either' you're saying neither do I," said Rose. She stretched her arms above her head. "And you're right. My father didn't want you on the force. Nobody did. Except your mother."

"I guess, then, he wouldn't have wanted me behind the chief's chair, wearing the chief's uniform," said Potter. "But that's where I'll be when Charlie's gone. So you better get used to it."

"My grandfather got sent to school when he was eight," said Rose. "Three teachers and twenty kids, all in one room. The school bully was one of your great-uncles; a mean little brat named Ambrose Fletcher. He started picking on Gramps right away, because Gramps was little and because his mother and father were Dutch. Finally Gramps had enough. Every day, whenever Willie was least expecting it, he punched him in the nose. The first few times, he took some bad beatings. But he kept it up until finally Willie would whine and start running anytime Gramps came near him."

"That's why your father didn't like me?" asked Potter, concentrating on his doodle. "Because of Uncle Willie?"

"Something like that," said Rose.

Potter put his feet back on the desk.

"Doesn't it bother you, a pretty white girl like Katy snuggling up to an Indian?" asked Potter.

"I always feel like I've made a point when you get nasty and change the subject," said Rose.

She stood up and glanced down at Potter's doodle. *TQ* in block letters.

He looked up.

"Someone else not to like," he said.

Twenty

"MY FIRST TIME AT KUTCHER'S, IT WAS just a farmhouse," said Martin. He was standing in the pebbled drive facing the elegant Tudor-style mansion that had replaced the original summer boardinghouse.

"In those days we ate on the front porch when the weather was right. Once a month at least. The best food in Sullivan County. That was more than thirty years ago."

"Still the best food," said Carl proudly. He was standing next to Jacob, holding Sarah's hand.

Inside, the entryway was unusually busy for a Monday night. A pretty girl standing in a makeshift cardboard booth was offering photographs and leaflets about places to see in the Catskills. A charity raffle was advertising a free winter weekend with three meals a day for two. Beyond the open doorway leading to the dining room, a strong high-baritone voice, backed by an even stronger piano, was singing a song in German.

" 'Ich bin von Kopf bis Fuss auf Liebe eingestellt. . . .' "

"I know that tune," Martin said, frowning, trying to recall.

"In English, it is 'Falling in Love Again,' " said Jacob.

"From a musical film, *The Blue Angel*," Carl added. "About a foolish professor who loses first his heart and then his head."

Sarah looked up quizzically.

"Not really loses," Carl assured her. "Only about what love can do."

The spacious, brightly lit dining room was more than half-filled, mostly with older couples and small family groups. It extended from the front of the building on one side across a wide span in the back, where a row of windows and glass-paned doors provided a view of Kutsher's Lake.

"We would like to be near the water," Carl said to the head-waiter, who led them to a round table decorated with pink roses in the far corner of the room. The piano player, hidden behind his upright at the opposite side, had shifted into another song.

" 'Jonny, oh, Jonny, wie schön war die Nacht. . . . ' "

"He sings special one hour a week for the Germans who come here," Carl explained, gesturing toward the other tables. "Many are new in America. Safe now, but homesick for the things they left behind."

"They are hungry for the music," said Jacob in agreement.

"The piano man plays the old songs. Very sentimental. About loneliness and lost love. But also the new songs, being sung in the cabarets right now."

Sarah sat next to Carl, her hands folded primly on the edge of the table, her lips moving silently to the words of the song.

Jonny, oh, Jonny.

She seemed studious, withdrawn. Martin wondered whether she understood German or was trying to learn it. A smart kid. He tried to imagine her up against Charlie and the others the next morning. He wasn't worried.

The piano rippled without a break into another pensive melody.

" 'Ich hab' noch einen Koffer in Berlin. . . . ' "

"See how they listen!" Carl exclaimed. "This song tells us that someone still has a wardrobe in Berlin. A closet filled with clean clothes. He dreams he will return someday. So foolish."

"Dreaming is not forbidden, Carl," said Jacob.

"Some dreams are nightmares," he replied.

"Is this the Sarah we hear so much about?" asked a jovial voice behind them.

Carl turned quickly, then pushed his chair back and rose awkwardly to his feet.

"Mr. Mark Kutcher, our host," he announced excitedly. "These are my guests: Mr. Martin Collins from Chicken Corners, and from the city Mr. Jacob Kaufmann, his first time to Kutcher's. And, of course, you are right, this is my Sarah."

"Welcome," said Mark with a special smile for the girl. "Please sit, Carl. I have only a moment. Martin I already know. We are old friends. The family is well?"

"Very well, thank you," said Martin, half rising as they shook hands. "We'll all be over soon. And not only for the food but to enjoy this new tummler we hear so much about."

"Sid Caesar!" said Mark in a stage whisper, as if he were protecting a secret. "The man is a genius, a star-to-be. I advise you, come quick while I still can afford him."

He and Martin laughed, and at the same moment the sound of another song filled the room. The words were crisp. The beat was military.

" 'Vor der Kaserne, vor dem grossen Tor . . .' "

"Ah, 'Lili Marleen,' " Mark whispered. "This is a new song, very popular. It is an old poem put to music just this year."

"I remember the poem," said Jacob. "A soldier goes off to war. He thinks he will come back someday. That he will rejoin his girlfriend, under the lamppost where they kissed good-bye."

"Another fool," Carl grunted.

Sarah stared carefully at Carl for a long moment, then with the others turned toward the drumming piano. The diners were mesmerized by the music. The beat was a strangely gentle march. Some of the men rose to their feet. Individual voices, men and women, joined in, unable to keep silent. They sang very softly, careful not to overwhelm the piano man.

Mark explained the lyrics for Martin between the lines.

"This Lili has promised to wait, but still the soldier wonders," he whispered. "Who will be standing under the lamppost with her if something happens to him?"

"Perhaps not such a fool after all," Carl said in reply.

As the song ended, the diners laughed with pleasure and applauded politely. The singer, a small, thin man, rose from behind his piano to take his bow. He was dressed in a white tuxedo, a wing collar, and a red bow tie. He wore minstrel blackface, ready for his next appearance. He lifted his hands high. Smiling, teeth and eyes shining. The applause swelled.

Mark's eyes moved slowly around the room, measuring the crowd. An elderly woman was crying. The man at her side tried to comfort her, but she pulled away.

"*Auf wiedersehen* is sometimes difficult," Mark said. "More so for some than others." He waved and walked away.

Jacob sat back in his chair, looking straight ahead.

"The poem is called 'The Song of a Young Sentry,' " he said. "It was written by Hans Leip, a soldier, in 1914. Soldiers on both sides wrote poetry in that war. So romantic. His poem was about separation. A poem for soldiers. Any soldier, anywhere."

"And now it is a song for Nazis?" Carl asked. "So romantic."

"Wait. We will see," Jacob replied.

"Wait too long and we will die," said Carl.

Martin broke the silence.

"Just a farmhouse," he said again. "We came here. Clara. My son, Edmund, before he went away. Another world."

"Another world," said Carl. "Just so."

"Everything changes in time, Carl," said Jacob. "We thought we were Germans. So, what are we now?"

Twenty-one

"THE FIRST I EVER HEARD ABOUT TOM Quick coming back was in 1928," said Rose. "From my father, just before he died. He heard the story from someone in Treasury."

It was after nine, Monday night. It had been a long day. Charlie was pouring beers for Rose and himself at a back table at the Coach & Anvil Lounge. Potter sat across from them, drinking sarsaparilla. The drinks were instead of overtime pay.

"It happened a few years earlier, in the early twenties, when everything was falling apart, really corrupt."

"Worse than now?" Potter asked.

"Fifty bucks if a cop didn't see a truck that shouldn't be there. You remember. Easy money all over."

Charlie signaled for a second pitcher of beer. It came with a basket of pretzels.

"An ocean of booze was coming down from Canada. They were using speed boats, coffins, the inner tube on the spare. Anything that didn't leak. But mostly trucks.

"The bootleggers were always switching routes, trying to fool the highjackers. Any truck that left Canada, some highjacker usually got tipped off. When, where, and which way."

"No honor among thieves," said Potter.

"So one of the mobs set up a route through Fredericktown. He figured he could supply the big resorts on the way, and he knew they'd hide his trucks if he asked. The first shipment went okay. The second got hit. But not by who they were expecting."

"Three guesses," said Potter. His eyes had a faraway look.

"It happened at the old iron span on the Neversink, over Devil's Chasm. Dynamite. Pop said whoever did it knew his stuff. It flipped the truck over the side without hardly scratching the bridge. Halfway down, the fuel tank and all that alcohol went blooey. The ravine caught fire on both sides."

"I know the place," said Charlie. "Nothing grew there for a long time."

"A week later, two guys from the city get picked up in Wurtsboro. They're showing everyone in town this postcard with a Wurtsboro cancellation. They want to meet the sender."

"Do not come back. Signed, Tom Quick," said Potter.

"Yeah. Something like that," said Rose. "It's addressed to the big man, himself. Dutch Schultz."

※   ※   ※

He remembered how silently his father walked, how he could hear things miles away, how he could see in the dark. On the Neversink Bridge, with no light and no moon, Fletcher had rigged a triple charge of dynamite. Two in the center, one on the side, with a two-second delay. He had slipped over the side and back underneath the girders, trailing the lead wires back to the detonator. He rose in front of Potter like a roll of smoke, the coil of wire clenched in his teeth. He could hear the truck coming.

"Right on time. Let's scarify a sinner, boy," he said.

※   ※   ※

As they were leaving the Coach and Anvil, a Fredericktown police car squealed to a stop. Charlie reached him first. Potter and Rose trailed behind.

"We've been looking all over for you," the driver said. "Someone tried to torch your house. An hour and a half ago."

"Katy's there," said Charlie.

"We took her to the hospital, but she's okay. Smoke was all. No burns. It was a bottle bomb. Gasoline and oil."

"I'm going to Katy," Charlie said to the others. "You two cover the desk."

He turned back to the driver.

"Did you get him?"

"Sorry, Sheriff, he was long gone," the driver said, "but he left his initials on your back door. *TQ.*"

   ⚓ ⚓ ⚓

Fredericktown Hospital was tucked into the hill above the high school playing fields, facing the town park. Charlie started to run diagonally up the hill, but the patrol car honked loudly and gave him a ride. It was almost eleven when he eased himself silently into the white wooden chair at the side of Katy's bed.

The top of the bed was tilted up. Katy's dark brown hair was spread out on the pillow, and her eyes were closed. They opened when a nurse in a gray-and-white uniform came in to check the pressure on an oxygen tank set up against the wall. She gave Katy a few whiffs from a face mask.

"Hi, Charlie," Katy whispered. "I'm okay."

The nurse placed the face mask connected to the tank on the bed near Katy's hand.

"Take a big sniff whenever you need one," she whispered loudly. "Just press the button."

On her way out she hissed, "No smoking!" at Charlie. He nodded obediently, even though he didn't smoke.

"I worked real hard," Katy said in a tired voice. "The window broke in your father's bedroom. I thought it was a bird, like that grouse last year. Except, not at night. Maybe a burglar. Before I had time to get scared, there was this *whoosh* and the whole hallway lit up."

She coughed to clear her throat.

"Don't talk if it hurts," said Charlie. "You gulped a lot of smoke."

He pushed a strand of hair back from her forehead.

"Maybe some papers got burned, Charlie, but it couldn't be much. It's lucky we moved the files. Was that what they wanted? To burn your father's files?"

"Could be, I suppose. But I can't guess why."

"To keep me from reading them, silly," she replied.

ᗺ   ᗺ   ᗺ

Potter stuck his head into the room, at the same time knocking gently on the open door.

"Anybody home?" he asked hesitatingly.

"Come on in," said Charlie, surprised to see him. Potter wasn't close to Katy. Maybe tomorrow, but not tonight.

"How's she doing?"

"They want her to stay the night. But she's in good shape. She'll be home tomorrow."

"I put a night watch on your place," said Potter.

He pulled up the other chair.

"You look better than I thought you would," he said.

"Thanks for nothing," said Katy. She didn't know what to say next. They looked at each other.

"Do you remember anything that might help?" Potter finally asked. He sounded anxious.

"The window broke and there was this *whoosh*. I threw the bucket of water from the bathroom, but it just got worse."

"Gasoline and oil," said Potter. "It would."

"Then I threw the bucket of sand. That slowed it down."

She smiled at Charlie.

"All those buckets you have everywhere. I used to think you were overdoing it. I yelled a lot. The neighbors came."

"You had it licked by then," said Potter. "The report says no real damage. Just a mess to clean up."

"Main thing, you're all right," said Charlie, touching the tip of her nose. He could feel the dread receding.

"Did you see anyone? Hear anything else?" asked Potter.

"No," said Katy.

"Before the window broke, maybe? At the back door? A voice?"

She shook her head.

"How about a car?" He was pushing hard.

"She'd tell you if she had, Potter," said Charlie softly.

"Yeah, I know. I'm sorry. It's just that it's important."

"It was him again," said Charlie. "Tom Quick."

"Looks that way," said Potter. "I want to check it out myself. Suppose I stop by your place early in the morning and wait for the lab crew."

"I'll be there."

"We've got that meeting tomorrow at ten. Okay if I'm not there?"

"If that's what you want," said Charlie. "Rose and I can handle it."

"The desk says he used a white crayon or something this time," said Potter. "*T* period, *Q* period. Script, not stick printing like the last time."

"He's full of surprises," said Charlie.

"Isn't he, though," said Potter.

🖐   🖐   🖐

That night Katy dreamed about Charlie.

It started in the halfway world. She dissolved slowly into a place where there were upside-down waterfalls and puffs of nightgowns and mellow pools of friends who changed into crystal spears of light that burst into sticky letters of the alphabet and woke her with her heart pounding, although in a speeding second she forgot everything and began to drift away again.

After two or three or a million toppling times she was deep inside and rolling around with Charlie. What a nice guy! And so big! It was hard to hold on to him. He was grinning and trying to push away. Why did he want to push away? They tumbled and it was like being underwater, but it wasn't wet, and Charlie was calling for his father. Did he like his father? Did he miss him? He never said so. The bats came when he called. He liked bats. He wouldn't kill them. Their big, black leather wings glided down the rippling walls from Jarvis's attic and tried to wrap around her.

Paper. It was piled around her and under her and there was only a small dish of light far away at the very top. No matter how much paper she sent arching so slowly from here to there, there was always more. She would never get away if she had to read them all.

"Don't be silly," said Charlie, "throw a bucket. It's only sand."

She wrapped around him until they were one person and then he wasn't there at all, just her, exploding like a bomb.

"I love you, Charlie," she tried to explain. "I'm sorry I can't cook."

And he ran his crazy fingers between her legs and Marjorie looked at her and Marjorie had all the papers squeezed in her arms and she looked at Charlie's fingers and began to laugh.

Twenty-two

MARTIN AND HIS GUESTS ARRIVED AT
Collins House from Kutsher's after ten. He had called his daughter-in-law Sunday night from the Baronet to tell her who was coming.

"We'll put the two Jewish gentlemen in the west wing and the little girl in Agnes's room," Mary said. Her words fluttered with excitement.

Martin started to say that Agnes's room might be a bit much for someone that young, but he heard how pleased she was and held his tongue. A child was a rarity at Collins House, and it had been a long time since Mary had sounded so full of life.

ψ　　ψ　　ψ

Sarah had no room for the cookies and lemonade.

"Let's show you where you'll be staying, then," said Mary, picking up the small valise.

Sarah kissed Carl and Jacob good night. Jacob placed his hand gently on Carl's shoulder to keep him from following.

With Sarah at her side, Mary led the way up the center staircase to Agnes's room by candlelight. When the heavy oak door opened,

Sarah took a step backward and drew her breath in sharply, dazzled by the softly lit bedchamber. Mary thought it was simply surprise.

"This room was fixed up by Mr. Collins's mother sixty years ago," she said in a hushed voice. "Her name was Agnes. Do you like it?"

The high ceiling was a froth of plaster flowers, encircling a crown-shaped cut-glass chandelier. The walls were covered with a French floral-trellis paper. Heavily carved rosewood furnishings were combined with a half-canopied, burled-walnut bed and a Renaissance bureau. The carpet was a Persian garden on a burgundy background. A small wood fire crackled in a white marble fireplace. On the mantel tall candles burned steadily inside glass chimneys. Vases of pink roses stood by the window and the bed.

"It is very beautiful," Sarah replied carefully.

She knew Mary was proud of the room and was trying to please her. It was important not to let her know how cold she felt inside.

"It is like a place I used to live," she murmured.

"Like this? Where was that?" asked Mary, not quite believing.

"Warszawa," Sarah said, so low Mary could barely hear her.

"Well, doesn't that sound far away."

She helped Sarah to unpack and put her things away.

"There's a basin and towels on the washstand and a toilet down the hall when you need it," Mary said. "I'll leave the door open a crack. Sweet dreams."

The mattress was very soft and very high. The colors shimmered in the firelight. In the half-darkness Sarah remembered Warszawa, the piano music rising from downstairs, half smothered by waves of tinkling laughter and occasional screams of rage or pain. There the bedroom lights had always been on. The floorboards had creaked, and eyes had watched her through the walls.

Tired as she was, it was a long while before she again was Sarah Spray and fell asleep.

⚚　⚚　⚚

The three men sat in a semicircle of leather chairs facing the fireplace in Martin's den. It was a brown, masculine room: wainscoted walls, floor-to-ceiling bookcases, tan braided rugs, mica lampshades, a smell of pipe smoke. On the walls were portraits in oil of Matthew and Agnes Collins by Thomas Rossiter and views of Lake Repose by Thomas Doughty and Asher Durand.

A leather-bound author's edition of *The Complete Works of Harriet Beecher Stowe* stood on a small oak table behind the desk. The first volume lay open. The inscription, to Agnes Collins, read, "God bless you. Harriet."

Martin puffed at a clay churchwarden. Jacob rolled a brandy snifter between his hands. Carl stared past him at the dead ashes in the grate.

"Our meeting with your sheriff went well?" Jacob asked Martin.

"Well enough. Charlie was accommodating."

"He is finished with us?"

"You folks are all he has, Jacob. That means you're it until he finds someone else."

Someone like my grandsons, he thought.

"Mr. Washington suspects me," said Carl. "I was in the house. I did not like her. I have guns. I am a Jew."

"For such a strong man, you are easily upset," said Jacob.

"I don't think he suspects either of you," said Martin. "But he doesn't believe you've told him everything."

"So, what did I not tell him?" Carl asked, sounding amused, as if he would enjoy a challenge.

"You are an intelligent man, Mr. Rozkopf. You are not naive. You wouldn't get involved in a thing like this—Mrs. Brown, a phony foundation, the farmhouses, the refugees—without knowing what you were doing. More than you've told us."

"That is true, Carl," said Jacob. "You would not let her lead you by the nose."

Carl turned to Martin. His voice softened.

"There are things they did not ask."

He seemed more relaxed, not as defensive.

"*Bitte*. So. From the first, I knew Emma Brown was a lie. Even rich charities do not throw money away." He snorted contemptuously.

"Then why did you get involved?" asked Martin.

"She was a mystery. I had to know if she meant harm."

He smiled, remembering.

"We went shopping together in the neighborhood. Shopping for people. Up and down the streets. She pointed at the kind she wanted. Foreign looking, and not so clean. She wanted long hair and black beards."

Jacob made a scolding noise with his tongue.

"Shopping for people, Carl? Our people?"

Carl shrugged, raising his shoulders high.

"Her money was good. It could be put to good use."

He turned to Martin.

"Summer in the city is very bad. I looked at the houses she had for them. They would enjoy, and I would learn."

"About what she was doing?" Jacob asked.

Carl smiled.

"*What* she was doing I knew from the beginning, Jacob. I did not know *why*. I had seen Jews used this way before. To give fright. You have seen this also, Martin? I may call you Martin?"

"If I may call you Carl. Yes, if it's what I think you mean, I've seen it before. And not only Jews. But why would you get mixed up in a thing like that?"

He waited while Carl searched for an explanation.

"Do you listen on the radio to the League of the Little Flower? The National Union for Social Justice? Does your Mr. Washington believe that Eddie Cantor, who sings and dances and makes jokes, is the most dangerous Jew in America?"

"Father Coughlin is it?" said Martin. "Just how does that peculiar man fit in?"

"When first I heard this Coughlin on the radio, my mind went back there again," he said. "The same fine words from the heart. Justice. Honor. Decency. Expose the conspirators. Protect the weak. Defend your country. Such noble ideas. Like Drexler and Strasser before."

"Nazis?" asked Martin.

"The first ones, the schoolteachers. Later it was Rohm and Hitler and Goebbels, not such nice Nazis. In the beginning they had many faces, many voices. Drexler taught twenty-five points of social justice. Did you know that?"

"I don't think I did. And Father Coughlin reminds you of this?"

"Divide the wealth. Abolish poverty. Expose the international bankers. Purify the world. A Pied Piper. First he is a rat catcher. Later he steals your children."

"For this you fill your house with guns?" said Jacob.

"When I saw "The Protocols of the Elders of Zion" in the father's magazine, I asked, is it happening again? Will they hammer on my door? Who is this Bernard Baruch he warns us about? What is this Jewish plot? Does he mean me?"

"Why did you leave Germany?"

"To stay alive. To escape my *kamerads*."

He took a deep breath, closed and opened his eyes.

"Let me tell you. My father was a ragman in Frankfurt am Main. A fine business, rags, after the war in Germany. We were the lumpen proletariat.

"I told you I was Reichswehr, yes? But only late in the war. When there were not many men left. When German men were dying fifty thousand a day, and the generals were happy to see a Jewish boy. I was a good soldier. I faced the Americans in France."

Martin flinched. *He faced Edmund in France.*

"I was decorated. Many years later, in a café in the Schwartzwald, a man from my old group remembered my face. I joined his table. We sang the old songs. Later we went into the city to salute the *Alte Kampfer*, the old soldiers who were betrayed at Versailles. Do you know Frankfurt?"

"I have been many places in Europe, but I have avoided Germany," said Martin.

"They took me to a brewer's warehouse by the river. I thought for a reunion, but it was only politics. I was not political then. We were drunk and happy. We listened to speeches and sang more songs." He laughed. "Such a bad mistake. My comrade, we discovered, did not know I was a Jew. I did not know he was Sturmabsteilung."

"The SA, a Brown Shirt," said Martin.

"We fought. I am a strong man, Martin. I broke his head, and some others also. My father and I quickly left Germany. It was 1927. He was able to bring money out. A few years more, it would not have been possible."

"So Martin, you understand Carl's guns," said Jacob. "Please, now, we will talk about the murder of this woman. How do Jews give fright, Carl? Make sense of this for me."

"Land," said Carl. "She wanted land. Much land. Cheap land. For what reason I do not know. But I knew her method. I helped her in many places for more than a year. We agreed when she had what she wanted, she would find land for me."

"You have land already," said Jacob.

Carl shook his head as if he were explaining to a child.

"For when the others come. There must be places for them."

He leaned out of his chair.

"Can you guess how many are coming, Martin? Millions."

"Coming here?" said Martin warily. "Millions?"

"When he lets his prisoners go, there must be places for them. Clean, dry, warm. Not in the tenements learning to steal. Camps, villages, towns. We are already making them. Space we can defend. For the children. Where we will not have to run again."

"So it was a swindle," Martin said quietly. "She was using your refugees to push the prices down. A real estate swindle."

Carl shrugged.

"It was justified. You said you have seen this before. 'Sell! Sell! The Jews are coming!' "

"To be frightened by Jews," Jacob muttered.

"Not the fancy doctors and professors, Jacob. Not their fancy wives. The other Jews. The ones who shake their fists at the sky. With the beards and the long hair. Emma Brown's refugees. *My Jews.*"

"Justified," said Martin. "I've used that word often in my time. A swindle is a swindle."

"There were six houses back and forth," said Jacob. "You kept us busy."

"Six!" said Carl. "There were twenty! Your buses were not the only ones. There would be sixty houses if this woman needed them. She had money. She had the will. She had land for me."

"Is it over now, Carl?" asked Jacob. "That she is dead?"

"I cannot answer. Shofar was many people, doing many things. I only knew her."

"What in God's name was she after?" Martin asked. "What was the land for? Who killed her? Who shot at the house?"

"She never told me what the land was for," Carl answered. "Who killed her, I do not know."

Twenty-three

CHARLIE THREW THE LIGHT SWITCHES gingerly, expecting sparks. They all worked. The wiring didn't seem to be damaged. The house smelled of woodsmoke, wet ashes, and oily gasoline. The night-watch patrolman snoozing in his car outside declined Charlie's invitation to come inside.

"It's the asthma, Sheriff," he explained. "I wouldn't be able to breathe."

Charlie sent him home.

Still, it was not as bad as it might have been. Charlie raised all the windows and pushed up the trapdoor in the hallway ceiling to give the peak vents a chance to suck the odors out. He propped the back door open with a kitchen chair and stepped outside to read the scribble on the pane of glass: T. Q. In cursive script with periods, like Potter said. Nothing like the block capitals without periods that had been scratched on the piece of black slate.

Got to photograph it before it rains, he thought.

His father's bedroom was a charred and soggy mess. Sections of the fiberboard walls and ceiling were hacked open. The window was gone. The rag rug, the curtains, the mattress and bedding, and some of Jarvis's clothes that had been in the closet were piled on the ground outside the window.

Right on top of T. Q.'s shoe prints, maybe, he thought. *Hope they left something for the lab.*

Someone had dumped two boxes of Jarvis's papers in the bathtub. They were partially burned and soaked through.

Salvageable, he thought. *Some of it, anyway.*

Jarvis had kept his files in the bedroom, packed in dozens of marbleized black-and-white cardboard boxes. Weeks earlier Charlie and Katy had stacked most of them in the small office next door. It was easier for Katy to work on them there.

The fire had not reached the office but the firemen had. Jarvis's desk had been swept clean. There were boot prints on the surface, probably where someone had climbed up to test the ceiling temperature. Charlie replaced the desk lamp and the small oscillating fan and switched them on. The fan immediately pulled more of the acrid smell in from the bedroom, so he turned it around to face the open door.

When he lifted the leather-cornered desk pad off the floor, the large sheet of brown blotting paper pulled loose on one end, and a single piece of paper slipped out. He picked it up carefully. It was a letter, finely hand-written in copper-colored ink on heavy paper with a feathery edge.

October 12, 1855

To my wife, Elizabeth,

  We are both guilty. We have betrayed each other. I will raise the child as my own. That will be my punishment. To it and to Ann shall pass all my possessions.

  Our marriage will be a pretense. I will never speak to you again.

Samuel

At the bottom penciled lightly in Jarvis's neat hand were two questions: "John Carpenter? More?"

Charlie fell into bed at three and slept soundly for two and a half hours. At five-thirty he sat bolt upright.

Katy was coming back Wednesday! It was already Wednesday! He had to pick her up at the hospital between noon and one!

He wanted her to stay with him, but she might not want to with the house looking the way it was.

Wearing only his shorts and rubber galoshes, he emptied the bathtub, cleaned the bathroom, and mopped all the floors except the one in Jarvis's bedroom where the lab crew might find something. He tacked a half sheet of old fiberboard over the missing window, and generally straightened up. He was not worried much about destroying evidence. Whoever threw the bomb had not come inside.

When things felt under control, he thought some more about Katy and himself together, took a shower, and made breakfast.

Twenty-four

POTTER PARKED HALFWAY UP THE DRIVE at seven-thirty and walked the rest of the way. Charlie was sitting on the front steps, finishing a fried-egg sandwich and sipping a second cup of coffee.

"Smells good," said Potter.

"New recipe. Brazilian mocha and wet ashes," said Charlie. "I'll get you one while you look around."

※　　※　　※

Potter came back out of the bedroom and sat next to Charlie on the porch step.

"I'll ask Danny to stay out here the next few days," he said. "You'll want to be in town."

"The sleepy guy with the asthma?"

"Rose is keeping him on until he makes his twenty-five. She's too soft, but he's okay."

"I don't know what he'd have to guard. Could he put in a window while he's hanging around? We might get some rain."

"I'll send someone out with a window. It'll cost you, though."

"Can't claim line of duty, huh? Charge it to TQ?"

"You'd never get that one past Rose. But we'll do what we can."

"Every little bit helps."

※　　※　　※

Coffee cups in hand, they circled around to the back of the house, watching their feet as they walked. The firemen had trampled the ground. There was nothing there to see.

The single pane of glass in the kitchen door was two feet by three. Tom Quick's initials almost filled the space. T. Q.

Potter stared at the letters, his gut tightening.

That was not me, he told himself. *I did not do that.* Someone was playing games with him. He felt lightheaded.

"You okay?" Charlie asked.

"Yeah, fine. Not used to good coffee. Or good ashes."

He put his nose close to the pane of glass and sniffed. Then he wet the tip of his finger with saliva and rubbed the edge of the top of the *T.*

"Not too much," Charlie said. "The scientists haven't been here yet, and I want a photo of that."

"Soap," said Potter, sniffing again. "Scented. Cashmere Bouquet, I think."

"The lab wouldn't have figured that out in a month," Charlie said with real admiration.

"I know the smell," said Potter.

"Katy thinks the bomber was after my father's files."

He said it casually and carefully, watching for some kind of reaction. He didn't get it.

"What for?"

"I hoped you might have some idea," said Charlie. "You're detecting good today."

"Not a clue. What makes her think so?"

"Just a feeling. She's been going through the files on and off, trying to make sense of them. If there's anything there, she'll find it."

Potter took a last look at the initials and turned away.

"Let her keep looking," he said, unconcerned. "Women are good at files."

In the kitchen, Potter paused to study the long row of pots, pans, and skillets that were hanging from game hooks attached to the ceiling along one wall.

"You got a lot of pots," he said.

"I cook," said Charlie. "You need them."

"That used to be my nickname," said Potter. "Pots. I hated it. When I'm sheriff I'll make nicknames illegal."

"You are not going to be sheriff," said Charlie.

Potter stood with his back to Charlie, thinking about that. He drummed a few notes on the bottoms of some pots with the fingertips of his right hand.

Finally he said, "You told me you wouldn't run again."

"I've changed my mind."

"Too late for that. It's all arranged. It's time for a change. I'm next."

Charlie knew what he meant. Potter knew a lot of people in town. Many of them had worked for his father at B & W when times were good. A few were still there.

"Sorry, Pots," said Charlie. "I can't let that happen. I get the feeling you're one of the bad guys now."

He was surprised to hear himself say that. Maybe it was a mistake, telling him. He had no proof, just a feeling. But it made him feel better. He'd know soon enough anyway.

"How bad is bad?"

"That's what I'm working on."

Potter poured the dregs of the coffee into the sink and placed the cup carefully in the center of the drain board.

"Don't waste your time, Charlie," he said. "The cowboys always win."

Twenty-five

MARTIN DROVE HIS GUESTS BACK TO Fredericktown from Collins House for the ten o'clock meeting in the briefing room. Rose had a message from Potter saying that he would miss the meeting, that he wanted to work with the lab crew at Charlie's house. The meeting went more smoothly without him.

"You have all been very helpful," Charlie said when it was over. "You especially, young lady."

Sarah acknowledged the compliment with a tiny nod. She had told her story about the men on the hill without emotion, occasionally glancing up at Carl, who sat at her side smiling encouragement.

Charlie turned to Martin. "It will take a few days to get this typed up. Copies for everyone, Rose."

"We are free to go?" asked Jacob.

"Whenever you want," said Charlie. He looked at Carl. "I may want to see you again."

Carl nodded. His face was blank.

"You are all welcome back at Collins House," said Martin. "It's a long trip back to the city, and everyone's tired. Why not stay another day and rest up?"

"You are very kind," said Jacob, "but I have much to do."

"And I have a farm," said Carl.

"I would like that very much, Mr. Collins," said Sarah.

She was sitting with her hands folded primly on her knees, ignoring the effect her announcement was having on the four men.

"You could stay with her, no?" Jacob asked Carl. "I would go back to help August."

"Vegetables do not grow by themselves," said Carl. He turned in his chair to face Sarah. "School begins soon. You have much to learn."

"Mrs. Collins will teach me to bake," Sarah countered.

"We'd love to have her," said Martin. "The house is so empty without children. The boys are away camping. Let her stay through the weekend."

He turned back to Sarah.

"You could pick a bouquet for me."

"I will do that," she replied.

"Then it's settled."

Carl's uncertainty showed. He took Sarah's hand in his.

"I will buy a present for when you come home. What should it be?"

"I would like a crystal chandelier," she said.

⚘   ⚘   ⚘

After the meeting was breaking up, Rose gestured Martin into Charlie's office and closed the door behind him.

"I'll have to be quick," she said. "I don't know how much you've heard. Three things. First, Tom Quick tried to burn down Charlie's house last night. Katy got the fire out. She's in the hospital, but she's okay."

"Why Charlie's house?"

"That's second. Katy thinks it was to burn Jarvis's files. No reason, she just thinks it. She's been sorting out the files for Charlie."

"Well, Katy's a bright girl. If that's what she thinks, there might be something to it."

"Third, Charlie thinks there might be two Tom Quicks. Like one isn't enough."

Martin groomed his mustache with his forefinger.

"Charlie's moving pretty fast on this. Soon he'll be wondering about the boys. I need something to trade him with, before he gets too far ahead of me." He paused, fingers on chin. "Do you have keys to Marjorie's office?"

"I have keys to everything," said Rose, "except your heart."

"This afternoon. I'll meet you there. Two o'clock?"

"It's a date."

"You're a love."

"Don't I wish," she replied.

Martin reached for the phone on the desk.

"Use the one on the side table," said Rose. "It doesn't go through our switchboard. I'm here if you need me."

She said it like she meant it.

Ψ   Ψ   Ψ

Martin's first call was to Mary at Collins House.

"I've got to be quick. Sarah will be with us until Saturday or Sunday. Get word to the boys to stay away until I send for them. Never mind why. I hope they've got enough food."

"I'll get some up to them. Anything else, Judge?"

"Yes. Sarah wants to bake a cake. And pick flowers. Looks like you've made a friend."

His second call was to Talmadge House, Patrick Cardinal Hayes's vacation retreat at Lake St. Joseph in Forestburgh.

"I would like to speak with His Eminence if he is there," he said to the soft male voice that answered. "This is Martin Collins. We're old friends. It is important."

Minutes later another voice, high-pitched and concerned, was on the line.

"Hello, Martin. It's Frank. How can I help."

Frank? Ah, Francis Spellman. I thought he was in Boston. Where could Patrick be?

"Frank. How are you? I should say Bishop. Your Reverence. It's been a long time."

"Too long."

"I was hoping to speak with the cardinal. I have a bit of a problem."

"I'm sorry, Martin. He isn't well. I've been taking some of the weight off his shoulders."

So, he's been picked to take over.

"I didn't know. I should have inquired. I've been out of touch."

Could he trust Spellman? He wasn't even from New York. From somewhere in Massachusetts, and sure to be spoiled by all those years in Boston.

"Perhaps I can help."

"I need a favor, Frank."

"Please ask. We owe your family many."

"My grandsons are into some kind of trouble up here. Chicken Corners, Fredericktown. I don't know how bad it is. There's not much to go on. Something about it reminds me of the Tammany shenanigans my father used to mastermind."

"Ah, shenanigans. Irish venial sins."

"They could be mortal this time, Frank. A lot of downtown money with the city and state people in for their share. And, of course, some kind of grand scheme behind it all. I have some of the names, and I hope to have more soon. One piece should lead to another."

"You will want to talk to Tim Cavanaugh. You know him, I'm sure."

"Monsignor Cavanaugh. The Chamberlain. I do indeed."

"The sobriquet is not official, but he's the man. He's here with us now. We are all scheduled to leave this afternoon, but I will ask Tim to stay over."

"That's very kind of you."

"You'll come down to St. Joseph's, then? Tim will be expecting your call. Now, give me whatever background and names you have."

※   ※   ※

On the way to the garage, Rose spotted Charlie and motioned him aside.

"Something's bothering me, Sheriff," she said.

When she used his title, he knew she was serious.

"Let's hear it," he said.

"Red right. Red left," she said, as if it meant something.

"Uh-huh," said Charlie, not really understanding.

"Not *red*, Charlie. *Ready!* The range command. *Ready on the right! Ready on the left!* Potter says that all the time. Like when we were talking about the targets in Rozkopf's room. *Ready on the firing line!*"

Charlie inhaled, held it a moment, then exhaled. *One of the bad guys.*

"Worth thinking about," he said. "You know what that might mean."

"It's only an idea."

"Let's keep it to ourselves."

Twenty-six

MARJORIE BINGHAM'S JOB AS RECORDS clerk had been to accumulate and record data on deeds, titles, liens, property sales, tax assessments, and so forth for the township. It took her no more than an hour or two a day. The rest of the time she was free to handle real estate and personal business.

Three days before she was shot and killed, the building switchboard had transferred one of her personal calls to Katy by mistake.

"Anyone here know someone named Emma Brown?" Katy called out to the two clerks in the bullpen.

When no one responded, she said, "Sorry!" and hung up. After the switchboard operator called to apologize for the error, she scribbled a note to Marjorie: "Someone called you on my line looking for an Emma Brown. No message. Katy."

Katy forgot about the call, but the next day Marjorie told the town clerk that she would be moving her real estate business out of her records clerk office at the end of the month.

"It's getting too small for me," she explained. "Much too small."

"What are we looking for?" Rose whispered.

"I'll know it when we find it," Martin whispered back. "And let's stop the whispering. If anyone comes in, we want to look like we belong here."

It was two o'clock Tuesday afternoon at the Public Records Building. Rose was working her way through a ringful of keys, looking for the one to Marjorie's office door. The words Senior Records Clerk with M. Bingham underneath were painted on the inside of the pane of frosted glass. To the left of the door was the L-shaped cubicle Katy had formed out of filing cabinets to house the editor-in-chief of *This Month* magazine.

"Got it," said Rose.

Inside the office an oak desk with a matching slat-back swivel chair faced a shaded window at the center of the outside wall. Dark brown filing cabinets spread out around the room. Martin moved slowly from one cabinet to another, checking the index cards slotted on the faces of the drawers.

"These two," he said, finally, "the property transfer records for '37 and '38. And over there, her real estate files. You take these, I'll take those."

"Looking for what?" Rose asked again.

"Anything that suggests what she was up to."

The drawers glided quietly on bar runners. They thumbed quickly through the folders.

"Lots of names here I don't recognize," said Martin, puzzled. "They're not locals. Mortgage sharks maybe, asking about defaults. They move in fast."

Rose passed him an open folder.

"Here's a carbon of a note to Carl from Emma Brown."

"Directions to Frank McBride's place in Thunder Mountain and a description of the house," Martin said.

"The McBride house is empty," Rose said. "Frank's doing six in Ossining. B and E. Annie took the kids back to Kingston."

"That's our fate, too, if we don't hurry," said Martin.

Most of the Emma Brown files were in a shipping box on the floor, next to boxes marked Bingham Real Estate. Rose selected a legal-sized folder, bound tightly with heavy rubber bands and labeled Confidential.

"Clever way to hide something," she said as she took a seat in the swivel chair.

Halfway through she said, "This might mean something. A three-page list of properties, each marked Buy or Option in capital letters. And there's some notes clipped on, her handwriting."

"Read some of them to me."

" 'Send space info to Rozkopf. Find another bank. Ask Steve for a better map. How much to shut Jarvis up?' "

She looked up.

"There's only one Jarvis I know. Charlie's father. I don't like the sound of that."

She passed the folder to Martin and went back to the boxes. He began checking the list against sheets he had been pulling from his files.

"Marjorie bought seven of these places as Emma Brown," he said. "Bingham Real Estate acted as agent. Some others went to Mr. Stephen Collier, a trustee of the Shofar Foundation, on options to buy with a fifty percent penalty on the advance."

"Whatever that means," said Rose. "Wasn't Collier the Presbyterian who helped Marjorie find Carl?"

"It means Mr. Collier gets only half of his down payment back if the deal isn't closed by the deadline. It keeps things moving. And he could be Episcopalian."

He browsed through a lengthy memorandum.

"Here's a link to Ginnie Washington," he said. "She agrees to sell nine properties to nine different names in the city. I know some of them. Take a look at these numbers."

The total agreed payment to Ginnie was $612,000, but the bill of sale showed only $210,000.

"A tax dodge?"

"It's dirtier than that. It fits in with some other things Carl told me."

In a folder labeled "Maps," Rose found driving directions to five more farmhouses on the outskirts of Lake Repose. Eighteen properties on a township map were circled in red crayon. "Change Shofar to Repose Management?" was written in the margin. A list of ten names with New York City business addresses was stapled at the bottom.

"What were you up to, little lady?" Rose mumbled aloud.

"Ginnie gets a one hundred thousand dollars bonus if all the deals go through by June of next year," said Martin. "She's dumping more than eleven thousand acres at a price way below depressed market. Including the house and land in Chicken Corners and some of the quarries."

The seven properties sold to Emma Brown had been reentered in the town records under a variety of New York City names, some of them the same names Martin had not recognized on his first pass through. The dates ran from September 1936 to December 1937. None of the option-to-buy agreements had been recorded, a legal requirement, but a batch of proper-notification forms, backdated, was in a separate envelope.

"This goes beyond sloppy paperwork," said Martin. "She was hiding something big."

Rose pointed to the label on another file folder.

"Wonder what this means?" she asked. " 'Judas Goat.' "

Two hours into the files, Martin and Rose felt beat up. Some of it made sense, a lot was gibberish. But Martin had collected over two dozen names, and he was starting to get the picture.

While Rose was locking the office door, he studied a typewritten poem tacked onto the *This Month* bulletin board.

"That was the last poem Jarvis submitted to *This Month*," said

Rose. "Katy printed most of his, but she said that one sounded a little creepy."

Legacy

Doorways that we wandered through,
Forests where the hemlock grew,
Trinkets that our mothers blessed,
Hollows where our fathers rest,
Laughter, hunger, reverence, toil,
Lovers, mountains, singers, soil,
   Must you leave us? Pause awhile.
   Do not trust them. They defile.

Martin pulled the tack, folded the sheet of paper, and tucked it in his coat pocket.

"That's a real shame," he said. "It could be his best."

$\mathcal{T}$wenty-seven

KATY WAS UP, DRESSED, AND READY TO
go when Charlie got to the hospital just after noon. Her head felt
like it was stuffed with peanut butter, and her stomach was rolling.
She had not been able to eat the steamed lunch. The doctor made
her promise to rest.

As they were leaving the hospital she told Charlie a fib.

"I really feel fine. I want to get at those files. I'll take the nap
later."

She was pleased at the cleaning up. She didn't want to go home
to Thunder Mountain, and Charlie cleaning up meant he wanted
her to stay. She had an urge to say, "You're a nice guy, Charlie,"
but she couldn't remember why.

ψ   ψ   ψ

On the way to Chicken Corners Charlie asked if she had ever
heard the name John Carpenter.

"The abolitionist?" she said. "Sure. Why?"

"Dad wrote it down. On the bottom of an old letter. And then
he hid it. It may mean something. A well-known guy?"

"I don't know much about him. Your father was going to do a paper on him someday. He thought he'd been overlooked. Carpenter was from up here. The 1850s."

"Is there a file on him? Any letters?"

"There's probably a file, but I haven't seen it. I don't know about letters."

"Keep an eye open, will you? How about some people named Samuel and Elizabeth, man and wife? And Ann, possibly a daughter?"

"Doesn't ring a bell."

They drove through Chicken Corners with the war memorial on one side and Rudy's on the other. Charlie's thoughts went back to the French-Canadian kid and the jar of turpentine. *Merde*. The kid had scrubbed the plaque clean and shiny. He didn't want to talk, but finally he had described a teenager and a grown man with a whip. It sounded like Potter Washington and maybe the older Collins boy, Robert. Something to file and not forget. *How bad is bad?* The kid was gone the next day.

"What could it mean?" Katy asked. "John Carpenter's been dead a long time."

"Gone but not forgotten," said Charlie.

 ₩   ₩   ₩

They reached the house early afternoon. Potter and the lab crew were gone. They had moved the mattress and the pile of soggy bedding and clothing away from the outside wall. There were no signs of any footprints, no plaster-cast marks anywhere. Not very promising. The initials were still on the glass on the kitchen door. Charlie was taking a tally when the carpenter drove up with a new window, fully framed, in the trunk of his car.

While Charlie was trying to photograph the T. Q. initials with one of Jarvis's antique bellows cameras, Katy was re-marking the boxes she had already been through. The carpenter was hammering away.

"Wherever your father is, he's probably enjoying my confusion," Katy called to him.

"Why not? He always enjoyed mine," Charlie muttered in reply.

⚜   ⚜   ⚜

Jarvis had designed a filing system he hoped only he could understand. There were numbers, letters, symbols, and words, some of which rhymed, but what they meant was anyone's guess. Katy's challenge was to break the code.

What the hell was he hiding here? she asked herself. She thought she knew. Private lives. Jarvis had a thing about private lives.

Katy had decided to undermine Jarvis's defenses by overriding his system. She began by numbering the boxes, starting with the numeral one, and alphabetizing all the contents, starting with the letter *A*. Jarvis hated simplicity, so she would confound him with it.

I'll getcha yet, you old rascal. She smiled to herself.

⚜   ⚜   ⚜

Charlie's airing-out had left the counterweighted trapdoor to the attic open. It was an inviting place, filled with Jarvis's picker treasures—paintings, books, crockery, clocks, rugs, lamps, toys, enough of what the antique dealers call 'smalls' to stock a shop.

Katy would have braved the dust, the dirt, and the cobwebs for a chance to browse, but she drew the line at bats. There were legions of them up there. Sometimes one would flutter down when the trapdoor was left open. Knowing it was open now made her scalp itch. The window hammering might stir them up.

"Hey, Charlie, the trapdoor's open. The bats will get out," she called, but he was busy with his camera.

She pulled the five-foot wooden ladder out of the hall closet, opened it, and with flashlight in hand cautiously climbed up.

"Be nice, fellas," she whispered.

As she reached up to grip the edge of the lifted door, she dared a quick peek at the loot. There it was, a thin file sitting on the lower shelf of a one-drawer stand at eye level. She had forgotten that the attic was one of the old rascal's hiding places. She tucked the file under her arm, lowered the door as she climbed back down, and went outside.

"Hey, Charlie, guess what I found," she said triumphantly. "John Carpenter."

Twenty-eight

MARY TOOK SARAH TO THE HIGH GARDEN to learn the names of flowers. She promised that whatever or how many flowers Sarah picked, they would make bouquets from them. As a surprise, they would make a special arrangement for the Judge's room that night. With some oatmeal cookies and a glass of milk next to it.

Martin used the wallbox telephone at Collins House to ring up Monsignor Cavanaugh. The monsignor understood the niceties of party lines.

"An intriguing list of names you left me, Martin," he said.

"I have a lot more now."

"I thought you were through with this sort of thing."

"I am, Monsignor. You have my word. This is the younger generation's mess, not mine. I would greatly value your interpretation."

"What you've got reminds me of something I've been watching myself. Many of the names are the same. Can you get down here tonight for dinner?"

"I would be honored," said Martin.

"I don't know what magic you worked with the bishop, but I have the place practically to myself. A marvelous chef, the key to the wine cellar, a rare opportunity to pose as a prince of the Church."

"I wouldn't miss it for the world, Monsignor. What time are you serving?"

"Cocktails at seven, is it? We'll skip the white tie. Stay over if you'd like. The house is deserted."

"I would like that very much, Tim," said Martin.

ψ   ψ   ψ

Standing in the doorway to the kitchen, he told Mary, "I'll be dining tonight at Talmadge House. I'll probably stay over."

"You'll be missing a lovely cake," said Mary, not bothering to turn around.

Sarah carefully spread the armful of flowers she had picked across the kitchen table, surrounding the chocolate cake she had iced herself.

He would not be home for dinner and cake for dessert. Or be sleeping upstairs where he would see the bouquet and the cookies and milk by his bed.

She did not let her face show her disappointment.

ψ   ψ   ψ

When Martin arrived at St. Joseph's at seven Tuesday evening, Tim was waiting in the doorway. He and Martin had known each other more than twenty years, and the warmth of their reunion was genuine.

Timothy Cavanaugh's first assignment following his ordination in 1912 had been St. Benedict's. While there he acted as chaplain to the Algonquin Lodge of Tammany Hall, an uptown clubhouse of the Old Irish. Over the years his superiors moved him into increasingly important and influential posts in New York County, city hall, and finally Albany.

Tim had delegated powers and no illusions. He summed up his abilities modestly: "Whatever's needed, within reason. Whatever is required." Wherever he served, he got good marks.

In the midtwenties Tim was one of those assigned to help put Alfred Emanuel Smith in the White House. When that opportunity was missed, the Right Reverend Monsignor Timothy F. X. Cavanaugh resigned himself to the political limbo of a suddenly different and curiously alien state capital. There he gathered intelligence, brokered deals, adjudicated quarrels, ran errands, and as always got things done.

Six feet two and big boned with short-cropped, steel gray hair, Tim towered over Martin. His deeply lined, rectangular face could have belonged to a soldier or a scholar or a farmer. He was coatless. He wore black trousers with red suspenders, a billowy white cotton shirt, a black satin clerical bib, and a stiffly starched Roman collar. His sleeve bands, worn above his elbows, were decorated gold-on-red with diamonds, hearts, clubs, and spades.

The dining room was at the rear of the house. Two places faced each other at the center of the long table. A cheery fire burned in the Federal-style corner fireplace, just enough to take the chill off the evening air. The mahogany sideboard was covered with silver serving dishes, long-stemmed glasses, and crystal decanters.

"Not all for us, I hope," said Martin.

"All and more," said Tim.

"We haven't really talked since the great campaign," said Martin as they sat down.

Tim smiled at that.

"Al Smith for President," he said, as he carefully boned the smoked trout. "A grand joke, that. Making kings must be easier. With the right ancestors, you don't need friends. There might be a little more blood, but there's less competition."

He held up a Champagne glass, inspecting the contents against the light.

"You sound a mite bitter," said Martin.

"I don't like losing," said Tim. "Not the way we did. I wasn't ready for it. And there's not another of our crowd on the horizon."

"What's next for you, then? You're still young. Maybe you've been climbing too short a ladder."

The monsignor laughed. "I've been pigeonholed, Martin. Typecast. I'm the Chamberlain. The fellow you have to see to get to the fellow you'd rather see. I enjoy the part. I play it well."

A dark-skinned young man in a white jacket tended the table. Tim and Martin served themselves from the buffet. The rest of the staff was invisible. Tim recommended the Chablis. The offer was tentative. Martin declined.

"You were just a greenhorn when we met," Martin mused. "New to the collar. Dad was gone. I was in my prime."

"You had us all terrified, Martin. Did you know that? The Collins name, the Tammany connection, the history. And you were a comer. Thin and quick. They called you Stone Martin."

"Did they? A predator. Member of the weasel family. I think I remember that. The war was on and finally going well. Clara and Edmund were both alive. Robert was a toddler, Ted was on the way. And Mary was a treasure. God, she was. Laughter and sunshine all the time, before we got the news from France."

"Did they ever find him?"

"No. He's over there somewhere."

"Between the crosses, row on row. May he rest in peace," said Tim.

"The family once had a great future," said Martin. "Bright as buttons, everyone healthy, no one in jail. Those days, I knew who I was, what I was doing, where I was going. And why. Somewhere along the line I lost it."

Tim lifted the silver dome off the entrée, red snapper in a white wine sauce, surrounded by baby onions.

"Well, down to business?" Martin asked as he took his portion.

"Ready if you are," said the monsignor. "That little list of names you gave His Eminence was all I really needed."

"I have a few more now, borrowed from the dead woman's files," said Martin. He passed a folded sheet of paper across the table.

Tim talked as he read.

"There's some here I don't have, and I've been following this little game for half a dozen years." He looked up. "By the bye, Martin, you'll keep the Church out of this, whatever happens? Agreed?"

"Agreed."

"Well, where to start? Do you know Candlewood Lake?"

"In Connecticut? Man-made. Beautiful, I hear, but I've never seen it. An electric power project of some sort."

"A model project, cleverly done. I was put watching it when I was young and learning the ropes. The promoters flooded a valley, the Rocky River basin, ten miles long, above Danbury where the Berkshire foothills begin."

"I remember the area," said Martin. "Tobacco country. We bought good hardwoods there—cherry, oak, poplar, black walnut—forty, fifty years ago. The farming was in decline."

"The flooding is continuous. Some of it comes from runoff. The rest they pump up through gigantic turbines from the Housatonic River. They fill the lake when electric demand is low and draw it off when demand is high. It was the first big effort of its kind in this country."

"What was the date on it?" asked Martin.

"Hartford gave the go-ahead around '07, but it was a dozen years before they had all the permissions. Even then, construction didn't start until '26."

"It must have been a grand adventure," said Martin. "A lot of land changing hands, and a lot of money."

"All aboveboard as far as I know. Once they got the go-ahead, they moved fast. One year to strip the valley, a few more to flood it. The Rocky River vanished. Along with thirty or forty farms, some orchards, woodlands, summer cottages. A few good-sized ponds. Even the low parts of some nearby towns. They moved the cemeteries to high ground."

"Concerned about the dead," said Martin. "Aren't they always. Did it turn out the way they wanted?"

"Beyond all expectations. They got their kilowatts, and the lake as a bonus. Sixty miles of prime shoreline."

"And the owners? The previous owners."

"The company had authority to flood the valley. They offered thirty to ninety dollars an acre. There were families that had farmed there since before the Revolutionary War. Some were grateful to get out at any price. A few balked, but most caved in. The holdouts got flooded anyway. There's some private land under Candlewood Lake to this very day."

"Thirty to ninety dollars?"

"One year after the flooding, shorefront lots were going for a thousand dollars an acre. They're worth five times that now. Imagine another ten years. The early birds got the worms."

"Is all this going where I think it is, Tim?"

"At the bottom of Candlewood Lake is a little drowned village they once called Jerusalem. It might remind you of Chicken Corners. Would you care for some dessert?"

Twenty-nine

WHEN POTTER LEFT CHARLIE'S HOUSE midday, he followed the lab crew's panel truck a half mile into the village center. The truck went on to Monticello. He parked his cruiser in the lot next to Rudy's and went inside to call his office. He had to be sure the Jewish kid wasn't anywhere around.

He got Rose.

"Are those Yids gone yet?"

"Yids!" Short for people who speak Yiddish. And not "How did the meeting go?" but "Are they gone yet?"

"Sarah, one *s*, is spending the weekend at Collins House, two *l*'s," she told him. "Kaufmann, two *n*'s, went back to NYC to join Kaufman, one *n*. Rozkopf, one *ʒ*, went up to his farm."

When he got to be sheriff, Potter reminded himself, he would have to do something about Rose.

"Why didn't the kid go back?"

"She couldn't bear to leave town without kissing you good-bye," Rose said maliciously.

So it was Sarah he didn't want to see! Something else to add to Rose's Potter list.

"I'm going to stop by the house before I come in. Maybe I'll take a ride over to Monticello, see what they've found out."

"You do that," said Rose.

"Ready on the right. Ready on the left," she whispered after she hung up. It was starting to get interesting.

ψ   ψ   ψ

Potter killed most of the day driving from place to place, avoiding Fredericktown and his office, until finally late in the afternoon he felt it was safe. Back at his desk he shuffled papers, thought about what Charlie had said, and accomplished nothing. He felt burned out by the tensions of the past five days. It was late evening before he got home.

He eased his cruiser into the space between his mother's old Nash and the Plymouth two-door that he drove off-duty. There was a light on in Ginnie's bedroom. He hoped she was not having trouble sleeping. She was sixty, not so old, but she had lost some of her fire when Fletcher died. It was even worse after her car accident. She didn't seem able to shrug things off the way she used to. With Marjorie no longer around to cheer her up, he worried how she would get by. She had been looking long faced and hollow eyed ever since the services on Sunday.

The August moon was high in its sweep across the night sky. From where he stood on the hill above the boathouse, Potter could see bits of Lake Repose shining through the trees, stretching miles up the long, deep valley to the Collins tract at the darkened end.

T. Q., scrawled on Charlie Evans's back door. Why at Charlie's? Who was calling himself Tom Quick? Robert? Ted? Had they broken their promises? What should he do about the little Jewish girl? He had to be careful not to let her hear his voice.

The house was calm and quiet, the way it always seemed when Ginnie was sleeping. Potter was careful not to wake her. He stopped at the small lavatory by the back door to wash traces of soot from Charlie's house off his hands, and there it was in the soap dish: a brand-new bar of Cashmere Bouquet with one corner rubbed away.

⚜   ⚜   ⚜

"I was napping," said Ginnie. "It was such a lovely dream, but I forget what it was about."

She smiled sleepily. She was annoyed that he had come into her bedroom without knocking.

"Look what I found, Mother," he said, holding out his hand. "A bar of soap."

She reached out and took it from him. She rubbed the corner, frowning, then looked up and smiled sweetly. Her eyes were cold.

"Every Saturday night, Potter," she said, "whether you needed it or not."

"I'm not amused, Mother. That's your writing on Charlie's door. I should have recognized your fancy *T*."

"Fancy is as fancy does," said Ginnie, "and penmanship is a mirror of the soul."

"What were you thinking? Were you trying to protect me? Tom Quick burns a house down while Potter is at work, so Potter can't be Tom Quick? Was that it?"

"To protect you. Yes," she said. She was fully alert.

"But why Charlie Evans, Mother? Why his house? I don't want Charlie upset any more than he is. He's suspicious enough already."

"To protect you."

"I don't need protection. He'll calm down."

"To protect you."

"Charlie can't connect me to anything, Mother. I scarified those people only because you asked me to."

Ginnie had no reply.

"Katy was there in Charlie's house, Mother. Did you know that? She could have been hurt."

"To protect you."

"Just tell me why."

"To protect you, *Potter Fletcher Babcock Washington,*" she explained. That was why.

☙   ☙   ☙

Ginnie could not possibly discuss the bar of soap with Potter. He thought she'd made the fire because of Tom Quick. He knew nothing about John Carpenter.

After Potter left the house, she thought about the girl, Sarah, the one Potter said was listening on the hill. The one who was weekending at Collins House.

He should be more worried, she thought. Only a child, but a serious danger. So many problems to solve.

She walked from room to room, gliding her fingers over the backs of chairs, the tops of tables, things of metal, things of glass. She paused to read a framed sampler that had been embroidered by her grandmother.

Elizabeth Flint, Age of Ten,

Prepared for Death,

I Know Not When

ABCDEFGHJKLMNOPQRSTUVWXYZ

1234567890

1835

Ginnie wondered if anyone other than herself had ever noticed that the letter *I* was missing. Elizabeth was a good girl. Self-effacing. She knew only God was perfect.

These things belong together, she thought. *Every picture, every plate, every stick of furniture. The wealth of so many lifetimes.*

To protect you, Potter Fletcher Babcock Washington. All these

things will soon be yours. You must marry. You must father a boy and
name him after Samuel. To heal the wounds. To continue the line.

"You made it sound so simple, Marjorie." She sighed aloud.
"You were never afraid. He should have married you."

Thirty

IT ALL BEGAN WITH MARJORIE AND THE way Tuttles were brought up.

Ann Fletcher, Marjorie's grandmother, had married Ralph Tuttle. Their daughter, Mary, who was Marjorie's mother, had married Arthur Jones. Ann was Ginnie Washington's aunt, which made Marjorie and Ginnie first cousins, once removed.

Ginnie had never cared much for either Marjorie or her mother. Mary had been all sour grapes and envious, and Marjorie, even as a child, was wily and grasping.

"It's that Tuttle blood," Ginnie explained to her husband, Fletcher. "It shows."

Ginnie surmised that the Tuttles, being generally poor, valued nothing above money. In Marjorie's case this turned out to be a blessing. After the death of her husband, Wallace, the widow Marjorie Fletcher-Tuttle-Jones-Bingham had shown an unsuspected talent for finance. Ginnie, whose company, B & W Stone and Gravel, was being slowly strangled by economic forces she could not quite understand, had to give her credit for that.

Fletcher Washington married Ginnie Babcock in 1900. He selected her for her family fortune as much as for her bloodlines. Certainly not, as everyone knew, for her looks.

"She's small and she's plain," Fletcher's mother, Mildred, cautioned him. "She's got no curves and she's a tomboy, but she does have spirit. And all that Babcock land makes her a very good catch. She'll inherit more real estate than God."

The land was mostly stone and gravel.

"That's my kind of harvest," Ginnie's father, Eli Babcock, liked to say. "Don't have to plant it, doesn't need water, and never rots."

Ginnie grew up in the Babcock quarries. As a child she would sit in a niche at the top of a pit, coated with stone dust, watching the workers, and wanting to be one of them. She was drawn to stone, she was glad that her maternal grandmother had been a Flint.

"Flint strikes sparks," she told Fletcher on their wedding night. He was pleasantly surprised.

Ginnie's mother, Prudence, had been a Fletcher. Prudence's mother, Elizabeth, had been wife to Samuel, whose sister, Constance, had married Brewster Washington, Fletcher Washington's grandfather, in 1838.

"It's a complete muddle without those charts in the family Bibles," Eli explained. "We're all related to each other at least twice."

The Babcock fortune was made over three generations by quarrying bluestone, granite, and marble and by surface stripping gravel throughout the western Catskills. After graduation from Fredericktown High, Fletcher went to work for Ginnie's father, driving a dump truck. Eli singled him out in a hurry. In five years Fletcher could handle the quarry operations as well as Ginnie could.

"Look at her, the little imp, and him, spunky as they come," Eli boasted. "You can hardly tell which one's the girl!"

Together Ginnie and Fletcher walked every inch of Eli's hills and mountains. They could scribe a quarry line and run a cutting crew. They knew rock, tools, machinery, workers, explosives. They knew all there was to know about the outdoor part of the business. But they did not understand money.

They sent Potter, their only child, to college to learn business and accounting, but he took to geology and politics instead. In 1933, Fletcher's last effort to straighten out his twisted spine killed him, leaving Ginnie on her own. Four years later Ginnie had been readying herself to tell Potter that B & W was just about bankrupt when Marjorie Bingham, bless her avaricious Tuttle blood, had come by with a suggestion.

ψ   ψ   ψ

The first meeting between Ginnie and Marjorie was at Ginnie's house in June 1937. Marjorie brought a generous batch of her spring potpourri, tied nicely in a blue linen pouch. It was a secret blend of early-season blossoms passed down from her grandmother, Ann Fletcher, Prudence's sister. Ginnie had tried for years to duplicate the fragrance but had never entirely succeeded.

Marjorie got to the point of her visit over tea.

"Now, don't you deny it, cousin Ginnie. Just about everyone around here is feeling the pinch. Even Martin Collins. And I know you are."

Ginnie's heart chilled over.

"What makes you so all-knowing about other folks' situations?" she replied, calmly as she could.

"Well, first it was pillow talk with Wallace," said Marjorie. "Then the town records job. Taxes and mortgages and credit ratings and things like that. I know who pays on time and who doesn't. Lately it's from real estate. You'd be amazed the things people will tell you when they're buying or selling a house."

"Aren't you the lucky one," said Ginnie.

"Truth be told, cousin Ginnie, I'm more clever than lucky. Nothing ever fell in my lap. Look how Wallace died, playing with those little brats, leaving me to scrape by. I've had to fight for everything I've got. I'm doing well now, but I want lots more."

"How do you propose to get lots?" asked Ginnie.

"That's what we should talk about. Some of Wallace's old friends from the city met with me last year. They have this wonderful plan, and they asked me to help. Because I live up here and know real estate, and because I handle the town records and things. It's lots of money, cousin Ginnie, and there's lots for you, too, if you want it."

"How much is a lot?" asked Ginnie, half closing her eyes.

"Bushels. Thousands and thousands. Enough to pay all your bills and save the bluestone quarries down by Pond Eddy. Enough to fight off those people from Scarsdale."

"You do know a lot about my affairs," said Ginnie.

Marjorie beamed.

"Knowing other people's business is my business," she said. "But you mustn't tell any of this to Potter. It's a very secret secret."

"What would I have to do?" asked Ginnie.

Marjorie looked up from her teacup and met Ginnie's eyes without blinking.

"We need a Judas goat," she said.

"A Judas goat?"

"You know," said Marjorie, "the tame goat the butchers use to lead the sheep to slaughter."

☙ ☙ ☙

"It's really simple," said Marjorie. "In real estate we do it all the time. Owners are always worrying something bad will happen to their property, lower its value. You have to make them think something *really* bad is right around the corner. Scare them enough, and they'll sell."

"Scare them how?" asked Ginnie.

"Oh, there's lots of ways. Like rumors. Make them think a stinky factory might be coming because there's no zoning. Or a roadhouse with loud music and motorcycles."

"That would certainly worry me," said Ginnie.

"Or have people with thick foreign accents call the schools and churches to ask how to enroll or become a member. Or drive around town with niggers or chinks in the car and point at things."

"How clever," said Ginnie politely.

"Or you can leave stuff around. Like newspapers in languages nobody can read. Or piles of chicken heads and sheep guts on out-of-the-way roads or in the parks. To make the ones who live nearby think really awful people are moving in."

"Aren't you the busy little bee," said Ginnie with a hint of sarcasm. Marjorie ignored it.

"One of the best tricks is to use real niggers. First you move a nigger family into a white part of town, a part that's not doing too well. You pay the first white who sells to you real well, but he has to tell the others that he sold low and that more niggers are coming. They sell to you for practically nothing, and you resell to niggers and landlords. It's all in the commissions."

"We have very few Negroes around here," said Ginnie.

"It doesn't have to be niggers. It all depends. Spiks or chinks or wops. Anyone the owners are afraid of."

"Where did you ever learn language like that?"

"It's just shop talk, cousin Ginnie. We're using Jews this time."

"What time, dear?"

"I'll try to explain. The group I'm working with has been buying land in this area for the past six years. We have a lot, mostly around Lake Repose, inside a ten-mile circle. Most of it we got real cheap. Swamps and worn-out farms. High ground with no roads. Bankruptcies that I hear about before anyone else. The Depression helped. We're thinking ahead."

"Thinking about what?"

"About how values might improve if a swamp gets drained or a hilltop becomes waterfront. That sort of thing. Or if you know the government wants some land for an airport or an army base, and you get to it first. Some of us have ways of knowing things ahead of time."

"It all sounds very impressive, Marjorie, but why are you telling me?"

"We already have a good part of what we need. Not all in our real names, of course. I have to fake some of the titles. But we need another one hundred thousand acres, and some of the best land around here isn't for sale. Not at prices we're willing to pay."

"What land is that?"

"Oh, land like yours, Cousin Ginnie," said Marjorie. "And Martin Collins's. And all my stuck-up neighbors."

※ ※ ※

It was an attractive offer. Somewhat reluctantly, Ginnie said yes. There would be lots of money. Marjorie's friends would buy the valley land, the house in Chicken Corners, the quarries on the other side of Lake Repose, and the old gravel pits. Ginnie would keep some of the hillside above, which would become the new lakeside after the dams went in. Marjorie's records would show a lower sales price. The Judas goat money would be Potter's wedding present.

"A bag of silver," she admitted to herself. It couldn't be helped.

Then Jarvis Evans came along and spoiled the whole thing. Somehow he discovered what Marjorie and Ginnie were up to, and he told Ginnie he wanted it stopped. He said he had ways to make them stop. He knew the gossip about Prudence being illigitimate, and he could prove it was all true. Worse, he had those awful letters from Samuel and Elizabeth that spoke of things no one must ever know. Not Marjorie or Potter or anyone.

He said if Ginnie could not persuade Marjorie, he would tell everyone. Potter would never get elected to anything again

"That's blackmail, Jarvis," Ginnie complained.

"It's nothing compared to what you are doing," he replied.

Marjorie wouldn't listen to a word of it. She said she didn't care what Jarvis Evans wanted or didn't want or what he threatened to do. The land project was going ahead. Her friends would take care of Jarvis. Everyone had a weak spot, and Jarvis was no exception. He sold antiques in a part of town that wasn't zoned for business. He probably didn't pay sales or income taxes. There were ways to find these things out.

"We're not giving all this up because some old fool doesn't like it, cousin Ginnie."

"He won't give up either, Marjorie," Ginnie replied. "He likes these valleys the way they are. He doesn't want things changed. And he knows family secrets. He knows about my mother. About Elizabeth's baby."

"Oh, nonsense. We've heard that story about your mother since we were children. Anyone says Prudence was a bastard, just deny it. Samuel Fletcher acknowledged Prudence as his daughter, and that's that."

Ginnie couldn't tell Marjorie everything. She couldn't tell her about the letters. Prudence being a bastard wasn't the only thing. The other thing Jarvis knew was much, much worse. No one must ever know.

"If you insist, I will speak with Jarvis one more time," said Ginnie. "Just one more time."

⚜   ⚜   ⚜

Ginnie tried to tell herself that she ran Jarvis over in the parking lot because he wouldn't shut up and let her have those letters. But she knew that wasn't the only reason. It was her temper getting out of hand again, always getting her into trouble. It was especially upsetting because Jarvis was an old friend, almost an old love. But he had turned his back on her. It would have been harder to kill him, she supposed, if he had still looked handsome, the way he did when he was young. Dying didn't matter as much when one got old. Neither did killing.

The hardest part was turning him over. Both the front and rear wheels on the right side went over him, and he did not look like Jarvis anymore. And after all that trouble, the letters about Elizabeth and that other man were not in his inside coat pocket where he had kept them before. He must have left them at his house. Ginnie wondered if he had told Charlie or Katy anything. She would have to take her chances.

The whole land business with Marjorie had been a terrible mistake. Looking back, she was now sure she could have scraped enough money together. Her mistake was getting involved with a Tuttle and all those bankers and Jews.

If I could do something about those raggedy Jews from the city, she thought, *that would bring Marjorie around.*

Potter did not have to be told everything, only that the Jewish resort people were plotting to gobble up land around Lake Repose. That they were already moving their people into places like Thornton farm. That they needed to be taught a lesson. Tom Quick would scarify them. He would make them go away.

※　※　※

The morning after Ginnie killed Jarvis, she drove her Nash coupe up her driveway into the big copper beech at the top. She aimed carefully so the car would smash the tree in the same place on the right fender where she had smashed Jarvis when he had walked away from her.

She had not anticipated how suddenly the car would stop. On impact her body had whipped around the steering wheel, and she had banged her forehead hard against the divider post at the center of the windshield. The glass did not shatter.

Months passed before the dizzy spells went away and Ginnie was able to resume her conversations with Marjorie and her search for the missing letters.

"You are a very lucky lady," the doctor told her when he made his last house call. "You'll be fine, but that tree died."

Thirty-one

TUESDAY NIGHT, CHARLIE HEATED UP
some Campbell's tomato soup for Katy, with a side dish of celery
stalks, radishes, and Saltine crackers.

"Healthy food," he said. "Nothing fancy."

When she was finished eating, Katy opened the John Carpenter file.

"Why would he hide this away from us?" she wondered aloud.

For the first time since starting on Jarvis's files, she had the
feeling she might be poking around in something that might turn
out unpleasant.

"Not from us, for us," said Charlie. "Away from anyone else."

"If you say so," she replied, not all that convinced.

She spread the contents of the folder out on the dining-room
table. On top was a packet of small, cream-colored envelopes,
tied with a thin black ribbon. "Samuel" was written on the top
envelope.

Under the envelopes were four typewritten pages, pinned together. The first page was headed: "Notes for a Paper on John
Carpenter."

Next was a brown file envelope, hand addressed:

TO MY SON, CHARLES EVANS.
OPEN ONLY IF I AM DEAD.
JARVIS EVANS

"You were right," said Katy, pushing the envelope toward Charlie. "He wasn't hiding anything from us."

Charlie stared at the envelope but did not touch it. He did not like to think about the dead.

On the bottom was Jarvis's usual catchall envelope, labeled "Scrapes." Katy picked it up, shook it gently, and raised her eyebrows questioningly.

"May as well," said Charlie.

Katy described the contents as she took each item out.

"Newspaper and magazine clippings . . . some research notes . . . a Sinclair map of New York State . . . a list of books . . . a program for 'An Evening of Song and Dance' at the African Theater on Worth Street in New York City, dated 1823 . . . an invoice, Henry Carpenter, Fine Furniture, Tulip Street, Fredericktown . . ."

"Let me see that last one," said Charlie. He whistled as he read the invoice. "Henry is billing a lady named *Elizabeth* Flint nine dollars for repairs to three freight wagons."

"That may be our Elizabeth," said Katy, "but who's *Henry Carpenter?*"

"Let's have a look at Samuel's mail," Charlie said.

⚘   ⚘   ⚘

The letters to Samuel, five in all, were from Elizabeth. The first was dated December 25, 1855; the last, March 3, 1859. The paper was similar to that of the letter Charlie found under Jarvis's blotter, but the handwriting was more delicate.

"Should I read them?" Katy asked.

"They won't mind," said Charlie.

December 25, 1855

Samuel,

I do not blame you. We are both fallen. God will judge our sins. I will keep your house and raise our child, my children.

Happy Christmas.
Elizabeth

"Funny way to word it," said Katy.

April 28, 1856

Samuel,

She will be Christened Prudence. It will remind her to avoid what we did not. I love her.

Elizabeth

"Prudence. I never liked that name," said Katy.

January 5, 1859

Samuel,

The father wishes to see his child. I have refused, but he persists. It must not be. She must never know. If I cannot stop him, I must tell you his name.

Elizabeth

"Long time between letters," said Charlie

January 18, 1859

Samuel,

He vows to hold her in his arms before her third birthday. He has lost all reason. He is John Carpenter. Love her. Forgive me.

Elizabeth

"Sounds like the little lady was playing around," said Katy.

"And got caught," said Charlie.

"There's a lesson there somewhere," said Katy.

March 3, 1859

Samuel,

I have heard. John is dead. Where is Justice? Was he at peace? Death is forever.

Elizabeth

"They did him in?" asked Katy.

"Not conclusive but could be," said Charlie. "But who were they?"

Katy picked up the If-I-Am-Dead envelope.

"Maybe the answer's in here," she said. "You want to open it?"

"Later," said Charlie. "You know how I feel about ghosts. Time for your nap."

"Okay," said Katy. "My throat is kind of scratchy. Too much smoke."

"Smoke and mirrors," said Charlie.

ψ   ψ   ψ

Katy woke up after midnight with all of Charlie's pillows piled around her. Charlie was sitting in the wing chair by the window.

"Welcome back from the other world," he said. "A penny for your dreams."

"You always ask," Katy replied. "You know I never remember. Something about paper."

She sat up. Charlie was holding "Notes for a Paper on John Carpenter" in his hand.

"I couldn't wait," he said. "He was a runaway slave."

"Who was?"

"Henry Carpenter, John's father. From St. Kitts to Baltimore, a stowaway on a molasses boat."

He picked up the papers.

"He was trained to make furniture in St. Kitts. He took the name Carpenter after he ran away. When he got to New York, he built stage sets for the African Theater and got to know some abolitionists. He married a free mulatto woman from Virginia before he moved to Fredericktown. John was their first child. 1820."

It took a few minutes to sink in. Katy pushed the pillows aside and swung her legs over the side of the bed.

"Elizabeth's lover was a Negro?"

"You're getting ahead of me," said Charlie. "Henry owned a house up here with a shop in back, near where the school library is now. He had a good business, two apprentices. There's an obituary from *The Fredericktown Flame*. Total estate valued at four thousand dollars."

"A lot of money, then," said Katy.

"John was a good-looking kid. Light skinned, real bright. Henry had him educated in Newport by the Quakers. He went to the city and became an actor."

"A Negro lover," Katy repeated. "A hundred years ago. Wow!"

"Have you ever heard of John Fairfield?"

"Sure, he's real famous," said Katy. "Your father called him the Liberator. He raided the South to help slaves escape. He got hired by their relatives up North."

Charlie turned a few more pages.

"Henry Carpenter built secret compartments in some freight wagons for Mr. Fairfield. That was the repair bill Elizabeth paid. He kept one wagon in Fredericktown. John Carpenter went south with him twice."

"That fits," said Katy. "The Underground Railroad. The western Catskills was one of the escape routes. Through Pennsylvania and up the Delaware. Liberty, Troy, Lake George, Lake Champlain, and on to Canada. Some of the runaways joined the tribes along the way."

"John had a part in the stage version of *Uncle Tom's Cabin* at the Quaker meeting house, 1853 and 1854."

He looked up.

"You'll like this. Both productions were sponsored by a Mrs. Elizabeth Flint Fletcher and her good friend from New York, Mrs. Agnes Collins."

Katy braced her hands on the edge of the mattress.

"Elizabeth Fletcher was Ginnie Washington's grandmother."

"That's what I thought. Listen to what my father says:

" 'Elizabeth Flint, born 1825. Quaker. Worked in Abolitionist movement with John Carpenter starting in 1846 before marriage in 1851 to Samuel Fletcher, born 1810. Samuel contracted syphilis in Saratoga while Elizabeth was carrying their first daughter, Ann Fletcher, born 1854. An overdose of tincture of mercury prescribed by a quack doctor made him impotent. Elizabeth's second child, Prudence Fletcher, an octoroon, born 1856, was the daughter of John Carpenter.' "

"Prudence. Ginnie's mother, Potter's grandmother," said Katy, "an octoroon."

"End of story," said Charlie. "John Carpenter disappeared without a trace in 1859."

Thirty-two

SAMUEL FLETCHER AND BREWSTER
Washington were born the same day of the same month of the same year, October 18, 1810. They studied together at Bertram Preparatory in Oneonta from 1820 to 1826. Brewster had the muscles and the beard of a man at fifteen. He protected the smaller boys from bullying. He was fearsome even then.

He grew up a somewhat solitary man. He married Fletcher's younger sister, Constance, in 1838 and built a fortresslike log cabin for her on the bluffs overlooking the Delaware, north of Callicoon.

Although they were relations and lived not far apart, Samuel and Brewster did not see each other often after they had graduated from school. Constance died giving birth to Brewster's only child, Enoch, in 1840. Brewster never remarried, and Enoch never left home. In 1869 Enoch married the former Mildred Potter, and his bride moved in with them.

"Stay away from that lot, blood or no blood." Samuel's father told his family. "There is a strangeness about them. They mean trouble."

Those of Brewster's neighbors who had problems they could

not solve themselves sometimes sought out Brewster, as Samuel finally did, because no one else could help them.

ῷ   ῷ   ῷ

Samuel and Brewster met in 1859 in the town of Lumberland near the mouth of the Mongaup in a building the locals called Showers Tavern. John Showers had settled in the area before the Revolutionary War. He traded with the white and Indian trappers who drifted between the Mongaup and the Delaware, offering uncut grain alcohol for furs and hides. The tavern had been rebuilt numerous times, always on the same spot. It was low ceilinged, dark, and smoky. It smelled of trappers and decay.

"Tom Quick summered in this place," Brewster told Samuel. "He killed a Delaware in that corner by the wall. In 1769. He shot it in the head while it was sleeping."

"The Indian Slayer?" asked Samuel. It was a convenient way to begin. "Some people say he did good and that his spirit is still about."

Brewster stared at Samuel a moment, making up his mind.

"You sent for me. I am here," he said.

And so, obliquely, the purpose of their meeting was nailed down.

"His name is John Carpenter," said Samuel. "He is a mulatto, almost white. A stage actor and a musician. The young girls of Fredericktown are smitten with him. Some of us believe he serves the devil."

"Their fathers allow this? Their brothers?" asked Brewster.

"It is Abolition fever," said Samuel. "The Quakers are at fault. Their meetings bring together people who should be kept apart. Evil things happen."

"What things?"

"Women's heads turn easily. He has seduced at least one who has borne him a child. I believe he has his eye on others."

Not a lie, he told himself. *If one has fallen, others will.*

"Can he be frightened?" asked Brewster.

"He enjoys danger. He shows no fear. His sights are set high. He is full of himself, and he has kin and friends in town."

"Then he must be stopped another way," said Brewster.

He frowned at Samuel.

"How did you know to come to me?"

"Others have done so," said Samuel. "As they did with your father. It is whispered that you can do what others cannot do."

"You and I were schoolmates," Brewster said. "Your sister was my wife. Yet we did not remain close."

"That was my failing."

"You must come visit me in Callicoon. I would have you know your nephew, Enoch, better."

He placed his left hand on Samuel's right shoulder.

"Let us drink to the Fletchers and the Washingtons."

They drained their tankards.

"Will Carpenter die?" asked Samuel.

"That is for Tom to decide," said Brewster.

⚜   ⚜   ⚜

Brewster and Enoch killed John Carpenter without difficulty. They lured him into the stable behind the Coach & Anvil Inn and clubbed him to death. They carried his corpse out of town and hung it from a thick branch of a giant oak called the Color Tree. In the eighteenth century the tree was used to execute Indians and Negroes found guilty of serious crimes. Brewster pinned a note to Carpenter's coat. It said simply, "He broke sacred rules. Tom Quick."

The message was wasted. A frayed rope dangled from the branch for more than a year, but neither the note nor John Carpenter's body were ever seen or found. There were panthers and bears and other savage beasts in the forests around Lake Repose in 1859.

Brewster Washington died in 1878, grandfather to Fletcher, Enoch's only son, who married Virginia Babcock. Brewster died never knowing that he and John Carpenter were destined to be coupled throughout eternity as the great-grandfathers of Potter Washington.

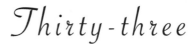

Thirty-three

"IF THAT WOMAN HADN'T BEEN KILLED, the shooting at the farmhouse wouldn't have attracted that much attention," said Tim. "It's the killing that's scaring the big shots away."

They were enjoying an early breakfast Wednesday morning on the screened-in veranda at the back of Talmadge House. A doe with twin fawns, still spotted, stood in the middle of the sloping lawn, watching the kitchen window.

Martin had not slept well. He'd had a dream about poppies. That probably meant Edmund. Tim's reference to rows of crosses had probably sparked it. Still, even a nightmare was welcome to Martin if it meant touching base with Edmund again.

"Scared of what?" he asked, although he thought he knew.

"Their objective was to panic local landowners. The mysterious shooting at the farmhouse wouldn't have set them back much. Perhaps they would have had to pull out of Chicken Corners for a while, but in the long run the brouhaha would have worked to their advantage."

"But Mrs. Bingham's killing was another matter," said Martin.

"It certainly was. She was a key member of the ring. A thorough investigation would have led straight to the leadership. Imagine all those prominent names mixed up in a killing. Small wonder the state police were told to stay out of it."

"May I see the names you've got?"

"If you promise to keep them to yourself."

"Agreed."

Tim passed three sheets of paper across the table. Martin read slowly, whistling softly as his eyes moved down the hand-written columns.

"They cover the spectrum, don't they?" he said when he was finished. "A list of names like this protects itself."

"It took a killing to make them run," said Tim. "There's a lot of money there."

"It makes me feel old," said Martin. "Dad and I once played great games with their fathers and mothers. We cornered markets, adjusted world currencies, made everything legal. It's not so easy now. But someone's put together a good cross-section here. New York, Boston, Minneapolis, St. Louis, D.C., upstate and down."

"The best kind of insurance. Spread the guilt around."

"New blood and old blood. Donkeys and elephants. City and farm. It's a peaceable kingdom."

"The lions made a deal with the lambs."

"All that land. What were they after?" Martin asked.

"The plan was to flood three valleys to make a huge new lake, Y-shaped with the Lake Repose basin as part of the north-south stem. There's plenty of fine, flat land up here. The Catskills are really a lifted plateau, not a mountain range. The new lake would have made a lot of the high land accessible."

"How big a project?"

"Bigger than Candlewood or any of the new reservoirs. More like a new Finger Lake. But better placed. Closer to the city and more valuable."

"Good long-term investment. All that prime real estate in just a few hands, Collins House included."

"Good short-term, too. Electric power, a hundred miles of waterfront, more resorts, golf courses, industry. The government was to buy in later. An airport on reclaimed wetlands, a state park. The plans are all drafted and under lock and key."

"And the military?"

"An army base, of course. And a training camp for a new kind of military police force, the War Disaster Military Corps. Elite units to be trained to control race riots and Bolshevik uprisings."

"Big money there."

"The whole thing should have netted a hundred million in just a few years."

Martin laughed.

"There was a time, a party this big, there'd always be a Collins invited. I should be hurt, not being on that guest list."

"That's what happens when you get out of touch," said Tim.

"A billion or more to be made in the long run, I suppose. And now it's all passé, like Marjorie."

The young man in the white jacket refilled their coffee cups.

"A shame about her," Tim said. "What a waste. She wouldn't have made much money, you know. The whole idea was doomed from the start."

"How so?" asked Martin.

"Bad timing. America's going to war again, Martin, and when the guns begin to thunder, schemes like this are quickly pushed aside."

"Another war?"

"Did the first one ever stop?" He snorted. "*Gallia est omnis divisa in partes tres*, Martin."

"All Gaul is divided into three parts."

"The European tribes are out to prove something again, and there are new madmen on hand to lead them."

⚓   ⚓   ⚓

Tim walked Martin to his car.

"Watch out for this fellow Rozkopf, Martin," he said. "He can get rough."

"You know him?"

"Only by reputation. He formed a partnership last year with an IRA gunrunner in the city whose brother wants to be mayor. The Irish vote can't swing an election alone anymore. Mr. Rozkopf is offering to trade Jewish votes for guns, FOB Palestine."

"Could he have killed Marjorie?"

"He has it in him," said Tim. "But anyone can kill with good enough personal reason."

He opened the car door.

"Another caution, watch out for Tom Quick."

"You know of him, too?" asked Martin.

"In my younger days, when I first went to Albany, I grew curious about him. I had great access to police intelligence, but I never could track him down."

"Some people around here think he was a hero."

"A protector of the ancient ways. Like Merlin. Barbarossa. Tecumseh. The Maccabees. Be careful, Martin. He can be dangerous."

Martin took his place behind the wheel.

"I understand he only scares, he doesn't kill."

Tim braced both hands on the lower edge of the car window.

"In 1828, near you in Vandenbergh, a widow named Charity Ames turned her house into a school for orphans. Some of them came from the towns and the churches, but she also took in strays. No partiality. Negroes, Indians. Boys and girls together. She wasn't particular enough for her neighbors. Stories got started. Tom Quick burned her out. She has died with eleven of the children. No one up there has ever made that mistake again."

"I'll keep both eyes open. Thank you for everything, Tim."

"My pleasure, Martin. It's a treat, you owing me for a change."

ψ　　ψ　　ψ

The narrow road north of Forestburgh rose steadily past tangles of trees and outcrops of rock. Tim's information was interesting,

Martin thought, but it didn't answer the primary questions, and it didn't address his particular problem.

It was time for a talk with Robert and Ted. If word had reached them, they would be waiting in the carriage house before noon.

As he drove past the courthouse in Monticello, he began his cross-examination.

How are your grandsons involved in this, Mr. Collins? "Well, it's clear the boys shot at the Thornton place, but I think that's all they did."

Boys, Mr. Collins? "I still think of them that way. Edmund lived to be thirty-three, but he's still a boy to me."

Isn't it time you put Edmund to rest, Mr. Collins? "I would if I could, but I don't know how."

Were the boys acting on their own? "Tom Quick was with them. And others may have been involved."

Who is Tom Quick? "An idea. An ideal. A revenger. A madman. The first one died one hundred and forty-two years ago. I don't know who the current one might be."

Any suspects? "One. But no evidence. Maybe I've picked him only because I don't like him. He was always hanging around when the boys were growing up. He took my place, Edmund's place."

Why do you drink so much, Mr. Collins? "A girl I was fond of got married to God, and then she died. The Germans killed my son. My wife died crying. Mary's mind isn't always with us. I lost the family fortune. I'm getting old. And besides, I like the taste of the stuff."

Why did the boys shoot at the farmhouse? "To scare the Jews away, I suppose."

Why would they do that? "I thought at first it was because of what Marjorie and her friends were doing. But how would they know about that? Unless Tom Quick told them. And if he knew, what was his interest? Why would he butt in?"

Did Marjorie know what Tom Quick was planning to do? "That would make no sense. She wouldn't have gone inside if she'd known."

Did the boys know she was in there? "Not likely. If they knew, I think they would have waited for a better day. I'll have to ask them."

Did Tom Quick know? "If he did, it didn't stop him."

Who killed her? "No one on the hill. Not August or Jacob. I'd swear to that. Carl, maybe, but how and for what reason?"

Do you care who killed her, Mr. Collins? Do you care about the Jews? "I'm ashamed to admit it, but all I'm worried about right now is the boys."

What have the years taught you, Mr. Collins? "Ah. That life's a fraud. A parlor trick masquerading as a serious puzzle. Nothing means anything. It's all been scripted in advance. When you're dead, nothing makes any difference."

ψ   ψ   ψ

"We thought we were helping you, Judge," said Ted. "It turned out badly. I'm sorry."

He and Robert were standing side by side in the back of the carriage house, looking clean but unshaven and sheepish.

"We will discuss remorse at another time," said Martin. "Let me make one thing clear. I am on your side, no matter what you did. That's because I love you, and we are family. I'll be with you, no matter what."

"We will not involve you," said Robert.

"I'm amazed you think you can control that," said Martin. "Right now I need answers to questions. First, were you alone?"

"No," said Robert.

"Will you tell me who was with you?"

"Tom Quick," he answered, without bothering to look at Ted.

"Will you tell me who he . . . or she . . . is?"

"We think it is better if you don't know," said Ted.

Lord, he's all grown up, thought Martin, *and I didn't even see it happen.*

"Let me tell you what I think," he said. "You wanted to frighten those people but not to hurt them. Tom Quick planned it. You each had a fixed number of shots and designated targets. You did what you were told. Is that about right?"

"Yes," said Robert. Ted nodded.

"You've done this vigilante thing with him before?"

"I have, a few times when I was younger, but not lately. Ted hasn't. There always seemed to be good reasons. I wouldn't have if there weren't."

"What was the reason this time?"

"Tom said you were in trouble. That the banks are after you. That you're badly strapped. Mother talks about it all the time."

"Does she? I didn't know she paid attention. I didn't want her worrying."

"I can't remember not worrying," said Ted. "When I was little I used to have a dream that the ground was covered with money. Nickels, dimes, quarters, half dollars. I picked it up all night. I filled my pockets so I could give it to you and mother in the morning. You wouldn't have your spells anymore. Mother could stop worrying. When I woke up and the money wasn't there, I was so disappointed. And tired. All that work for nothing."

"I know the money dream," said Martin. "I think it runs in the family."

"Tom said the resort people are ganging up on you," said Robert. "He said they were going to build more of those places like at Monticello and Liberty and Swan Lake."

He's got just a piece of the plot, Martin thought. *The story line. Maybe he didn't know the whole thing.*

"And this shooting was going to stop them?"

"Tom said they would back off. There are other places they can go. Just leave Lake Repose alone."

"Did you know Marjorie Bingham was inside?"

"No. Tom didn't either."

"Do you know who killed her?"

"No."

"Why won't you tell me who he is?"

"Well, first, because we promised," said Ted. "And, second, we figured if we don't tell on Tom, maybe Tom won't tell on us."

"When you're back in your camp, think it over," said Martin.

Thirty-four

ALONE IN HIS OFFICE AT NOON ON Wednesday, Charlie munched on a roast pork sandwich while he studied the package of transcripts Janey Planck had sent over. Janey and two of her operators had transcribed every word spoken on the Collins's party line, in and out, since Monday afternoon. Most interesting were Martin's calls sending the boys camping and instructing Robert to keep away from the house. And Monsignor Cavanaugh's invitation to dinner at Talmadge House.

It's getting hard to tell the good guys from the bad guys, Charlie said to himself. *Time to find out what Mr. Collins knows that I don't. And whose side he's on.*

Before calling Martin he called Katy, who was back at the house working on Jarvis's files.

"It's starting to come together," he informed her. "I'm going to try to see Martin Collins around three at Collins House. I think he may have located some of the missing pieces to this puzzle."

Or maybe he's one of the pieces himself, he thought.

He paused uncertainly. "You know Dad's letter, the one I've been avoiding? Take a peek at it for me, would you? If there's anything there I need to know, bring it up to Collins House around three-thirty. If I don't call again, it means the meeting's on. Don't say anything to anyone, especially Potter."

ψ　　ψ　　ψ

Mary and Sarah spent Wednesday morning baking. Sarah served Martin a big slice of chocolate cake with orange icing for lunch and was rewarded with a grateful smile. Around three o'clock, Mary filled a small picnic basket with cookies, fresh peaches, lemonade, and ice tea, and she and Sarah strolled out to the Wild Garden.

The Wild Garden was a semiformal maze of wild and cultivated flowers that stretched from the blueberry hedges lining Ravine Path in back of Collins House to the edge of the public road in front. Mary and Sarah picked slowly and selectively, searching for perfect blossoms with long, unbroken stems. Mary told Sarah the English name of each new flower they came across. She was chatty. She was having fun.

"When you come next spring, this will look very different, much more colorful," she promised. "That is, if you do come. I hope you will."

"I hope so, too, Mrs. Collins. Thank you," said Sarah.

"There will be bright yellow daffodils and tulips and iris. The colors soften in August. These field daisies and black-eyed Susans are wild, but we planted the marigolds. Doesn't the phlox smell wonderful? There's a wild kind that blooms earlier."

She had spread out a blanket in a small clearing for their picnic.

"That's globe thistle. Don't the bees love it? Don't swat. They won't bother you if you don't bother them."

The air droned and tasted like spiced water, and the sun was crispy hot. Sarah wore a floppy straw hat to keep the sun off and carried a wicker tray with a loop handle over her shoulder. It was slowly filling with flowers.

All afternoon Sarah had watched for flowers like those her mother grew in Poland, but none of those in the Wild Garden looked the same. The Polish flower she remembered best was sky blue with pale green leaves. It sprouted early in last year's furrows as they thawed. Her father turned them under in the spring.

"If you pull the petals off this one, you'll find out who loves you and who you're going to marry," said Mary.

Sarah smiled. She already knew who she would marry. His name was Eddie. But first she had to find him.

ψ   ψ   ψ

"Let's go down and face the music," said Ted.

After their meeting with Martin, he and Robert had set up a new campsite on the south side of Melting Mountain. They had moved partway down after lunch to the top of the Slide, where they had disposed of the Springfield. The Slide was a long, natural granite slope that chuted off a cliff into the waters of Lake Repose. Every male Collins since Matthew had careened down its polished surface at the age of sixteen seated on a slab of bark, a family rite of passage. Matthew had done it at forty-seven. Ben had pretended disappointment at being much too old.

"Why would we want to do that?" asked Robert.

"Mom's cooking."

"Good reason."

"No mosquitoes. A hot bath. A soft bed. Peace of mind."

"You make a good case," said Robert. "I suppose the Judge can tell us what to do. Okay, on one condition."

"What?"

"One more slide."

Wet and laughing, they packed their gear, scattered the cook fire ashes, and began the downward trek to the ravine that led to Collins House.

Thirty-five

KATY PICKED AT HER LUNCH AND STALLED
for an hour after she was finished. She could understand why a letter addressed like that bothered Charlie. A message from someone dead couldn't be anything but bad news.

"Dammit, Jarvis. You never did make it easy," she said as she tore open the envelope.

December 18, 1937

Dear Charlie,

If you are reading this, I guess I am dead. A difficult way to begin a letter. I will try my best to be cheerful.

Hi, Katy, if you are there, too! No tears, please. If there is life after death, wherever I am, I am sure to be fine.

I assume I passed away soon after writing this letter and went quickly. Otherwise, I would have burned it, along with the rest of John Carpenter's file, and no harm done.

If you are reading this, however, something must have gone wrong.

As you well know, collecting local history has often caused me trouble. I often run across things that maybe I shouldn't.

This latest thing I am involved with is sort of your fault, Katy. That question you asked me about Marjorie Bingham and the way she kept her land records set me thinking, so I sneaked a look at her files. I am worried. She is doing something very destructive, and I fear she is in pretty deep.

Marjorie and I never got on. Years ago I almost married her mother, Mary Tuttle, but at the last minute something scared me off. Whatever it was, Marjorie has it in spades.

I didn't go directly to Marjorie about the files because, to be honest, I find her hard to talk to. Instead, I went to Ginnie Washington, who clearly is in this with her somehow. I like Ginnie, although she too can be difficult. When we were kids she had a temper that could melt a nail.

I told Ginnie I knew what she and Marjorie were up to and that I wanted it stopped. They would defile and destroy our valley, Charlie. I will not let that happen.

Ginnie balked. Or maybe it was Marjorie. I put a lot of pressure on. I showed Elizabeth's letters to Ginnie and told her about John Carpenter, and she kind of crumbled. I told her to give it up or I would let the whole world know. It would ruin Potter, but this valley means more to me than Ginnie's genealogy.

I have a feeling she is coming around. I am meeting her tonight. If all goes well, I will be able to burn the file and leave you out of it. That would mean that I am not dead and that you have not read this letter—a pleasant way to end a task that began on such a sour note.

Love,
Dad

"It wasn't an accident," Katy whispered. "Poor Jarvis. Poor Charlie."

ψ   ψ   ψ

Killing Jarvis had not put an end to it. Ginnie needed time to find those letters. She had continued to plead with Marjorie for a delay, but the silly woman would not be reasonable. It was too bad about Jarvis, Marjorie had argued, but accidents do happen, and sometimes for the best. Jarvis was gone to his reward, and that was that. He couldn't reveal anything anymore.

"Sticks and stones," she said. Whatever the gossips said about Great-Aunt Prudence didn't matter anymore.

Early on a Thursday morning, after Potter had left the house, Ginnie called Marjorie at the records clerk's office to make another, more urgent appeal. It was really far more serious than Marjorie knew, she insisted, Jarvis had shown her some very damaging papers and had threatened to make them public. They might be anywhere. She let Marjorie think the papers were about the land project.

"We have to find them before someone else does," she argued, "and we must postpone all this agitation."

"Well, if we must talk, you will have to come to me," said Marjorie. "I'll be working at the Thornton place late this afternoon. Do you know where it is?"

Of course Ginnie knew where the Thornton place was. Billy, the Thornton eldest, had worked for Fletcher until the boy's legs were crushed in a rockslide. Ginnie used to visit him before the family moved away.

"I know it very well," she said.

"Be there at seven. Come to the door with the Private sign at the top of the stairs," Marjorie said, "and don't talk to any of the Jews."

When Ginnie went out to the garage at six that afternoon to get her car, she was surprised to find it gone. Potter must have taken it, she guessed, without telling her. How odd. But Potter's car was there, and the extra set of keys was on the nail behind the door.

She had not driven for eight months, not since the accident, and was not used to Potter's car, but she adjusted easily. It was a lovely August day, warmer than one might expect past midsummer, and there were wildflowers along the road in full bloom.

Marjorie's car was parked in front of the Thornton house, to the left of the front door at a slight angle. There was a small bus, green and yellow with a black roof, parked in the drive at the right, facing forward. Ginnie parked Potter's car next to Marjorie's, turning it around carefully so that she would not bruise the honeysuckle.

Two small boys and an elderly woman in black were standing by the door of the bus, staring at her. The boys had long brown curls dangling in front of their ears. Ginnie smiled and wiggled her fingers at them, but they did not wave back.

"How do you do," she said to the woman. "I won't be long."

She opened the front door and hurried through the hallway, glancing into the rooms left and right. The floors were covered with mattresses, but there were no people to be seen. She climbed to the top of the stairs, clutching her knit bag under her left arm. It was bulky and a bit heavy. She had brought along the little lady's gun that had belonged to Elizabeth. She did not think about why.

She knocked softly at the door with the private sign, and Marjorie's voice said, "Whoever you are, come in."

Thirty-six

CHARLIE ARRIVED FOR HIS MEETING AT Collins House at three, which allowed him a half hour alone with Martin before Katy arrived. They sat face-to-face on wicker chairs on the screened-in porch on the ravine side of the house. Mary had placed a tray with a mound of cookies, two pieces of chocolate cake, a pitcher of lemonade, and two glasses on the low wicker table between them.

Martin gestured toward the tray.

"Sarah," he said, "is baking up a storm. She has talent."

"I have a confession to make," said Charlie, munching on a cookie.

"Isn't it supposed to be the other way round, Sheriff?" said Martin. He poured the lemonade.

"I've obtained transcripts of all your phone calls. Shorthand."

"Janey Planck, I suppose," said Martin. "I hope we spoke slow enough for her."

"I think she got all the words, but some parts don't make complete sense. For example, the part about it being 'the younger generation that made this mess.' Would that be a reference to your grandsons?"

"I'm a little out of practice, Sheriff," Martin said, ignoring the question, "but isn't it illegal to monitor a telephone line?"

"Probably," said Charlie. "It's certainly impolite. And certainly not proper for people who are supposed to be working together."

"Is that what we're doing, 'working together?' My clients have first claim on me."

"Kaufman and Kaufmann, Rozkopf and Spray. Tell me, if you had information that would exonerate them, you'd give it to me right away. Right?"

"What kind of information?"

"Like the names of the shooters on the hill," said Charlie. "Like whatever Marjorie was up to. Like anything useful that Father Cavanaugh told you."

"The Right Reverend Monsignor Cavanaugh," said Martin. He sipped some lemonade. "Perhaps an exchange is in order. I'm sure you've made some discoveries of your own."

The sound of tires crunching on gravel interrupted as Charlie was nodding his agreement. A car pulled into the driveway and stopped at the porch steps.

"That looks like Katy," said Martin.

"With my father's ghost," Charlie replied.

♦   ♦   ♦

Martin started off with a summary of Marjorie's plot.

"Jerusalem and the Judas goat," said Charlie. "Good background. It explains some things. But it doesn't tell us who killed her or why."

"That's my contribution," said Martin. "Now it's your turn."

"Let's see," said Charlie. "Well, for starters, I think Potter was one of the shooters on the hill."

Katy was surprised. Martin wasn't.

"I also think he's Tom Quick. That's a name I've been after for a long time."

"He did act funny with that piece of slate," said Katy.

"Remember how relieved he was when he learned Marjorie was shot by somebody inside?" said Charlie.

"With a twenty-two," said Katy.

"Rose caught something, too. 'Red on the right. Red on the left.' It was Potter that Sarah heard on the hill."

"And he's been avoiding Sarah," said Charlie. "I couldn't get them together."

"It's not evidence," said Martin. "A good lawyer would rip it to shreds."

"What do you make of it?" Katy asked.

"I'm convinced," Martin replied. "But I haven't been a good lawyer for a long time."

"I think the other two shooters were your grandsons," Charlie said.

Again, Martin ignored the accusation. Charlie did not press it.

"There's still some pieces missing," Charlie went on. "Marjorie and Ginnie hire Carl to bring the Jews to the farmhouse. Potter . . . and two others . . . try to frighten them away. Marjorie doesn't know what Potter is up to, and somebody kills her for no reason at all."

"Not just her," said Katy in a very small voice.

She lifted her canvas bag onto the edge of the table and looked directly at Charlie.

"We should tell Mr. Collins about John Carpenter, Charlie. It all fits together now."

She took the letters and Jarvis's notes out of the bag and gave them to Martin. Then she held out the If-I-Am-Dead letter.

"First you have to read this," she said.

ψ　　ψ　　ψ

"I'm terribly sorry, Charlie," said Martin. He took Jarvis's poem out of his pocket. "He tried to warn us,"

" 'Do not trust them, they defile,' " Charlie read aloud.

"I knew Jarvis Evans as well as anyone," said Martin. "We were friends almost twenty years. I bought some furniture from him. A few paintings. We played cards. It's hard to imagine him blackmailing Ginnie. Why didn't he just tell me?"

"He had a dark side," said Katy. "He was a guardian of these mountains."

"Demons," said Martin. "I'm not the only one."

He gathered the papers together and put them all in the file.

"It's still not hard evidence," he said, "even with this. It's only assumptions. About Potter. About Ginnie."

He locked eyes with Charlie.

"Or anyone else."

"We can make it stronger," said Charlie. "If your grandsons would testify, that would convict Potter. And with the names you've collected, Marjorie's friends . . ."

Before Martin could reply, the screen door at the end of the porch banged open. Robert stood in the doorway, breathing hard, holding his side.

"Ginnie Washington took the little girl," he panted. "In the Wild Garden. She has a gun."

❦   ❦   ❦

Coming out of the woods at the top of Ravine Path, Robert and Ted had seen the three tiny figures—Mary, a small girl, and a woman in a blue dress—standing in the Wild Garden three hundred yards away. A black car was parked at the side of the road. The girl had a basket of flowers slung over her left shoulder.

The woman in the blue dress was talking and waving her arms. It looked as if she were asking directions. The girl moved between them. The woman held her left hand out to Mary, then grabbed at the collar of the girl's blouse and began to tug her toward the car, walking sideways. Mary stood still.

"She has a pistol," Ted said to Robert. "It's Mrs. Washington."

Ginnie had moved around the back of the car, still holding on to Sarah. She opened the door on the driver's side, pushed the girl in, and slid in beside her. Ted began to run down the path toward them.

"Take care of Mother," Robert shouted. "I'll get help at the house."

ψ   ψ   ψ

Mary had been startled to see Ginnie Washington pushing through the wild rose hedge.

"Don't make a fuss, Mary," said Ginnie. "I have killed two others already. Don't make me kill you, too."

A thorn had scratched her forehead, and a thin line of blood ran down the side of her nose.

"Who did you kill, Virginia?"

"That isn't important."

"What do you want?"

"Just the girl."

"You can't have her," said Mary.

She moved toward Sarah.

"That's what I meant by a fuss," said Ginnie, pointing the gun. "Don't make me."

She obviously meant it.

Sarah stepped between them.

"Don't worry, Mrs. Collins," she said. "Eddie said nothing bad can happen to me anymore."

Over Mary's head, Ginnie could see two men on the path, high up the hill. The Collins boys, watching.

"Give this message to Potter," she said, passing a folded piece of paper to Mary with her left hand. She swung her right hand, holding the gun, toward Sarah.

"Come along, child," she said, catching the collar of her dress. She kept her eyes on Mary.

"On one condition," said Sarah.

"You're in no position, child," said Ginnie. "What kind of condition?"

"That you let me keep the flowers."

※　※　※

Carl had called Jacob at Kaufmann Tours near closing time from his farm above Liberty.

"I should not have let her stay," he said. "She does not belong with them. They are not her people. She may become too accustomed. I could be there in an hour."

"This lack of trust bothers me, Carl," Jacob replied.

"This is not about trust, Jacob. We must stay together. They could never understand. In a week the papers will be final."

"So much pushing people away, Carl. She will be with Martin and Mary only three days."

"Half the universe was created in three days," said Carl.

Thirty-seven

"MRS. COLLINS SAYS IT'S A SMALL HAND-gun," said Charlie, "possibly a twenty-two. She knows how to use it."

"Ginnie's afraid Sarah might recognize Potter's voice," said Katy. "That's why she's taken her, isn't it?"

"Tell us again, Mary," said Martin. "Anything you think of. Try not to cry."

Mary couldn't stop sniffling.

"I wanted to stop her, Martin, but I couldn't think how. She was waving the gun. I was afraid she would shoot us."

"You did just right, Mary. That was the bad moment, and you got past it. Don't worry. We'll get Sarah back."

He turned to Ted. "Maybe she should lie down. Ask one of the girls."

Charlie telephoned the alert in to Rose, first making sure that Potter was not there. Rose said she thought he had gone to Chicken Corners.

"That's right, kidnapped," he told her. "Never mind by whom. If Potter calls in or comes in, don't say anything about it. Understand, *nothing*. Tell him I need him at Collins House, fast. You don't know why. And none of this gets radioed. Understand?"

Rose said she did, although she really didn't, and hung up.

"If Potter shows up here," Charlie said to Martin, "send him right back to Fredericktown. Keep him going in circles."

Robert and Ted volunteered to search the local roads. They knew them well.

"I'll have to deputize you," said Charlie. "I don't want vigilantes. Take guns. She won't listen otherwise. But don't use them unless you have to."

Martin looked pleased when Charlie swore them in. There was no more need for a trade. Charlie saw the smile, grimaced, and slowly shook his head.

"They're all I got," he said to Martin, justifying his action. "If I broadcast an alert, Potter might hear it. We don't want him linking up with Ginnie."

Martin and Mary agreed to stay at Collins House in case Ginnie called or came back.

"Arm yourself, Martin," said Charlie. "She's a killer."

"What about me?" said Katy.

"We'll go together," said Charlie. "Jarvis's over-and-under is in the trunk of the cruiser. It's lightweight. Use it if you have to."

He spoke quietly to the others.

"Rose said Potter went home around four. Katy and I will start there. If he's there alone, we'll hold him."

"What if they're both there?" Martin asked. *Poor Potter*, he thought. *Things fall apart.*

"Then I'll break silence on the two-way. There should be some backup around by then."

"Who can you count on?"

"Rose is telling every car that goes out to look for a black '29 Nash coupe. She sent one car to the Thornton place in case Ginnie goes back there."

"You think she killed Marjorie, too?" Katy asked.

"Probably. But I can't think why. It's twenty minutes to the Washington place. Let's go."

When they were all gone, Martin went to his den to select a handgun, shaking his head all the way. He took a Colt .45, U.S. Army issue, out of the bottom drawer of the gun cabinet and held it flat in the palm of his right hand. It was quite heavy. Someone at the armory once told him that the .45 had been invented for use in the Spanish-American War. The Moro wrapped strips of wet rawhide around their testicles before they went into battle. It shrank as it dried, and the pain was so intense it drove them crazy. A .30-caliber bullet didn't stop them unless it hit something vital. A .45 knocked them down no matter where it hit, even a hand.

Imagine me drawing against Ginnie Washington, Martin thought.

He tried to picture it. A dusty street, the two of them twenty feet apart, face to face.

She's probably faster than I am, he decided.

He put the gun back in the drawer.

He returned to the front hall just as Mary was putting the telephone earpiece back on its hook. In her left hand she held the note Ginnie had given to her for Potter.

Thirty-eight

"MRS. COLLINS WAS TELLING ME flower names," said Sarah. She was arranging the blossoms in the basket on her lap like a sunburst, stems to the center, heads hanging over the side.

"Wasn't that sweet," said Ginnie, "but we have a lot to do here. Put the basket down and help me with this lantern. It will be getting dark soon."

The wiring around the glass chimney of the old kerosene lantern was twisted and rusted. Ginnie shook it gently. The fuel chamber sounded almost full. She remembered Fletcher saying kerosene doesn't spoil like gasoline. Something about resins or phenols. She hoped that was true. Perhaps he meant that the chemistry was different for lighting than for cars.

"Hold the glass up straight while I get this wick right."

Sarah put the basket on the cracked linoleum floor and pushed it to the side. She cupped the chimney in both hands while Ginnie clipped the edge of the wick with her nail scissors and adjusted the height. When she had finished, she looked carefully at Sarah.

"Now, don't you go getting any ideas," she said. "I've got a gun."

"I know you do," said Sarah. "Am I your prisoner?"

The smell of kerosene reminded Sarah of her father trying to help the farmer in the next house start the old tractor that all the farmers shared.

"I suppose you are. Get comfortable," said Ginnie, pointing to the center of the daybed, which was pushed up against the back wall. "We will be here awhile."

She scraped a wooden match against the bottom of the lantern until it flared, then lit the wick and lowered the chimney.

"Lanterns make such a lovely light," she said with satisfaction. "So, Mary was telling you the names of flowers. That's useful. Do you know their names in the language you came from?"

"It was Polish. I only knew some. We did not have so many."

Every night in Warsaw they had put a great vase of red roses on the table by the piano, but she was not allowed near it. Some of the girls tucked white flowers in their hair.

"That is too bad. I'll tell you a secret. When I was a girl, younger than you are, I used to name rocks. That's right, proper names for rocks. Now, don't you laugh."

Sarah shook her head. She wouldn't.

"Names are important," Ginnie continued. "Anything worthwhile should have a name. Even rocks. Not science names, like quartz and feldspar. My father taught me those."

Sarah sat motionless with her fingers laced together, the way she sat in school.

"I mean personal names. I thought, mountains have names, like Everest and the Alps. So do big rocks, like Lovers' Leap on the Mongaup and Hospital Rock at Minisink where Colonel Brant murdered all our wounded boys. And the Rock of Gibraltar, of course. That's famous. But no one gives names to little rocks, even when they're worthwhile. I thought that wasn't being fair."

Sarah nodded in agreement. She had difficulty understanding what "being fair" meant.

"I thought, without names the poor things won't know who they are. Not just any old rocks. I meant rocks that were special."

As she talked she watched Sarah closely. The lantern was burning clean. The gun was resting lightly in her lap. Her finger was inside the trigger guard.

"I've never told this to anyone before," she said.

"What kind of names?" asked Sarah.

"Now, that was the hard part. I did *not* want to give them people names or names like pets have. And I did *not* want just sounds. I gave them noun names, words that seemed right after I stared a long, long time."

She fell silent.

"What kind of noun words?" Sarah asked. She did not know what "noun" meant.

"Oh, names like Song and Lace and Dipper. And Fist and Joke. Lace was light blue and covered with white lines. Dipper was just like a ladle. Joke was upside down. Fist had closed fingers. I can't remember why Song was."

"How old were you?"

"About nine, I suppose."

"I was nine when the great man came. How many did you name?"

"Oh, at least a hundred. I wrote them all down. Mother found the notebook, and of course the names made no sense to her at all."

"What did she do?"

"She asked what they were about, but I couldn't tell her. She might have thought I was addled."

"What's addled?"

"Not right in the head. I was afraid she might laugh at me, and that is something I absolutely cannot abide. So I took my punishment and kept my secret to myself."

"I keep secrets, too," said Sarah.

Ginnie was twisting the adjustment screw on the lantern. The wick was smoking, blackening the chimney on one side.

"You can tell me one of your secrets if you want," said Ginnie. "I told you one of mine."

Sarah did not reply.

"Oh, don't bother then," said Ginnie, miffed. "How many secrets could a little thing like you have anyway?"

"Many," said Sarah thoughtfully. "Uncle Carl says that if I do not speak of them they will go away. But I remember everything."

Sarah sat tight-lipped with her ankles crossed, making up her mind.

"Two days after the great man came to our *gospodarstwo*, I ran away to Warszawa," she said finally.

"Speak English," said Ginnie. "What does 'gospowhatever' mean? And that other word?"

"*Gospodarstwo* is like a little farm here but not so nice. A great man owns it. We had three rooms and our roof was made of grass. Warszawa is the capital of Poland."

"Oh, you mean Warsaw. Why did the great man come?"

"To see my father. There was another man with him. The great man had a long coat with a black fur collar. Father sent me with my mother and my brother to the small room, but we could hear them talking."

"What did they say?"

"The great man said he wanted us to go away. He said father must give him money if we wished to stay. Father called me to come out so the great man could look at me. He told father we could stay two more years if he gave them some money. And if he gave them me."

"Gave them you? That's outrageous."

"For two days I waited. Father looked angry. I thought he did not want me anymore. I did not want to go to the great man, so I ran away."

"To Warsaw?"

"Yes, but they caught me on the way."

"Eddie took care of me," said Sarah. "That is not his real name. He is Polish and very handsome. He lives with his mother in Warsaw. In the District Muranow. I write to him, but he does not answer."

"Perhaps you need to use more stamps," said Ginnie. "Are you sure you have the right address? The District Muranow?"

"Yes, where the Jews live. He works in the house they took me to. In the afternoon he comes to play the piano until the other man comes at night. He tells stories, and he sings songs. In English sometimes. The girls like him very much, and the men give him money. He is my best friend."

"I never had a best friend," said Ginnie. "The girls said I was too rough." She smiled. "Even the boys were afraid of me."

"He is saving his money to go to Hollywood. If he does, I will go with him. Sometimes with the other girls we sang the English songs. One was about Mammy and another was about showers and flowers."

"I know those songs," said Ginnie. "A man on the radio sings them all the time."

"Eddie sings them better than anyone," said Sarah.

"How old is your Eddie?"

"He was fifteen. I was nine. Now he is a man."

Ginnie had opened the windows but closed the louvered blinds. The air was hot and stuffy. She had piled the old blankets and cushions on the daybed. They smelled of mildew and cats and made her nose wrinkle. The lantern was hanging at the far end. The door was open a crack for ventilation.

The more Ginnie thought about it, the more Sarah's secret bothered her.

"Just what kind of place were you and Eddie in?" she asked.

"From the parlor windows, I could see the river. It was called the Vistula. The house was very beautiful. It had a chandelier like Collins House. It is a famous place. Eddie said it was a pleasure house. He said King Stanislas and his knights had parties there a long time ago. The king paved the street with wooden blocks because the carriage wheels were too noisy when he was with his girls."

"I suppose that would be a distraction," said Ginnie.

"Eddie said it was a bad place. At night the men came to look at me. One man had no hair. I sat on his knee. When I was in bed I could hear what they did, and there were little holes in the walls. Eddie said I should leave, but they said they would hurt my mother if I did."

"Families can be a trial," said Ginnie.

"He said when I saw him singing the 'April Showers' song and rolling his eyes at me, it was time to go. Or else they would take all my clothes away and the men would gamble for me."

"I know that song," said Ginnie. "I hope you listened to him."

"I put my things in a pillowcase, and I jumped out the window when the others were eating. Eddie caught me. He only had a little time, but the railroad station was not so far."

"You were very brave," said Ginnie.

"Eddie was brave. He gave me a letter and money to buy a ticket on the train. He said to go to Paris if I could, but not to Germany. I did not tell him I could not read the signs. That would spoil his plan."

"P-A-R-I-S," said Ginnie. "Paris is easy."

"He told me to say 'Jewish, Jewish,' in Paris, and people would help me."

"I suppose they might. You *are* Jewish, aren't you? You saw Potter at the farmhouse. And heard his voice. Oh, dear."

"Eddie kissed me on my head, and then he had to go back. I was reading the numbers on the signs when the ladies asked to see my letter. It said I was a Jew, so they brought me to a place where Jews were, and they sent me to my uncle Carl."

"That certainly was an adventure. Warsaw, Poland. Imagine. And a house like that. You must have been very frightened."

"I was not, truly," said Sarah. "Eddie said nothing bad can happen to me ever again."

※　※　※

"When I grow up, I'm going back to Warszawa," said Sarah. "If Uncle Carl won't take me, I'll go by myself."

"What in the world for?" asked Ginnie. "It sounds like an awful place. Aren't you happy here?"

She looked down at the gun in her lap and then at Sarah's face and suddenly felt tired. This was not working out at all.

To protect you, Potter Washington, she thought.

"I'm going to find them all," said Sarah. "My father and mother and brother. The great man and the man who was with him. And the man with no hair. The ladies at the train. And Eddie, unless he's in Hollywood. If he is, I will go there."

"What will you do when you find them?"

"I will marry Eddie. For the others, I am not sure. I will kill most of them. But not the ladies at the train or my mother or my brother."

"Well, aren't you the little Tom Quick," said Ginnie.

"Why did you take me away from Mrs. Collins?" Sarah asked. She had pulled the basket back between her feet and was fashioning a bouquet. The flowers were wilting.

"It's all because of names again," said Ginnie. "Family names this time. Potter is my son. I want to protect him, but now I don't know if I can. When I am angry enough I can always do something, but I'm not angry with you. Even if I were, it wouldn't help. He will find out about Elizabeth no matter what I do."

She was shifting the pistol from hand to hand, as if it were growing hot.

"Who is Elizabeth?"

"My grandmother. Elizabeth Flint. A lovely, foolish woman who got mixed up with a colored man. Imagine that." She laughed. "He was my real grandfather. Flint strikes sparks."

"What is it your son will find out?"

"That he isn't what he thinks he is. He'll wish he'd never been born. He will say it was my fault."

"Maybe if you say you're sorry?"

"Sometimes that doesn't work."

She struggled to her feet.

"You hold this while I hang up the lantern."

She gave the .22 pistol to Sarah.

"Don't point it at me, you little goose," she said sharply.

Sarah pushed it down between her knees.

"Hide it under the flowers," said Ginnie. "He will be here soon."

Thirty-nine

FOR THE FIRST TIME IN POTTER'S MEMORY, Rose could not or would not tell him where Charlie was. She just grumbled, "I don't know," and kept on typing.

"Is this some kind of a game?" he demanded. "Look at me!"

"I said I don't, and I don't, Potter. And I can't work and look at you at the same time. He's out there somewhere."

It was true. She was just as mystified as Potter, although she wouldn't admit it to him. At 2:27 Charlie had walked out of the building in full gear without stopping to mark the location book, an absolutely strict rule. He had never done that to her before. Rose had called after him when he reached the front door. He had looked back, put his index finger over his lips, winked, and left. That meant, *Don't say anything to anyone.*

She telephoned his house a half-hour later, but all she got was Katy, working on the files. She waited another ten minutes, then called Collins House to let Martin know that something strange was going on. He thanked her, but that was all. From the sound of his voice, Rose could tell he already knew.

"Well, I won't let Charlie's truancy ruin my day, babe," said Potter, trying not to sound bothered. "When he does show up, call me at home."

Rose made a face. Some people she didn't mind calling her babe, but not Potter.

"Ready on the firing line," she snapped when she was sure he was gone.

ψ   ψ   ψ

When Potter arrived home, his mother was not there. For the first time since her accident she had not answered when he called to her upstairs. There was an echo. The house sounded empty, the way abandoned houses do.

A day for firsts, he said to himself.

He searched everywhere, in closets, behind couches, under tables, thinking she might have fallen and could not get up. The cellar door was latched on the outside. That meant she could not be down there. He was prepared for anything. There was a hollow feeling in his stomach.

"Mother, where are you?" he heard himself asking.

On the way to the garage, he recalled being small and feeling this way, remembered how frightening it was, not knowing where his mother was. And how good it felt when he finally found her, when he sat snuggled on her lap with her arms around him, the gas lamp hissing, her voice calm and warm.

"Between the dark and the daylight,' " he heard himself reciting, "When the night is beginning to lower . . ."

The garage doors were wide open, and her Nash was not inside. She must have taken it for a drive. The car was old but in excellent condition. Potter started it up regularly to keep the battery charged. He had taken it into the shop to have the dented fender repaired and repainted after her accident.

The only time he had driven it himself in recent years was on Thursday with Robert and Ted to go out to Thornton farm. His mother must have used it Monday when she set fire to Charlie's house.

"To protect you," she had said. From what? he wondered.

He thought of calling the office, asking Rose to have the patrols watch for the Nash. But what would he say? *"I can't find my mother?"* Better not. Rose might see a weakness there. He needed to be strong with Rose.

Back in the house he stretched out on the porch glider where he could hear the telephone if Rose or Charlie rang. There was no cause to worry. He would deal calmly with whatever was going to happen.

" ' . . . comes a pause in the day's occupations, that is known as the Children's Hour.' "

Lying quietly in the glider, his thoughts drifting aimlessly between rabbits in overalls, firebombs, and soap, Potter had a sudden, stiffening thought.

He went upstairs to his mother's room and opened the top center drawer in her bureau where she kept her special things—her pearls, her opera glasses, her long kid gloves, and her guns. The long-barreled, single-shot target pistol was there. But the antique lady's handgun was not. It had once belonged to Elizabeth Fletcher. It was a short-barreled, seven-shot Smith & Wesson revolver with a mother-of-pearl grip. It fired .22-caliber rim-fire cartridges. He searched the other drawers quickly, but he knew it would not be there.

It was beginning to make terrible sense.

When Potter promised to get rid of the Jews, he had not told his mother how or when. She had not known what he was planning. He used her car that afternoon. She must have taken his.

Ginnie was an excellent shot. Eli had taught her to hunt. A regular tomboy, he used to boast. Killing and blood did not bother her. She could gut a deer as well as any man.

She was in there when the shooting started. At the top of the stairs. Rapid-fire, *bang-bang-bang*. One slug exited above the forehead. Two stayed inside and rattled around.

His mother killed cousin Marjorie. But why?

The phone rang, two rings repeated twice for the Washingtons.

"Oh, Potter, I'm so sorry," said Mary Collins. "Your mother took Sarah away. She has a gun. Charlie and Martin are out looking for her. They were trying to find you. It must be because she hit her head that time she ran into the tree."

"Please slow down, Mrs. Collins."

"She gave me a note for you. I forgot until now. It says, 'My Country 'Tis of Thee.' I don't know what that means."

Robert knew what "My Country 'Tis of Thee" meant.

He and Ted had crisscrossed the back roads for almost an hour. When they returned, Martin was trying to call Rose so that she could relay the words of Ginnie's strange message to Charlie. Martin had tried to reach him at the Washingtons' but there was no answer.

Robert explained about the song.

"He was the tramp kid who painted that dirty French word on the memorial, Judge."

He paused.

"It was Potter with us on the hill. He's Tom Quick."

"I guessed that," said Martin. "But I'm glad to hear it from you."

Forty

"POTTER CALLED IN FROM HIS HOUSE," the duty man told Rose. "He wants to know where everyone is. He says if we can't handle whatever's going on, he'll handle it himself. Handle what?"

"If he calls again, or radios, tell him you don't know what's going on," said Rose. "Which you don't, so you're not lying. Tell him the sheriff wants him at Collins House."

"The sheriff's not at Collins House," said the duty man.

"Do what you're told," Rose ordered. "We're on the firing line."

*   *   *

There was no longer any reason to keep radio silence.

"Rose, this is Martin. Get word right away to Charlie. Don't worry about who's listening. Tell him Ginnie has taken Sarah across the lake to the old house trailer. Yes, that's what I said, Ginnie Washington. The trailer near the gravel pits where that squatter family used to be. Tell them Ginnie got a message to Potter, so he may be there, too. I'm leaving now, with Robert and

Ted. We'll take the logging road over the top. It's rough, but it's fastest. Say a prayer, love. I don't know what happens next."

* * *

Potter moved quickly after Mary's call. The little girl was the only witness against him, and his mother had her. Robert and Ted wouldn't talk. They were in it as much as he was. He slid out of his driveway quietly, lights out, and drove south on the old shore road toward the tip of the lake. He felt surprisingly good. Ready for action. The young braves were hunting Tom Quick again.

Mother is lost. I can't save her. But she can save me.

He hid the cruiser a quarter mile from the trailer behind a high mound of gravel siftings at the edge of an abandoned gravel pit. In the spring, rain and melting snow filled parts of the pits to overflowing. By August, fed only by seepage and light showers, most of the quarry was dry. At the bottom of the pits, moonlight glazed the surface of the remaining puddles, making them look like polished ice. The moon was almost full. The mountains were carbon black shadows against the evening sky. Fractured clouds sailed by.

Potter hugged the shadows as much as he could, not knowing who might be ahead of him or what to expect. He was shivering with excitement. The evening breezes in the quarry sounded like the hissing of arrows and the honing of knives. Two hundred yards from the trailer, he took cover behind a spinney of second-growth white birches. Between the lean trunks of the trees, he could see a sliver of vertical light at the edge of the trailer's metal door and sparkles of light behind the two windows on the right. They were both in there. Even at this distance, he could smell kerosene.

He slid his Colt Detective Special and holster under the front seat of the car and tucked a cheap, untraceable .38 revolver into the waistband of his pants. Had his mother killed the girl yet?

Why hadn't she done it at Collins House? Perhaps she needed more time. A difficult thing, he imagined, to kill a child. Not like a deer. Not like a grown-up. Not like Marjorie.

What had Marjorie done to deserve it? he wondered. He might never know. It didn't always have to be deserved. Sometimes it just couldn't be avoided.

I'll give her ten more minutes. If she doesn't do it, Tom Quick will.

☙   ☙   ☙

"I am all alone splitting hickory rails for old man Westbrook in the Mamakating Valley," Tom told the boys at Decker's Tavern. "I work so hard, I don't pay close attention. Seven of them snuck up behind, and just like that they got me.

"They can't make up their minds to kill me right away, like they could easy if they wanted, or better take me back to where they camp to show me off. I say, 'Do what you must, but I don't want to die owing Westbrook half a day's work. Help me split these rails if you in such a goddamn hurry.' And so they do.

"This long hickory trunk, I got it half split with a wedge to hold it open. 'Grab on to the two sides and pull,' I tell them. 'Then it goes faster.' Three of them grab hold on one side, four on the other. I knock out the wedge, and the split snaps closed with their fingers caught inside.

"I sit and laugh at them awhile. Then I cut their throats, one at a time."

☙   ☙   ☙

On his deathbed Tom begs those gathered around to bring him just one more Delaware so that he can die certain that he has killed a full one hundred. They bury him with his Pennsylvania flintlock at his side wrapped in soft deerskins. It is a massive rifle with a forty-inch barrel. The maple stock is so worn that the ramrod shows through.

The Delawares dig his body up and cut it into pieces. Their sachems send chunks to all the encampments so the clans can celebrate his death. But Tom has died of smallpox, and an epidemic comes. The corpse of the Indian Slayer purifies the valley.

ψ   ψ   ψ

It was getting dark. Potter slipped from behind the birches into the shadow cast by a moving cloud. He moved silently across the pebbled yard toward the trailer, like Fletcher, like Enoch, like Brewster, like Tom. *He was hunting again. His beard was tangled. His braid was knotted on his neck. Wood lice were living in his hair. Panthers were coughing in the distant hills. Feathers were brushing against the leaves of low trees. He could smell wet buckskin.*

He tugged gently at the slightly open door. The door swung halfway open. The low-burning lantern was hanging from a hook at the right.

"You sent for me," he said. "I'm here."

Forty-one

"IS THAT YOU, POTTER?" GINNIE ASKED lightly. "You got my message? I'm glad. Come in where I can see you."

Potter slid through the half-open door, pulled it closed behind him, and turned left toward his mother's voice.

Ginnie had hung the lantern to the right of the doorway at the kitchen end of the trailer, above a countertop littered with rodent droppings. On the countertop a small two-burner stove with cast-iron cabriole legs squatted next to a sink. Two wooden cabinets hung from the ceiling on either side. A galvanized fuel tank was cradled on perforated metal straps between them.

Ginnie and Sarah were huddled at the other end of the long narrow room on a sagging daybed. Ginnie was on the left, Sarah on the right. Their spines were curled against the cushioned rear wall. More cushions and blankets were piled around them. Their legs were drawn up. Their toes peeked out from beneath their skirts. Ginnie's hands were at her sides. Sarah's were in her lap, buried in flowers.

The lantern at Potter's back threw his shadow over the daybed.

"You were clever to remember this place," he growled. " 'My Country 'Tis of Thee.' That was a long time ago." His voice was raspy, the way Fletcher's voice had sounded when he talked about God's work. *Time to scarify a sinner, boy.*

"The child is still alive?" Potter asked softly.

"Don't talk like that," said Ginnie. "She's just fine. We've been having a nice conversation. We're so pleased you are able to join us. Sarah, you've met my son, Potter. Potter, you know Miss Spray."

"You said you would protect me," he replied.

The lantern cast a ring of blurred light around his head. His hair at the edges looked like spiderwebs or fine black fur. Sarah recognized the voice. *"Red on the right." "Shoot to kill."*

"Stand up, girl," Potter said. "Come here."

In the *gospodarstwo* the great man's face had been half covered by a black fur collar. Sarah's father had called her back into the room. She had done what the great man asked. *"Turn around, child, slowly. Lift your arms. Now back, the other way. Very nice, Jew. Very nice."*

"Stay still," Ginnie snapped. "I want her next to me, Potter. Whatever you think I came here for, I've changed my mind."

She pushed her heels back against the side of the lumpy mattress, feeling for the edge of the bedframe with her toes.

Sarah cradled the barrel of the pistol in the palm of her left hand and very slowly tipped it up. Her right hand glided around the grip, her index finger searched for the trigger. The flowers rippled. Phlox perfumed the air.

"They are looking for you, Mother," said Potter, sounding official. "They are not stupid. They must know about Marjorie by now. And about the fire. Charlie knows you took this little girl."

"In time they will know everthing, I suppose," said Ginnie. "I tried to protect you. I can't do it anymore."

"Protect me from what?"

"From finding out you are not what you think you are," said Sarah.

Potter's eyes moved quickly to Sarah, then back to Ginnie.

"What is that supposed to mean?" he asked. "You're crazy.

What are you doing? Why Marjorie? She was our own blood. What did she ever do to you?"

"She wasn't the only one, Potter. I had to kill Jarvis, too."

"Jarvis Evans? The accident," said Potter slowly. "I had the fender fixed."

"There is no way to protect you anymore. Everyone will know."

"Know what? This child is my only worry," said Potter. "Whatever else has been done, you did."

"You don't know about Elizabeth," said Sarah.

"They'll put you away," said Potter.

"I might like that," said Ginnie. "This is the worst day of my entire life, Potter. From beginning to end, nothing worse than today can happen."

The backs of her legs were beginning to cramp. She stared at the butt of the pistol pressed into Potter's belly above his belt.

"Tell me why," he said. "She was family."

"I wasn't going to tell you anything," said Ginnie. "I tried to keep it from you. But you're bound to hear it someplace. Better from me. Now, stop fussing and listen."

She hunched forward, curling her toes around the metal bar.

"It started with a Judas goat," she said, "and Grandmother Elizabeth."

Forty-two

UPSTAIRS AT THORNTON FARM IN THE
room with the Private sign, sitting straight up in the pressed-back
chair with her knit bag on her knees, Ginnie carefully explained
all of it to Marjorie again, right from the beginning. But Marjorie
would not pay attention. She nibbled on a piece of toast and sipped
a cup of tea, never offering a crumb or a drop to Ginnie. She kept
fiddling with papers in a box on the floor, taking them out and
putting them back, making it clear that Ginnie was wasting both
their time.

Ginnie was annoyed by the rudeness, but a part of her admired
the confidence, the style, the strength.

Finally Ginnie said his name, John Carpenter. Almost immediately, Marjorie looked up and stopped whatever she was doing.
Ginnie had not intended to say that much, only enough to make
her understand how serious it was. But once she started, it all came
out in a rush.

Marjorie listened to the story of Prudence and John Carpenter
without expression, without saying a word, and then she smiled.
Just a little turnup at the corners of her mouth at first, and then a
grin.

"You and Potter? Negroes?" she said. "And Prudence? Mother would have died." And she began to laugh.

"Don't do that, Marjorie," said Ginnie. "You know I will not abide that."

"All your fancy Babcock ways, treating us like back-door dirt. And you're nothing but Negroes!"

At that moment the first bullet from Robert's Springfield came through the outer wall. It punched a hole above the corner window, exploding a ball of plaster, and went out near the top of the opposite wall.

Marjorie stood up, looked down at the box of papers, and pressed her lips tightly together. Someone downstairs screamed. Another bullet came through, above the other window. She walked calmly to the door and looked back at Ginnie.

"Come on, nigger," she said. "We're leaving."

At the top of the stairs, when Marjorie was down one step and their heights were the same, Ginnie shot her three times in the back of the head.

Forty-three

ROSE'S VOICE WAS CRACKLING ON THE cruiser radio, and the telephone started ringing behind Charlie and Katy as they clattered down Potter's front steps.

"You've got to be there somewhere!" Rose was squawking. "Say something, dammit."

"I got the two-way," Charlie told Katy. "You get the phone. Pick up but don't talk. It might be Potter calling home."

Katy came back out running.

"It was the duty desk," she gasped. "Rose told them to call. Ginnie's at that old trailer in the gravel quarry."

"I know. I just heard it from Rose direct. Martin and his grandsons are on their way. Let's go."

ψ   ψ   ψ

The county kept the logging road clear of rocks and fallen trees so that the firefighters could get equipment through, but it was deeply rutted and almost washed out at low points where rain had coursed down the mountain. Robert drove, Martin beside him, Ted in back. The car careened down the long, winding slope, bouncing, rocking, and tipping, its body lifting off the leaf springs one moment, slamming hard against the chassis the next.

"Hang on to Grandfather," Robert yelled to Ted. "He's too old for this."

"Don't be impertinent," Martin said through clenched teeth. "Just drive."

Robert turned the headlights off before they reached the gravel flats and rolled slowly the rest of the way. He stopped when he saw Potter's empty cruiser parked behind a hillock, bathed in moonlight. Charlie and Katy were standing behind it, facing them, waving their arms.

ψ   ψ   ψ

"I don't know what's called for," Charlie whispered to Martin, "moving or waiting. We haven't heard a thing. She's had time enough for anything."

"Or he has," said Katy.

They were huddled behind the same spinney of birch trees that Potter had used for cover.

"We can't wait any longer," Charlie decided. "We'll spread out and move in real quiet, ten feet apart. I'll take the center with one of the boys on each side. Katy, you stay behind the trees with the over-and-under. Train it on the door. Use your own judgment. Martin, you're in back of me."

"What am I back there? The rear guard?"

His legs were numb from the hammering ride. He was leaning heavily on his ebony walking stick.

"Back me up. Watch for something I don't see," said Charlie.

He wanted Martin where he couldn't get in the way.

"Let me go first," said Robert. "I know the layout. I've been inside before."

"Makes sense," said Charlie. "You lead the way."

When they were in position, Charlie said, "Wait for a cloud. Don't trip on anything. No noise."

Katy propped the small rifle-shotgun in the crotch of a lower branch, her fingertip lightly stroking both triggers, the two muzzles centered on the door. When the sky darkened, the men moved forward.

Forty-four

THE EXPRESSION ON POTTER'S FACE DID not change while Ginnie told her story. He looked slightly amused.

"Prudence was a Negro, Potter" she explained gently. "Nothing can change that."

When she was finished his lips twisted in anger.

"It's a lie," he said. "They always lie. They said the same thing about Tom. That his mother was a squaw. To make his friends desert him. I'm as white as he was."

He backed deeper into the the kitchen area, twisting his head from side to side, pushing something unwanted away. His shadow spread wider.

"John Carpenter was my grandfather, Potter. Like it or not, there it is. Wishing he wasn't won't change it."

"This is a holy war. Father warned me. He prepared me."

She thought of the sampler. *Elizabeth Flint, age of ten, prepared for death, I know not when.*

"Marjorie was right, Potter. She called me a nigger, and I killed her. But she was right. Prudence, myself, and you, we are niggers. I can't say it plainer than that. We are descendents of John Carpenter."

"We killed John Carpenter!" Potter screamed. *"Brewster and Enoch and father and I."*

"That was just your father's talk," said Ginnie. "You weren't even born."

Potter smelled the wet buckskin again. The reeds, the warm embankment mud. He heard the soft swish of the paddle. He combed his callused fingers through his beard, loosened the knots in his long black hair. His eyes glowed. His nostrils flared. He could hear crows squawking in the trees. The river water was above his knees. A baby was crying.

"We spat on him," he said calmly. "We gutted him. We tied a rope around his feet. We hung him from a tree."

He crouched lower. At the far end of the trailer the lantern glowed above his head. He twitched his shoulders, like an animal preparing to spring. Ginnie did not recognize him now.

"Nothing matters anymore," she said.

Potter sucked in his stomach, pulled the pistol from his belt, and moved forward.

"Cry if you want, girl," he growled. "Nits make lice."

The moment Potter's fingers touched the butt of the gun, Ginnie uncoiled. She thrust hard against the mattress and frame with her hands and feet, spraying flowers everywhere. Her body stretched out like a diver's, filling the space between her son and Sarah.

"No!" she screamed. *"No! No! No! No! No!"*

Forty-five

CHARLIE AND ROBERT WERE THIRTY FEET from the wooden steps, Martin behind them, when Potter screamed, *"We killed John Carpenter!"* They froze, eyes fixed on the metal door.

Robert was at the top step, tugging the door open, when Ginnie screamed. Inside, two gunshots snapped from the left, a third barked from the right. The sound of the gunshots were joined by a flash of light and a blast of searing hot air that shoved Robert backward into Charlie and Ted, pushing them to the ground.

Potter was braced in the doorway, facing out. His shirt and pants were smoking. A burning curtain from a window behind him had blown across his right shoulder, and small flames were licking at his hair. Both his hands were wrapped tightly around the silver pistol. He poked it down and sideways, dazed, then swung it arm's length back into the trailer.

"Get him!" Martin yelled.

Charlie lurched upward from the steps and wrapped his arms around Potter's thighs, pushing him back and down. Robert struggled to his feet, blinking at the white flash spots that floated in front of his eyes. Ted pushed up to his hands and knees, head down.

"Get them out! It's on fire!" Martin called from behind them. He stumbled toward the steps, waving his walking stick.

Inside, the fire near the door had burned out, but the kitchen cabinets were blazing and a thick layer of sooty smoke was forming at the ceiling. Candle-sized flames danced on the splintered plywood shelf below the place where the fuel tank had been hanging.

Charlie wrapped his arms around Potter, heaved him over his left shoulder, and hauled himself to his feet. Body bent forward, he began to back out the trailer door. Potter's toes were dragging, his elbows were braced on Charlie's back, and the gun was clenched in his right hand. On the top step, when they were clear of the doorway, Potter raised his head, squinted his eyes, and pointed the gun at Robert.

"Tom Quick," he muttered. "You?"

He sounded confused. The gun dipped and rose again.

Martin yelled, "Don't!" and pressed the release button on his walking stick.

Hopping forward on wobbly legs, he placed his right foot in the small of Ted's back and lunged over Robert, pushing him aside. The blade of the short sword entered Potter's shoulder at the joint, cutting through nerves and cartilage, instantly deadening the arm. Potter screamed and twisted. The silver gun bounced off the top step and fell to the ground. Potter pulled loose from Charlie's grip and fell to the floor. Martin rolled off Ted's back, landing on his feet.

"Ginnie and Sarah," he shouted. "Them first."

He recovered the lower section of his walking stick and returned the short sword to its sheath.

Charlie covered his nose and mouth with his kerchief, stepped over Potter, and went back inside. Robert followed.

Before joining them, Ted turned to his grandfather.

"Don't punish Potter anymore," he told him. "That's enough."

Martin did not challenge the command.

Charlie was first out, carrying Sarah. Twists of black smoke curled around them. Ginnie's pistol was in his left hand. He passed the girl into Katy's waiting arms.

"He shot his mother, Katy," Sarah said matter-of-factly. "He tried to shoot me."

Ted appeared in the doorway with Ginnie wrapped in a blanket, cradled in his arms.

"I think she's still alive," he said. "But just."

Charlie found a grassy spot clear of stones away from the trailer door. Martin folded his jacket into a pillow for Ginnie's head. When she was as comfortable as they could make her, Charlie showed the pearl-handled revolver to Martin.

"Two rounds left," he said. "Five used out of seven. It was on the bed between them."

"Well, well, well," said Martin.

"One more to go," said Robert. "I don't think we should move him very far."

Potter's forehead was red and very swollen. Blood had run down between his eyes. Ted straddled him, hooked his hands beneath his armpits, and lifted him by his shoulder blades partway off the floor. Robert and Martin each grabbed a leg, and, together, they brought him out and lowered him onto the gravel outside.

ψ   ψ   ψ

They were spread out in the area in front of the trailer, too damaged or too weary to move.

Potter was propped at the side of the wooden steps, his arms at his sides, his legs straight out, staring blankly at the moon that flashed above him between the broken clouds.

Martin sat forty feet away next to Ginnie, holding Sarah in the curve of his arm. Ginnie was lying on her back, her eyes closed. Katy was holding Martin's folded jacket underneath her head. Ginnie was sucking air through her mouth and through a hole in her chest.

Ted was standing above Martin. Robert was kneeling, facing the smoking trailer.

"We should move back," Charlie said in a loud, tired voice. "The inside is all wood. It's like a big furnace."

He dropped on one knee next to Martin.

"A bullet must have hit a fuel tank," he muttered. "Can we move her farther away?"

"She's pretty bad," Martin said.

"You don't look so hot yourself," said Charlie. "Why don't you wait in the car?"

Martin rose and with Sarah's hand in his began walking back to where the cars were parked.

"We can't wait for an ambulance," Charlie said to Ted. "Give me a hand."

He and Ted lifted Ginnie gently between them. Katy supported her head.

Behind them the flames suddenly flared in the louvered windows, twisting and spinning like a top inside the open door. The roof pushed up and split, sending a fountain of sparks into the summer air.

"We've got to get Potter away from there," Robert called to them. "It's getting hotter."

The heat on his face made him realize that he must have been burned when the fuel tank blew. He pushed himself to his feet, wondering if he could manage Potter without help. Just as he started forward, the gasoline drum that Mrs. du Sault's men friends had stored behind the trailer eight years earlier exploded with a throaty roar.

Wrapped in a sudden ball of fire, the trailer bounced sideways off its cinder-block foundation. A wave of fiery gas, blasting forward from underneath, tore the steps away, lifted Potter to his feet, and held him upright for a moment, arms and legs spread, fingers curled, before it pitched him forward.

Robert, lying where he had been thrown by the explosion, could smell embers smoking close by. Too exhausted to move, he watched Potter burn.

"My Country 'Tis of Thee!" He could still hear the boy crying, *Don't! Don't!*

"You little half-breed bastard," he whispered, "that's what I call getting even."

ψ   ψ   ψ

Katy and Ted were sitting on a wooden bench in the emergency room, waiting for news. Martin had taken Sarah back to Collins House.

Charlie came through the swinging double doors, looking stone-faced and grimy but in better shape than the rest of them.

"Ginnie died on the table," he reported in a flat voice. "Potter's still alive, but he won't last the night. Robert's burns aren't serious, but they want to hold him a day."

"Did Ginnie say anything?" Katy asked.

"Nothing that made much sense. In the car she said to Rose, real clear, 'Fussing won't change anything.' And just before she died, she said, 'Al Jolson,' very pleased with herself, like she remembered something she'd forgotten."

Forty-six

AT CHARLIE'S REQUEST, THEY ASSEMBLED in the briefing room at noon the next day—Martin, Mary, Ted, Katy, Rose, and Carl, who had driven down from his farm early that morning. Rose stood behind Charlie's chair with her steno pad. With Charlie and Potter out of the office, she had more or less run the operation until dawn, and she was still too wound up to sit down.

Katy had beaten out the flames on Robert and Potter with Martin's jacket. But Robert had blister burns on his face, hands and arms, and the internist had been cautious about infection. He was due to be released at one o'clock.

Sarah was asleep in Agnes's room at Collins House. Carl had kept watch in a chair by the side of the bed before driving with Martin to Fredericktown.

"We didn't try to question her last night, Mr. Rozkopf," said Charlie. "If she's up to it, Rose and I will stop by later in the day."

He turned to a chalk outline of the quarry pit and trailer sketched on the blackboard behind him.

"Sarah was lucky. Potter and Ginnie were in front of her when the first fuel tank exploded, and she was hunkered down low. The open door took some of the blast. That kept most of the flames at the other end until after she was out."

"She told me you went into the fire for her," said Carl. "I wish to thank you."

"My pleasure," said Charlie. "Robert Collins went first."

He opened his notebook and placed it on the table.

"While it's all still fresh in our minds, let's see what the rest of us can remember."

Mary and Ted started with Ginnie coming into the Wild Garden, and one at a time they reconstructed the events that led to the quarry pit.

"From this point on, it gets confusing," said Charlie. "Potter yelled something about killing John Carpenter, and the shooting started just as Robert was opening the door. Sarah's the only one who may know what started it or who fired first."

"She does not remember everything," said Carl.

"Not surprising," said Charlie, glancing at Martin.

"The shots sounded all together," said Martin. "Three, I think. Simultaneous."

Charlie nodded his agreement.

"Potter's bullet, thirty-eight caliber, hit his mother in the chest. One of the shots from the twenty-two hit him in the forehead. We think another one hit a small fuel tank hanging over the sink near a lantern. It exploded. Probably a camper's mix of gasoline or alcohol in kerosene. They do stupid things like that for quick heat."

"What about the second explosion?" asked Ted.

"A drum of gasoline someone must have put there years ago," said Charlie. "The fire broke through the back of the trailer and heated it up."

He returned to his notes.

"The twenty-two fractured Potter's skull, just above his eyes. The doctor said it didn't penetrate. It's a funny old gun. Handmade rim-fire cartridges, low velocity, and it hit a thick part of his head. I don't know how he stayed on his feet."

"He got stuck in the doorway," said Ted. "He was only half-alive."

"He pointed the gun at Robert, but your grandfather skewered him before he could fire. That was quite a stunt, Martin."

"Like an acrobat," said Katy.

Martin closed his eyes and shook his head. He looked worn out.

"How are you planning to report all this, Sheriff?" he asked, in a tone that suggested maybe he shouldn't.

Charlie could feel everyone's eyes on him.

"That's something we ought to talk about," he said. "Suppose I put the pad away."

"Okay if I stay?" Rose asked.

"Sure, if you want," said Charlie, "but no notes. What we say from now on didn't happen."

"Thanks," said Rose. "I hate to miss the endings."

"Three points I want to make," said Charlie. "First, there are some things we don't know and never will. Second, most of what we do know we can't prove. And third, except for Sarah, all the people who might have first-hand knowledge of the killings are dead."

"We know Ginnie killed at least two people," said Katy. "Three if you count Potter. And Potter killed her."

"That's what we *think*," said Charlie. "And we think we know why she did it, like we think we know why he did what he did. But it's only conjecture."

"He went there to kill Sarah," said Katy.

"Probably. But I could as easily argue he's a hero. Suppose I claim he went there to stop his crazy mother from killing Sarah and died trying. My loyal deputy."

"That's pure nonsense and you know it," said Rose. "Loyal? He wanted your job so bad it was unsanitary."

"Or turn it around. Ginnie took Sarah there to hide her from her crazy son. Or they were working together."

"More nonsense."

"I couldn't prove that," said Charlie. "Neither could you."

"He pointed a gun at Robert." Ted said.

"He'd just killed his mother, been shot in the head, and survived an explosion. That would explain a certain amount of confusion."

"But you don't believe that," said Katy.

"It won't matter much what I believe."

"What do the powers in Albany want you to believe?" Martin asked.

"They haven't told me yet. What's your guess?"

Martin arched his back in the folding chair. Every muscle ached. He could not get comfortable.

"I think, whatever you believe, you have to make some kind of decision soon. If you don't wrap this up quickly, you will make a lot of people nervous."

"So, why don't we just let it be?" said Charlie. "No conspiracy, no blackmail, one unsolvable homicide, no kidnapping, a suicide pact, no Tom Quick. The investigation turned to ashes."

He turned to Rose.

"Just forget it?" Rose asked. "Marjorie was the fairy god-mother? Potter was the Lone Ranger? And Ginnie was Florence Nightingale? What about Jarvis?"

"Nothing will bring my father back, and Potter was the last of the Washington line. Let it be."

Rose snorted her disapproval.

"They'll put up another monument," she said. " 'The Savior of Chicken Corners.' For Potter this time."

"Over Aunt Copper Pot's dead body," said Charlie. "And mine."

"If you don't look like you're digging deep enough, there could be an independent inquiry," said Martin.

"It wouldn't get very far. Nobody up there wants one. Ask the state police. Potter, Ginnie, Marjorie, my father—they're all dead. Let it be."

"How does that sound to you, Mr. Collins?" asked Carl.

"Worthy of Solomon," said Martin.

He looked around the room. Rose shrugged her shoulders. It was decided.

"I wish to take Sarah home," said Carl.

"No reason not to," said Charlie. "I just need a short statement."

"Why don't you stay the night at Collins House, Carl? Leave in the morning," said Martin. "We can tie up the loose ends."

"I would like that, Martin," said Carl.

♦   ♦   ♦

Charlie and Rose drove to Collins House after lunch at the diner. Sarah's statement took ten minutes. She said she couldn't remember much. She and Ginnie had talked about rocks and flowers. Charlie said he was satisfied.

Martin walked Charlie back to his car. Rose accepted Mary's invitation to spend the afternoon.

"Will you be running for sheriff again?" Martin asked.

"If I can't avoid it," said Charlie. "It's become more difficult to tell the good guys from the bad guys."

"What about my clients?"

"No problems there I can see. Some formalities, that's all. Jacob and August are clear. Carl has more important things to keep him occupied. If all those Jews in Europe show up in the Catskills, he'll need someplace to put them. Now he's got the inside track on some cheap land."

Sitting at the wheel with the engine running and Martin standing by, Charlie seemed reluctant to leave.

"Off the record," he asked, "last night, did you ask Sarah who shot who?"

"Why would I?" Martin replied. "Her adoption will be final next week. She'll be a citizen. Why make trouble?"

"How about accidental or on purpose? Or who shot first? Him or one of them?"

"Does it matter, Charlie?"

"Like I said, it's getting more difficult."

☙   ☙   ☙

Before going to bed that night, Martin and Carl agreed that Sarah should keep her answers simple if anyone asked any more questions. Ginnie shot Potter. Potter shot Ginnie. She did not know who fired first or why. She had been too frightened to notice anything more than that.

At breakfast, Sarah listened carefully.

"If you want me to say I was frightened, I will, but I was not," she said. "Nothing bad can happen to me anymore."

"I wouldn't doubt that," said Charlie.

"Amen," said Martin.

Carl and Sarah left for the city before lunch.

Forty-seven

"FEELING SORRY FOR YOURSELF?" KATY asked.

They were sitting side by side on his front porch in matching Adirondack rocking chairs, sipping cider from jelly jars, and popping sunflower seeds.

"Yup," said Charlie.

"Nobody to arrest?"

"Nope."

"You could arrest the Collins boys."

He pretended to consider that.

"I made them my deputies. Might make me look silly."

"No credit for all that brilliant police work? The man who caught Tom Quick?"

"Not even a thank-you. Nobody knows."

"You sound like you don't care."

Charlie sat up straighter.

"Maybe that's it," he said. "The minute you start caring, you're in trouble. Too little or too much, it doesn't matter. You're in trouble either way."

"More's got to be better than less."

"Does it? No one cared more than my father and Ginnie Washington, and look what it got them."

"That wasn't just caring. That was loving."

"Love's the worse kind of caring. You stop worrying about yourself."

"That's sweet," Katy said. "I love you, too."

She leaned over and kissed his nose.

"What matters, Charlie, is what you care *about* and the kind of person you are."

Charlie twisted sideways, reached across, and put his hand over hers.

"I know what I care about," he said. "It scares me half to death. What kind of a person am I?"

"You are Lord of the Catskills and a Wolf of the Delaware, Charlie Evans," she said. "And don't you ever forget it."

ⱴ   ⱴ   ⱴ

Late that afternoon, the Collins family strolled out to the Wild Garden. Rose was with them, walking next to Mary. Martin walked between his grandsons, his hands resting lightly on their shoulders.

"Someone I know recently told me that anyone can kill, given enough reason," Martin said to Robert. "I didn't think I agreed, but he was right. When I thought Potter was going to shoot you, I tried to kill him."

"I'm grateful," said Robert, "but I don't think he would have pulled the trigger. He thought I'd be the next Tom Quick."

"So that's what he meant," said Martin.

"He decided on me that night the Klan burned the cross on our lawn."

"Poor man," said Rose disgustedly. "All he wanted was a son of his own."

They stopped at the place where Sarah had been kidnapped. Wilted flowers were scattered on the ground.

"It will be quiet here without her," said Mary.

"Your sense of humor approaches the outrageous," Martin replied.

Mary smiled. "Still, I hope she comes back. She was different. We need a change."

"Wishful thinking," said Martin. *"Plus ça change, plus c'est la même chose.* The more things change, the more they remain the same."

"Another way of saying we never get anywhere?" Ted asked. "We just keep going in circles?"

Rose was picking the petals off a field daisy. She winked at Martin. He winked back.

"You be the Judge," he said.

ᴪ   ᴪ   ᴪ

Two weeks later Martin was sitting on a stone bench inside the sunlit courtyard of the chancery building of the Roman Catholic Archdiocese of New York. The palatial, Renaissance-style building was on the east side of Madison Avenue, across from the cardinal's residence, which was behind St. Patrick's Cathedral. There was no cardinal in place at the moment. Patrick was dead, and Frank Spellman was only an archbishop. On the other side of the cast-iron gates, the shapes and shadows of people flickered by.

Martin was there to see Tim Cavanaugh. To thank him again for his help. To tell him how it ended.

While he waited, he thought about how alike and how different he and Tim were.

How in the world can someone as smart as Tim disagree with me so completely? he wondered with immodest amusement. *It takes all kinds, I suppose. The one and the many.*

The New York Times on his knee said WAR!

Gallia est omnis divisa in partes tres. What would it be like if we were all the same?

He stared at the shadows beyond the railings, moving both ways. *From nowhere, going nowhere. An infinite ending, a bottomless beginning. What really is important? Trinkets that our mothers blessed? Hollows where our fathers rest? Anything? No answer. Not even a decent question. A joke without a joker. A trick masquerading as a puzzle.*

"And why not?" he said aloud. "Where's the harm?"

ψ   ψ   ψ

Tim swept into the courtyard in full regalia, a sash with a fringe wound around his cassock, his gray hair glinting in the filtered sun. He had just finished the reading of his Latin breviary, a daily canonical obligation he often failed to perform. This day, perhaps because of Martin Collins's visit, he was reminded of an ancient credo. The words tolled slowly in his mind, like the last tones of a bell:

> . . . He ascended into Heaven,
> And sitteth on the Right Hand of God
> the Father Almighty;
> From thence He shall come
> to judge the Quick and the Dead.